Matt Jensen, the Last Mountain Man:
Torture Town

Matt Jensen, the Last Mountain Man:
Torture Town

William W. Johnstone
with J. A. Johnstone

PINNACLE BOOKS
Kensington Publishing Corp.
www.kensingtonbooks.com

PINNACLE BOOKS are published by

Kensington Publishing Corp.
119 West 40th Street
New York, NY 10018

PUBLISHER'S NOTE
Following the death of William W. Johnstone, the Johnstone family is working with a carefully selected writer to organize and complete Mr. Johnstone's outlines and many unfinished manuscripts to create additional novels in all of his series like The Last Gunfighter, Mountain Man, and Eagles, among others. This novel was inspired by Mr. Johnstone's superb storytelling.

All Kensington titles, imprints, and distributed lines are available at special quantity discounts for bulk purchases for sales promotions, premiums, fund-raising, educational, or institutional use. Special book excerpts or customized printings can also be created to fit specific needs. For details, write or phone the office of the Kensington special sales manager: Kensington Publishing Corp., 119 West 40th Street, New York, NY 10018, attn: Special Sales Department; phone 1-800-221-2647.

ISBN-13: 978-0-7860-3342-3
ISBN-10: 0-7860-3342-8

First printing: February 2014

10 9 8 7 6 5 4 3

Printed in the United States of America

First electronic edition: February 2014

ISBN-13: 978-0-7860-3343-0
ISBN-10: 0-7860-3343-6

Prologue

The artillery rolled across the field like claps of thunder, first the distant thump, then the sound of the shells coming in . . . a rushing noise like a unattached railroad car rolling down a track . . . then the sharp boom of the explosion, followed by the whistling sound of the shards of shrapnel, flying out from the bursting shell.

Ben Ross and Morgan Poindexter were part of the 38th Illinois Infantry, and they were moving to plug up the middle of the Union line. When their company was moved, it opened up a gap that the Confederate forces exploited, and men in gray came pouring through.

Ben went down and a Confederate soldier rushed over to him with the intention of thrusting his bayonet into Ben's defenseless body. Morgan shot the Confederate, then ran back toward Ben, dodging bullets until he reached his friend.

"Get out of here! Leave me be!" Ben shouted. "There ain't no sense in both of us gettin' kilt."

"Hush up," Morgan said, bending down to pick up his friend. With Ben draped over his shoulder, he ran as quickly as he could to get off the open field and into the relative safety of a grove of trees. There were enough Union soldiers there to keep the Confederates at bay.

The battle continued for the rest of the day and into the next, before the Union Forces withdrew back to Chattanooga. The result of two days of fierce fighting was horrendous, with a total of thirty-four thousand soldiers killed and wounded.

Ben was one of the wounded, and Morgan stayed with him until he received treatment from the doctors.

"It is good you got him to me when you did," the doctor who treated Ben said. "Had you delayed even an hour longer, the wound would have had time to fester, and I would have had to take off his leg. I heard what you did, rushing out on the battle-field like that. He must be an awfully good friend for you to take a risk like that."

"Doc, I don't have a better friend in this world," Morgan said.

Franklin, Tennessee—November 30, 1864

Ben Ross and Morgan Poindexter, both now first lieutenants, stood behind their barricaded men as they watched the Confederate brigades advance across the open field. When the Confederates drew within four hundred yards, the Union batteries began firing canister shells, each shell containing twenty-seven large balls. The deadly blasts cut down the attacking rebels like a scythe through wheat.

Despite the terrible firepower used against them, General Cleburne managed to lead his troops all the way up to the Union defensive line, and even penetrated it, before Cleburne was himself killed, and his troops were finally repulsed.

Morgan Poindexter had been shot, and as the Confederate troops began to withdraw, two of the Rebel soldiers grabbed Morgan, one on each leg, and they started pulling him back across the field with them, dragging him across the ground.

"We might be leavin', Yanks, but we ain't leavin' alone!" one of them shouted.

Ben Ross jumped over the parapet and started after the two Confederates who were dragging Morgan away.

"Lieutenant Ross, you get back here!" Major Baker called. Baker had assumed command of the 38th Infantry only six days earlier, when Colonel Chapman had died.

Ben paid no attention to the major, pursuing the fleeing Rebels on foot with his pistol in his hand. He shot both of the men who were dragging Morgan with them. Then, precisely as Morgan had done for him a year earlier, he picked up his friend, threw him over his shoulder, and started back to his own lines, cheered on by the men of Company B.

Springfield, Illinois—January 15, 1866

"There's land to be had for free out in New Mexico," Ben said. "All we have to do is go out there and file a claim on it. Come with me, be my partner. We'll start a cattle ranch."

"Cattle ranch?"

"Sure, why not? The war's over, I've got a feeling that the country is going to get mighty hungry for beef. We'll make a ton of money."

"You can't make money without money. How much do you think we'll need to get started?" Morgan asked.

"I'd say no more than five hundred dollars. We only have to come up with two hundred fifty apiece."

"Right now I'm about forty dollars short of that," Morgan said.

Ben laughed. "You're ahead of me. I need about sixty dollars. But I know how we can get the money."

"How?"

"The Atchison, Topeka, and Santa Fe Railway is paying five dollars a day to workers. They also feed and house you, so we won't have to spend a cent. One month of working on the railroad, and we'll have enough to start our ranch."

Morgan smiled broadly, and stuck out his hand. "All right, Ben, you've got yourself a partner."

"How soon will you be ready to go?"

"Is an hour too long?"

Ben laughed. "We'll tell our folks good-bye, and leave tomorrow."

Rio Arriba County, New Mexico Territory—May 1866

Ben and Morgan discovered that if each of them would file an independent land claim, they could get more property. They filed adjoining claims, and because the county was so sparsely populated at the time they arrived, they were able to stake out two hundred and fifty thousand acres apiece, which they joined to create the half-million-acre R&P Ranch.

The first thing they did was build a cabin. The first night they were able to sleep inside, they sat at the table they had made, drinking whiskey and staring into the crackling flames in the fireplace.

"We've got us a cattle ranch," Morgan said. "But we don't have any cattle."

"Yeah, that's the next thing we need. I guess we have enough money to buy us a couple of seed bulls and some heifers," Ben said.

"It's goin' to take a long time to build up a herd that way."

"You got any better ideas?"

"Maybe," Morgan answered. "I've been hearing about something called cow hunts, down in Texas."

"Cow hunts?"

"During the war, a lot of the cattle down in Texas left the ranches and started wandering all over the place. Now there are huge, unclaimed herds down there. All we have to do is go down there, round some of them up, and bring them back here."

"Just the two of us?"

"I think if we go up to Denver, we'll be able to find someone to help us," Morgan said. "If we can figure out how we are going to pay them."

"Suppose we cut one cow out of every ten that we collect, and use those cows as payment. If we can round up five thousand head, that'll give us five hundred head of cattle to use for working capital. If we only got five dollars a head, that would be twenty-five hundred dollars," Ben said. "That should be plenty enough."

"Damn!" Morgan said. "That's a good idea, Ben! Why didn't I think of that?"

"Because I got the brains and you got the looks," Ben teased.

In Denver, Ben and Morgan rounded up ten people who agreed to their terms of being paid when they finished the round-up. The youngest of the drovers was fifteen and the oldest was twenty-one, though they did hire a cook who was in his late fifties.

Buying a chuck wagon and filling it with possibles, they started south.

When they began their "cow hunt" in Texas, they weren't particularly careful as to whether the cattle were wild or not. Several of the cows had brands, but often there were many different brands mixed into the same herd, that they used that as justification that the cattle were now free-range cattle.

When they had three thousand head, it was Ben who suggested that they start back.

"I thought we were going to round up five thousand head," Morgan replied.

"You want to hang around until a posse comes?"

"What posse?"

"The kind of posse Texans send after cattle rustlers."

"We aren't rustlin' cattle," Morgan said.

"More than half of these cows are wearin' brands," Ben said.

"Yes, but all different kinds of brands. We didn't go onto any ranch land, every cow we took was from open range," Morgan insisted.

"You want try and explain that to a necktie party?" Ben asked.

Morgan was quiet for a moment; then he smiled, sheepishly. "No," he said. "I think you're right. We need to get back to New Mexico."

June 1868

Within two years the R&P Ranch was the largest and most productive ranch in the entire county. Ben Ross and Morgan Poindexter had become wealthy men, and the nearby town of Thirty Four Corners profited from the business the R&P Cattle Ranch brought in.

"Do you remember me tellin' you that we might want to get married someday?" Ben asked Morgan a couple of months after they had left the cabin and built two houses, one for each of them.

"Yes."

"Well, for me, that someday is coming sooner than later," Ben said. "Look at this."

Ben showed Morgan an advertisement in the *Rocky Mountain News*.

MARRIAGE BROKER
~
Let us find a Bride for you
Only Women of Finest Character

"I've ordered me a bride. She'll be arrivin' in Denver in two more weeks. What I'd like you to do, if you would, is go meet her for me, and bring her to Thirty Four Corners."

"Wait a minute, Ben. She's goin' to be your wife. Shouldn't you be the one to go get her?"

"I'm not goin' to have time. I'm goin' to have to be gettin' the house ready for a woman. And I got to make arrangements with the preacher for the wedding."

"What's her name?"

"Her name?" Ben looked puzzled. "I don't know her name."

Morgan chuckled. "Ben, how do you expect me to pick her up, if I don't know who I'm lookin' for?"

"Wait, I got a letter from her. I haven't read it yet, but more'n likely her name is in the letter."

"What do you mean you haven't read it yet? The woman is going to be your wife for crying out loud—the least you can do is read her letter."

"Yeah, okay, let me get it, and we'll read it."

"I don't need to read it. It's a personal letter to you."

"How can it be personal? She doesn't even know me."

A few moments later Ben returned with the letter.

Dear Sir,

You may be wondering what sort of woman would submit herself to the indignity of a brokered marriage. Let me assure you that it is not a character flaw that has driven me to this point of desperation. Both of my parents have died, and I am left in a condition of severe financial need. I am twenty years old, tall, fair, well-educated, accomplished, amiable, and affectionate. I am a good woman, and I will make you a good wife. I ask only that you treat me well.

Sincerely
Dorothy Clay

"Her name is Dorothy," Ben said. "So now that you know it, you can go get her for me."

"All right, I'll do it, because you're my friend,"

Morgan said. "But I tell you true, Ben, it just doesn't seem right that I'm the one to go meet her."

"Who better to send than my best friend?" Ben asked.

According to the marriage broker, Dorothy Clay would be arriving on the two o'clock train, so Morgan was standing on the depot platform when the train rolled in. He watched all the passengers detrain, and saw only two women get off alone. One of the women looked to be in her late fifties, short and stout. The second woman was considerably younger, and with a pinched face and beady eyes.

He had no idea which of the two women it would be, but neither one was what you could call a "looker." *Poor Ben*, he thought, as he started toward the two women. But what else can you expect when you get a pig in a poke?

Just before he reached the two women, the older woman smiled broadly as a man approached her. The two hugged, then walked off together. That left only the pinched face woman.

Morgan touched the brim of his hat. "Would you be Miss Clay?" he asked.

"Get away from me, sir, or I shall call an officer of the law!" the woman replied in a shrill voice.

She turned and walked quickly away from Morgan, who, with his back to the train, watched her storm off. He still didn't know if this was Dorothy Clay or not.

"I am Miss Clay," a soft, well-modulated voice said from behind him.

Turning toward the train, Morgan saw one of the most beautiful women he had ever seen in his life standing on the bottom step.

"You?" he asked in a disbelieving voice.

The woman stepped down from the train and extended her hand. "Am I meeting my future husband?" she asked, with a big smile.

"No, ma'am, but I sure wish to hell you were," Morgan said. "I'm just here to pick you up for my friend Ben."

There was only one church in the town, and it served all denominations. This morning the church was filled because there was about to be a wedding.

Ben was waiting in the pastor's office with the preacher.

"Looks like the whole town is here," the Reverend E. D. Owen said.

"Don't you go preachin' now, just 'cause you've got a big crowd," Ben joked. "All I want to do is get married, and get back out to the ranch. I got some calves to brand."

Owen laughed. "That's some honeymoon you're going on."

"Dorothy knew when I sent for her what she was gettin' herself into."

"I suppose so," Owen said.

* * *

Dorothy Clay was waiting in the narthex with Morgan Poindexter. There had been some discussion as to whether Morgan should be used as a best man, or as a surrogate father of the bride, so he could give her away. At Dorothy's request, Ben decided to let Morgan act as her surrogate father. At the moment, only the two of them were waiting in the narthex.

"I don't want to give you away," Morgan said.

"What do you mean?"

"I mean, I don't want to give you away," Poindexter repeated. "Truth is, Dorothy, I love you, and I've loved you from the moment I saw you get off the train in Denver."

"Oh, Morgan," Dorothy said. "Why didn't you say something before? When you came to pick me up, I thought you were the man I was to marry. You've no idea how disappointed I was when I learned that you weren't."

"Don't go through with it, Dorothy," Morgan said.

"I have to go through with it. It's too late, don't you see? Ben paid for my passage out here."

"I'll pay him back."

"But what . . . what would you have me do?"

"Come with me. We'll go to Denver and get married."

"We can't do that."

"Do you love Ben? Or do you love me?"

"I . . . I love you," Dorothy said.

"Dorothy, if you go through with this marriage with the way you and I feel about each other, we're going to get together. You know it, and I know it. And if you're married to Ben when that happens, one of us is going to wind up dead. I don't want to kill Ben, he has been my best friend since we were boys. We fought in the war together. But if it came right down to me or him, I'd have no choice.

"So, don't you see it would be better if you came with me now . . . before you are married?"

In the church the organist started playing the music, and, nervously, Dorothy looked toward the closed door to the nave.

"All right," Dorothy said, quickly. "God help me, all right."

With Morgan holding her hand, and with the train of her wedding gown trailing behind her, Morgan and Dorothy left the church, and ran toward the buckboard Morgan had brought into town today. He helped her in. Then, untying the reins, he hurried around, climbed into the seat, and urged the horses into a gallop.

In the pastor's office Reverend Owen, hearing the music, opened the door and looked out toward the sacristy.

"It's time for us to go wait for your bride," Owen said, with a broad smile.

"Hurry the wedding up, will you, preacher? Like I said, I got work that needs to be done," Ben said.

"This is your wedding day, Mr. Ross. It will be conducted with dignity," Owen said, as he led Ben out to the altar.

The organist began playing the bridal march and everyone in the congregation turned toward the front door, which was still closed. The organist was halfway through the music and still, no bride. One of the ushers looked toward Reverend Owen, who gave him a nod, suggesting that he open the door and hurry the bride along.

The usher opened the door to the empty narthex, then saw that the front door was also open. Stepping out through the front door he saw the buckboard racing away from town, the bride's gown flowing in the wind.

"Lord have mercy, Preacher!" the usher shouted. "The bride's done run away with Morgan Poindexter!"

"What?" Ben shouted. He ran down the aisle to the open door of the church and saw the buckboard, now a quarter of a mile away.

"Morgan! You son of a bitch!" he shouted at the top of his voice.

Chapter One

One week after Morgan and Dorothy ran off to get married, they returned to Thirty Four Corners. It was obvious, as they drove down Central Street, which was the main street of the town, that they were the center of attention.

"Hey, Poindexter, after what you done to a good man, why did you bother to come back to Thirty Four Corners?" someone shouted from the front of Sikes's hardware store.

"Don't let Hancock get to you, Poindexter," someone called from the front of White's Apothecary, which was just across the street. "It ain't like you run off with another man's wife. . . . They wasn't married yet. You 'n' your new missus had ever' right to get married if you wanted to."

For the entire drive down Central Street, Morgan and Dorothy were assailed by such calls, some accusatory and some supportive. They stopped in front of the Homestead Hotel.

"I'm going to get you checked in here," Morgan said. "Then I'm going out to the ranch and make things right with Ben."

"Oh, Morgan, do be careful," Dorothy said, laying her hand on Morgan's arm.

"Don't you worry about it, darlin'," Morgan replied, patting her hand. "Ben and I have been best friends from the day we were born. We'll get things patched up, all right."

R&P Ranch

"I can't believe you would have the nerve to come out here," Ben said angrily.

"Ben, what can I say? I'm sorry it happened like this. It isn't something that Dorothy or I planned. We fell in love. You didn't love her—you know you didn't. She never was anything more than a mail-order bride to you, and that's all she ever would be. Hell, you can order another bride." Morgan laughed, trying to lighten the situation. "I'll even pay for it."

"I have already sent for another mail-order bride," Ben replied. "I don't want you to pay for it. In fact, Morgan, I don't want anything at all from you. I don't want anything to do with you ever again."

"That's going to be sort of hard to do, isn't it?" Morgan replied. "We are equal partners in this ranch. How are we going to work together, if you never want anything to do with me again?"

"I've already spoken to a lawyer," Ben said. "He

has drawn up a plan that will divide the ranch into two separate ranches. You can have everything north of Bacas Ridge, I'll stay south."

"But my house is here, not more than a hundred yards from this house."

"I'll be buying your house, and your interest in all the other structures. That will give you enough money to build your own place."

"I don't want to do that, Ben. Why can't we just keep things the way they were, as partners and friends? I'll live in my house just the way I have been doing, and you can live in yours. You said yourself you've already sent for another mail-order bride. I'm sure she and Dorothy will be as good a friends as you and I have been for all these years."

"Please meet me in Lawyer Norton's office tomorrow afternoon," Ben said.

Dan Norton had thinning hair that had once been red and a face with freckles that had faded over time. He sat behind his desk and looked at the paperwork that lay before him, three matching documents, one for Ben Ross, one for Morgan Poindexter, and one for the county files.

"You have both read the documents," Norton said. "Do you have any questions?"

"Yes," Ben said. "What is this right here, this hatch-marked piece of land?"

"That is fifteen thousand acres that was not claimed in the original land grant," Norton said.

"So, file on it, and we'll divide it."

Norton shook his head. "I can't file on it," he said. "It has already been claimed."

"Claimed?" Ben replied. He looked at Morgan with an angry expression on his face. "Morgan! You son of a bitch!"

"Mr. Poindexter isn't the one who filed on it," Norton replied, quickly.

"Well, who did?"

"Kyle Stallings," Norton said.

"Stallings? Impossible," Ben said. "He rides for me."

"Not anymore," Norton said. "I understand he is starting his own ranch now."

"Ha! You can't have much of a ranch with only fifteen thousand acres," Ben said.

"As I understand it, he just wants enough land to be able to survive. And, because his ranch is situated between the two of you, he also hopes it will keep the peace between you. He says that he likes both of you, and doesn't want to be put into the position of taking sides."

"His land doesn't completely divide us," Morgan said. "It comes to a point up here. From here, all the way out to the Navajo Range, our two properties are adjacent."

"I propose one last partnership enterprise between us," Ben said.

"What would that be?" Morgan asked.

"That we build, and share in the cost of, a five-mile-long barbed wire fence."

"All right," Morgan agreed.

The papers Norton had drawn up for the two men divided not only the land, but the cattle. The cowboys who had worked on the ranch were also divided as to which of the two erstwhile friends and partners they would work for. About half of them chose the one they wanted to work for; the others, with no particular preference, were divided by lot. What had been the R&P Ranch, became two ranches. Ben Ross owned the BR Ranch. Morgan named his ranch the Tumbling P.

Shortly after the division of the property was made, and even before Morgan had managed to build his new house and outbuildings, Ben Ross's new mail-order bride arrived. Her name was Nancy Malone, and she came from Georgia, ironically from Chickamauga, the place where Morgan had saved Ben's life.

Morgan had hoped that getting a new wife would mellow Ben to the point that they could make up and resume their friendship. In order to accomplish that, he and Dorothy went to the church on the day of Ben's wedding, but they were met by some of Ben's riders, all of whom were armed.

"Sorry, Mr. Poindexter, but you can't go into the church."

"Dean, what are you saying?" Morgan asked. Dean Kelly was Ben Ross's foreman, a man that Morgan had known since he and Ben had started the ranch.

"Like I said, you can't go in. Mr. Ross, he's done give me orders to keep you out."

"Would you shoot me, and my wife, to keep us from going into a church?"

"I wouldn't want to," Kelly said. "But Mr. Ross, he's real serious about you not comin' in to spoil his weddin'. And you know me, Mr. Poindexter. I'm loyal to whoever I'm workin' for."

"I had hoped that we could end this silly disagreement," Morgan said. Then he sighed, and put his hand on Kelly's shoulder. "But I'm not going to force the issue. You're right. You are a good and loyal man."

"I'm sorry, Mr. Poindexter."

Morgan nodded, then turned to his wife. "Come on, Dorothy," he said. "Let's go out and see how the builders are doing with our house."

Within a year after they were married, Dorothy gave Morgan a son, who he named Nate. Six months later, Ben was blessed with a son, who he named Rex. One year later, Morgan and Dorothy had a daughter whom they named Sylvia.

Then, when Sylvia was twelve years old, Dorothy died, and Morgan sent his daughter back to Illinois to live with his sister.

"Please, Papa, I don't want to go back," Sylvia begged. "I want to stay here with you and my brother."

"You're going to be a woman someday," Morgan said. "And I intend to see to it that you have a woman's touch while you're growin' up. I loved your mama more than I can say, and I wouldn't feel right raisin' a tomboy."

Despite her protestations, Sylvia went east.

Over the next several years, animosity grew, not only between Ben Ross and Morgan Poindexter, but also between those who supported one side or the other.

The Lewis Ranch, Freemont County, Colorado

Fourteen-year-old Claire Lewis was standing in a kitchen that was redolent with the aroma of the biscuits her mother had baking in the oven. Claire was holding a hand mirror, extending her hand, then bringing it up for a closer examination, turning her head one way, and then another. She was also holding her lips in various ways, smiling, and puckering.

"Mama, am I pretty?" she asked.

"Of course you are, darling. You are a beautiful girl."

"I know you are going to say that, because you are my mama. But am I really pretty?"

"Is the horse that Matt Jensen gave you pretty?" Martha asked.

"Sparkle is beautiful," Claire replied.

"Are you saying that just because he is your horse?"

"No, I'm saying it because . . ." Claire stopped in midsentence. "I know what you are doing," she said.

"What am I doing?"

"You're showing me that I can say Sparkle is

beautiful because he really is, and not just because he is my horse."

"And that means?"

"That means you can say that I am pretty, and not just because I'm your daughter."

"But I didn't say you were pretty," Martha said.

The smile left Claire's face.

"I said you were beautiful."

Claire laughed again.

"Go out to the barn and tell your papa to get cleaned up to eat. As soon as the biscuits come out, supper will be ready."

Claire started toward the back door, but before she reached it, it was suddenly opened, and three men came in.

"Who are you? What are you doing here?" Martha asked, fright causing her voice to rise in pitch.

"Now, is that any way to greet company?" one of the men said. He was a big man, with a bald head, a flattened nose, and an unkempt red beard.

"I'm going to call my husband," Martha said. "Jim! Jim!"

"Oh, would this be your husband?" the red bearded man asked. Reaching back out onto the porch he grabbed something, then brought it in to show to Martha.

It was Jim Lewis's severed head.

Martha fainted.

James had been decapitated, and Martha and Claire had both been slaughtered. Jim Lewis had been one of Matt Jensen's closest friends, and Matt's friends were particularly important to him, because his lifestyle of wandering from place to place limited the number of friends he had.

Matt Jensen was particularly close to the Lewis family. He had spent last Christmas with them, and he had given Claire a horse as a Christmas present. He remembered how excited the young girl had been about the horse, a handsome palomino.

"Oh! He is the most beautiful horse I have ever seen in my whole life!" Claire had said excitedly, running her hand over the horse's unblemished gold coat. "What is his name?"

"He doesn't have a name," Matt had said. "He's been waiting for you to name him."

"I'm going to call him Sparkle," Claire had said. "Because his gold coat sparkles in the sunshine."

Claire's father had laughed. "Sparkle? I hope the other horses don't start making fun of him with a name like that."

"Oh, pooh! Sparkle knows he is a beautiful horse, and he won't care what the other horses think."

Matt had been particularly stirred at having been invited by them to participate in what was, normally, a personal time for family. And since Matt had no family of his own, being included in their Christmas made him feel very welcome. When he'd learned that they had been killed—and not only killed, but killed in a way that was brutal and senseless—he had been consumed with rage. That was when he'd made up his mind to find the killers, and bring them to justice.

The three men who had done this were Rufus Draco, Muley Ferguson, and Garth Hightower. A reward of one thousand dollars had been offered for each of them, but for Matt, who lived a nomadic life and had done some bounty hunting in the past, it wasn't the money that had put him on the trail of these three men. This particular quest had become personal.

There had actually been a fourth man, Merlin Morris, who'd started out with them, when their only purpose had been to rob the Lewis ranch. But when Morris had seen the other three go into a killing and raping frenzy, he'd run away . . . as much in fear of his own life as in revulsion for what he was seeing. Feeling a sense of guilt and remorse for even associating with men who could do something like that, he'd turned himself in to the law, and given the names and descriptions of the other three.

Draco, Ferguson, and Hightower were already wanted men, and for the same kind of crime they had perpetrated at the Lewis ranch, so Morris's story rang true.

"Draco and Ferguson went one way 'n' Hightower went the other," Morris said. "Hightower is mounted on a horse that he stoled from the ranch. It's a real purty palomino horse."

"Sparkle," Matt said, feeling a renewed sense of sorrow as he thought of how excited Claire had been over the gift.

Chapter Two

Working with all the available evidence he had, Matt trailed Garth Hightower to Conejos, Colorado. Although it was in Colorado, the small settlement could well have in Mexico. It differed from most of the other towns Matt was familiar with in that the buildings were mostly adobe, and there were more signs in Spanish than in English. Matt caught a break when he saw a golden palomino tied in front of the Niña Bonita Cantina. It was the same horse he had given Claire Lewis for Christmas.

"Hello, Sparkle," Matt said quietly, as he stroked the horse on its forehead. The horse, recognizing its name and Matt, nodded its head in appreciation of the friendly and familiar contact.

"As soon as I take care of a little business, I'll get you out of here," Matt said. "I promise you."

When Matt stepped into the cantina he saw that all the customers, as well as the bartender, were Mexican. He stepped up to the bar.

"*Buenos días, mi amigo. Veo que tienes tequilla. También tienes cerveza?*"

"Yes, I also have beer," the bartender answered in English.

"Good, then I'll have a beer."

The bartender drew a mug of beer and set it in front of Matt. Matt paid with a dollar and when the bartender gave him his change, Matt slid it back toward him.

"There is a palomino tied up out front," Matt said. "It is being ridden by a gringo who is missing half of his ear." Matt put his hand to his left ear to demonstrate. He had gotten the description of Hightower from Merlin Morris.

"Is the gringo your amigo?" the bartender asked.

Matt hesitated for a second. If he lied and said that Hightower was a friend, would the bartender be more cooperative? He took a chance and answered truthfully.

"He is no friend," Matt replied. "He killed a friend of mine, then he murdered and raped . . . *asesinada y violada* . . . my friend's wife and young daughter." He spoke the words in Spanish to make certain that the bartender understood why he was looking for Hightower. "Has such a man been in here?"

The bartender said nothing, but he raised his head and looked toward the stairs at the back of the room.

"*Gracias,*" Matt rumbled. He finished the drink,

then looked toward the flight of wooden stairs that led upstairs to an enclosed loft.

Matt pulled his gun as he started up the stairs. The others in the saloon, seeing Matt going up the stairs with a gun in his hand and realizing that he must be going after the gringo they had seen go up earlier, stopped their conversations to watch.

When Matt reached the door, he listened for a moment, and heard sounds that made it evident what was going on in the room. Putting his hand on the doorknob, he turned it, but when he pushed against the door, he discovered that it was locked. He knocked on the door.

"Go away! We're busy in here," a gruff voice called.

"Hightower, you murdering, raping bastard, I'm taking you back to hang!" Matt shouted through the door. As soon as Matt yelled, he jumped to one side.

"The hell you are!" Matt heard the explosion of a gunshot, and a .44 caliber slug, energized by the pistol shot, punched a hole through the door.

Almost immediately after the shot, Matt heard the crash of breaking glass, and kicking the door open with a splintering smash of wood he rushed inside. A naked woman had jumped from the bed and was now standing in the corner, trying to cover her nakedness with her arms. Her eyes reflected her terror.

The window had been broken out, and Matt ran over to look outside, expecting to see someone down in the alley, but there was no one there.

"I've got you now, you son of a bitch," a gruff voice called from behind him, and Matt turned quickly to see that Hightower had set a trap for him. A broad smile spread across Hightower's face as he realized that he had the drop on the man who was coming after him.

But Hightower made a huge mistake. He didn't know who had come after him, and he'd badly overestimated his advantage. The smile on his face vanished when he saw how quickly Matt recovered. Even as he was thumbing the hammer back on his pistol, Matt was shooting. The bullet hit Hightower in the middle of his chest, and slammed him back against the wall. Without having fired a shot, Hightower slid down, leaving a streak of blood on the wall behind him.

"Who are you?" he asked in a pained voice.

"I'm a friend of the little girl you raped," Matt said. He could have saved his breath, because Hightower was already dead.

"He raped a little girl?" the woman who had been with him asked.

"She was fourteen years old."

The woman walked over to Hightower's body and looked down at it. "*Y te dejo dormir conmigo, hijo de puta!*" Angrily, she spit on him.

At that moment, the sheriff and several others came clomping up the stairs and running into the room, their guns drawn.

"Is he dead?" the sheriff asked, looking down at Hightower.

"Yes," Matt said. He pulled out the dodger he held on the man and showed it to the sheriff. "Here is the reward poster, and there is the body. I want the money."

The sheriff looked at the dodger for a moment, then at Hightower. "Oh yes, I heard about this. It happened up in Freemont County, didn't it?"

"Yes," Matt replied without elaboration.

The sheriff studied the dodger on Hightower for a moment; then he nodded. "All right," he finally said. "I'll validate that this is Hightower. It'll probably take a couple of days, though, to get the money down from Denver."

"That's all right," Matt said. "I can wait."

Taos County, New Mexico Territory—1891

Leaving Sparkle in a livery stable in Conjos with enough money to keep the horse comfortable for at least two more months, Matt continued with his search. With one down, and two to go, he managed to pick up the trail of Rufus Draco and Muley Ferguson, following them down into New Mexico.

The metal bit jangled against his horse's teeth. The horse's hooves clattered on the hard rock and the leather saddle creaked beneath the weight of its rider. Matt Jensen's boots were dusty and well worn, the metal of his spurs had become dull with time. He wore a Colt .44 at his hip, and carried a Winchester .44-40 in his saddle sheath

He dismounted, unhooked his canteen, and took a swallow, then poured some water into his hat. He held it in front of his horse, and the horse drank thirstily, though Matt knew that the small amount of water did little to slake the animal's thirst. The horse drank all the water, then began nuzzling Matt for more.

"Sorry, Spirit," Matt said quietly. "But that's the best I can do for now. We'll reach the monastery before nightfall, and there'll be water there, I promise you."

The monastery Matt was referring to was the Brothers of Mercy. Records in the monastery indicated the Spanish had built it nearly two hundred years earlier, its location selected because of a year-round supply of water from Cottonwood Creek.

Matt reached the monastery just before dark. The abbey was surrounded by high stone walls and secured by a heavy oak gate. He pulled on a rope that was attached to a short section of log. The makeshift knocker banged against the large, heavy gates with a booming thunder that resonated through the entire monastery. A moment later, a small window slid open and a brown-hooded face appeared in the opening.

"Who are you?" the face asked.

Matt had been here before. He knew Brother Paul, the monk in the window, and he knew that Brother Paul knew him.

"I am just a traveler," Matt replied.

"What do you want?"

"I want to come in. I need food, water, and shelter."

"I'm sorry. You can't come in."

"But, Brother, how can you turn me away?"

"I am sorry," the monk said again. "God go with you." The little window slammed shut.

Matt had known from the moment Brother Paul had asked who he was that something was wrong. The monk was trying to send Matt a message, and, with an almost imperceptible nod, Matt let Brother Paul know that he understood. Matt remounted, then rode away from the gate.

Rufus Draco and Muley Ferguson were standing just inside the gate. Draco was peering through the crack between the timbers of the gate.

"What's he doin'?" Ferguson asked.

"He's ridin' off," Draco answered.

Draco chuckled, then put his pistol away. He looked at the short, overweight monk. "You done that real good," he said. "I don't think he suspects a thing."

"It is not good to deny someone in need," Brother Paul said.

"Yeah? Well, I'm in need now. Come on, let's go see if the cook has our supper finished. I'm starvin'."

The courtyard of the monastery was a verdant growth in the desert, lovingly tended to by the brothers of the order. Two centuries of monks had irrigated and cultivated a garden paradise that was lush with flowers, fruit trees, and vegetables. It was a never-ending task, and even now there were a dozen or more monks in the yard, gathering fruit, picking vegetables, and cutting flowers.

The building they entered was surprisingly cool, kept that way by the hanging ollas, which, by the process of evaporation, lowered the temperature by several degrees.

"Did I hear a knock at the gate?" Father Mordecai asked.

"Yes, Father, it was a stranger," Brother Paul said. "I do not know who he was."

"What did he want?"

"Water, food, shelter."

"And you denied him sanctuary?"

"I had no choice," Brother Paul said, nodding toward Draco and Ferguson.

"You prevented us from offering sanctuary?" Father Mordecai asked Draco.

Draco was a big, ugly man, bald headed with a bushy red beard. His nose had been broken more than once, and it was flat until it swelled out for the nostrils.

Ferguson was much smaller, with a ferretlike face, dead eyes, and skin that was heavily pocked from the scars of some childhood disease.

"Maybe the padre here didn't know who he was, but I knew who it was as soon as I seen 'im comin'. He wasn't no ordinary visitor. His name is Matt Jensen, and he's hot on our trail."

"Why is he pursuing you?"

"That ain't none of your business."

"I see," Father Mordecai said. "Still, to turn someone away is unthinkable. It is a show of Christian kindness to offer water, food, and shelter to those who ask it of us."

"You're being Christian enough just by takin' care of us," Draco insisted. "Now, what about that food? How long does it take your cook to fix a little supper?"

"Forgive me for not mentioning it the moment you came in," Father Mordecai said. "The cook has informed me that your supper is ready."

"Yeah, well, it's about damn time. Why didn't you say somethin'?" Draco said with a growl. "Come on, Muley, let's me 'n' you get us somethin' to eat."

Brother Paul led the two men to a rather austere-looking dining room, consisting as it did of nothing more than one long table and benches.

"If you gentlemen will just have a seat, I'll bring you your meal," Brother Paul offered.

A moment later, Brother Paul came back into the room with two bowls and two pieces of black bread.

"What is this?" Ferguson asked.

"This is your supper. Please allow me to ask a blessing."

Brother Paul bowed his head and, though his lips moved, his words couldn't be heard. Not until then did he put the bowls down in front of the two men.

"What did you bother to bless this for? Hell,

there ain't nothin' here but beans. Ain't you got no meat?"

Brother Paul shook his head. "In this order we do not eat meat."

"What do you mean you don't eat meat? I know you got some beef here. I seen some cows."

"The cows provide us with our milk, cream, butter, and cheese," Brother Paul said.

"Just eat your beans, Ferguson. It's better'n nothin'," Draco said.

Matt waited until after dark before he returned to the monastery. Leaving Spirit hobbled, he slipped up to one of the side walls, then climbed over it and dropped to the ground on the inside.

There were few lights to be seen, for there was no electricity in this remote place, and the residents of the monastery used candles and lamps sparingly.

Though the night was dark, it wasn't quiet. Matt could hear the long, high-pitched trills and low, violalike thrums of the frogs, the chirping of crickets, and the long, mournful howls of coyotes.

Moving carefully, and staying in the shadows, Matt moved toward the chapel, which showed a light through the window. When he reached the window and looked inside he saw Draco, Ferguson, and Father Mordecai. The priest was holding a chalice, the cup glistening in the flickering light of the single candle.

"What is it worth?" Ferguson asked, pointing to the chalice.

"What is it worth? There is no way to put a price on it."

"It's gold, ain't it? That means it's worth something."

"Yes, it is pure gold."

"So if I was to take it, and melt it down, I'd say there must be at least twenty ounces there, then it's got to be worth no less than four or five hundred dollars."

"Melt it down? How can you even think such a thing? No, that would be an unspeakable sacrilege! You would have to kill me first!" Father Mordecai insisted.

"Well hell, preacher-man, that ain't goin' to be no problem," Ferguson said, cocking his pistol. "I can take of that for you right now."

Matt leaped through the window, then fell to the floor and rolled. The sound of breaking glass got the attention of the two outlaws.

"Son of a bitch!" Ferguson shouted, turning his pistol away from the priest and toward Matt.

Matt fired at the candle, snuffing the light. "Run, Father!" he shouted.

As Matt was shooting at the candle, one of the outlaws was shooting at him, and Matt felt a hammer-like blow to his shoulder. He returned fire, using the muzzle blast of the pistol that had shot at him as his target. He heard a grunt, followed by the sound of someone falling.

He also heard someone running, then the crash of glass from the other side of the building, and he realized that someone had jumped through that window. He lay on the floor for a moment longer until his eyes grew accustomed to the dark, and, by the ambient light of the full moon, he saw Father Mordecai crouched in a corner. He also saw that one of the two outlaws was down, and the other was gone.

"Are you hurt, Father?" Matt asked.

"No."

Matt got up and walked over to the man on the floor and saw that, while not dead, he was seriously wounded. Matt picked up the wounded man's pistol, then moved quickly to the window. He looked outside, but saw nothing. The other man had gotten away.

Rufus Draco was the one who had leaped through the window and escaped into the night. Muley Ferguson was the man Matt had shot in the exchange of gunfire, and though Matt wanted, very much, to question him, Ferguson was unconscious and unresponsive.

Both Matt and Ferguson had been wounded in the shoot-out, and the Brothers, after tending to them, put them in the same room on side-by-side bunks. And even though Ferguson was an outlaw who had bullied the Brothers and had been in the process of attempting to steal one of their most precious artifacts, the Brothers gave him the best care they were capable of providing.

Over the next twenty-four hours, Ferguson's condition worsened, and Matt realized that there was very little chance that he would be able to question him to find out where Draco might have gone.

The Brothers buried him the next day. Matt, with his shoulder expertly bandaged, stood out with the others as Father Mordecai prayed over Ferguson's body. The outlaw was interred, not in the consecrated graveyard, but at least on the grounds.

"How can you pray for him?" Matt asked. "Don't you understand that he was about to kill you?"

"I wasn't praying for the body. I was praying for the soul," Father Mordecai said.

"What makes you think that a body like that even had a soul?"

"Oh, but you don't understand, Matthew. We aren't bodies with souls. We are souls with bodies," Father Mordecai explained.

It was two more weeks before Matt, with his shoulder nearly mended, stood beside Spirit just inside the front gate, ready to ride on. Brother Paul and Father Mordecai were there, along with all the other Brothers of the monastery. Matt lifted his left arm and moved it around.

"How is your arm, Matthew?" Brother Paul asked.

"As good as new," Matt replied. "Nobody has ever done a better job of patching me up."

Father Mordecai handed Matt a package wrapped in cloth.

"What is this?"

"I noticed that you developed a particular liking for black bread," Father Mordecai said. "So I asked the cook to bake up a couple of extra loaves for you to take with you. Also a jar of honey."

"Well, now," Matt said with a big smile. "It looks like I won't be hungry for a while."

"You will be going after Mr. Draco?" Brother Paul asked.

"Yes."

"I know what Mr. Draco and Mr. Ferguson did," Brother Paul said. "And I know that we are supposed to love the sinner and hate the sin, but I am finding that very hard to do so with someone as evil as Rufus Draco. I find myself hoping that you do find him, and I pray that, in any such encounter as may ensue from such a meeting, you escape unscathed."

"You do know, don't you, Brother Paul, that the only way I can escape unscathed is if Rufus Draco comes out the worse in any direct confrontation. And that means that I will probably have to kill him."

Brother Paul chuckled. "Yes, I know. In such a way I can pray that justice be done, without praying, directly, for any evil to befall the man."

Matt laughed, and reached out to put his hand on Brother Paul's shoulder. "Brother Paul, you are a most devious man," he said. "I like that in a person."

The gate to the monastery was opened, and Matt rode out, waving good-bye at the men who had nursed, fed, and befriended him.

As the gate closed behind him, Matt thought about the task ahead. Draco had escaped him this time, but Matt was sure he would catch up with him someday. And when he did . . . he would kill him.

Chapter Three

Pecato, New Mexico Territory

It had been three weeks since the incident at the monastery, and Matt had lost direct contact with Rufus Draco's trail. He wandered into Pecato, just on the chance that Draco may have come through there, and he tied up in front of a false-fronted saloon called Mad Dog. Inside, under the soft, golden light of three gleaming chandeliers, the atmosphere was quite congenial. There were a few men standing at one end of the bar, engaged in friendly conversation, while at the other end, the bartender stayed busy pouring drinks and cleaning glasses. Most of the tables were filled with cowboys, miners, and storekeepers laughing over exchanged stories, or flirting with one of the several bar girls whose presence added to the enjoyment of the evening.

Because it was mid-June, the two heating stoves

were now cold, though the distinctive aroma of
wood smoke from their winter's activity continued to
hang around these appliances. Mixed with that scent
were the smells of liquor, tobacco, and women's
perfume, and the occasional odor of too many men
with too few baths.

Matt took advantage of the ambience of the
saloon, getting into a game of stud poker with
three other players he had befriended. The other
three poker players were a doctor, the owner of a
livery stable, and a driver for the New Mexico Stage
Coach Company.

To the casual observer it might appear that
Matt was so relaxed as to be off guard. A closer examination, however, would show that his eyes were
constantly flicking about, monitoring the room,
tone and tint, for any danger. And, though he was
conversing easily with the others at the table, his
keen sense of hearing was listening in on snatches
of dozens of other conversations, listening to see
if he could find out anything about Rufus Draco.
Additionally, he possessed a sense that could not
be described . . . a kinesthesis developed by years
of exposure to danger.

"I believe it is your bet, Mr. Jensen," Dr. Dunaway
said.

Matt had two queens. He had hoped to draw
another queen but failed to do so. The doctor had
two kings showing.

"I fold," Matt said.

Joel Matthews, the livery stable owner, also folded.

That meant that Manny Crabtree, who was showing two jacks, was the only one left to challenge the good doctor.

"You know what, Doc? I don't think you've got those kings backed up. On the other hand, I might have my jacks backed up, but it's goin' to cost you to find out, so I'm raising you five dollars."

Dr. Dunaway smiled, and slid the money out into the middle of the table. "All right, I call," he said.

"Damn!" Crabtree said. "You ain't supposed to do that. . . . You're supposed to raise me back so's we can spar a bit longer."

"I don't need to spar. I've got you beat," Dr. Dunaway said. He turned over a third king.

Two men came into the saloon then, and they walked over to the bar. The men caught Matt's attention immediately. Perhaps it was because of the way they wore their guns, low and kicked out, or maybe it was how they looked at everyone in the saloon. Since Matt entered a saloon the same way, their caution was something that he immediately recognized. One of the two had a disfiguring scar that came down through his left eye and across his cheek. Matt had to look twice, before he realized that he didn't even have an eyelid over that eye. Though the other one had no disfiguring scars, he stood out because of dull gray eyes that looked lifeless.

But it was more than their looks that caught his attention. It was something else, though it was nothing he could explain. It was just a feeling that these two men meant trouble.

"Gentlemen, I hate to run away with my winnings, but I've got to get back home," Dr. Dunaway said. He chuckled. "My wife thinks I'm calling on patients."

"She's going to know better when you show up with all your winnings," Matthews said.

"Ha! And just what makes you think she's going to know about this money?" Dunaway asked, and the others around the table laughed.

"I tell you what, just to show you what a good sport I am, suppose I buy you three boys a drink before I leave."

"Well, now that's awful nice of you, Doc, seein' as you'll be buyin' me a drink with my money," Mathews said, though the tone of his voice was more teasing than angry. "Leastwise, what was my money."

Dr. Dunaway laughed again, then walked over the bar, left some money with the bartender, and pointed back to the table where Matt and the other two were sitting. A moment later one of the bar girls started toward the table carrying three drinks on a tray. She was smiling at them; then Matt saw one of the two men who had just arrived stick out his foot and trip the girl. She fell, and the drinks spilled on the floor.

"Damn, girl!" the dead-eyed man said. "Can't you walk?"

"You . . . you . . . ," the girl started, but the smile left the man's face, to be replaced by a snarl.

"I what?" he asked, tauntingly.

"You tripped her," Matt said, speaking the words loudly enough for all to hear.

"What did you say?" the dead-eyed man asked.

"You gents had better move away from the table," Matt said under his breath. Both Crabtree and Matthews got up quickly, and hurried away. That left Matt as the only one remaining. He made no effort to stand.

"You heard what I said, you fish-eyed, slack-jawed son of a bitch," Matt said easily. "I said you tripped her."

The dead-eyed man smiled, though the smile didn't reach his eyes. The scar-faced man moved away.

"Mister, I'm going to tell you who I am, then I'm going to give you an opportunity to apologize," the dead-eyed man said. "My name is Vargas. Eddie Vargas. I reckon you've heard of me."

"Can't say as I have," Matt said. Matt had heard of him, but he knew that it would irritate Vargas if he thought Matt hadn't.

The smile left Vargas's face, and Matt could tell that it bothered him.

"Well now, that's too bad. You see, if you knew who I was, you wouldn't have got yourself into this fix. Now, it's too late. I'm going to have kill you, and all because you couldn't keep your nose out of my business."

"I'm sitting down," Matt said. "Are you going to

give me a chance to stand up before we open this ball?"

Vargas laughed. "Why would I do that? Do you think this is some kind of a game we're playin' here? Killin' is my business, and it don't matter to me whether you are standin' or sittin'."

Now, inexplicably, Matt smiled, and his smile surprised Vargas.

"What? What the hell are you smilin' about?"

"I'm glad you feel that way, because when I put a hole in your chest, you won't have an argument coming, will you?"

"You're goin' to put a hole in my chest? Now, just how do you plan to do that?"

"You may have noticed, that my right hand is under the table, and it's been there since this conversation started. There's a .44 in that hand, and I've just pulled the hammer back. If you make one move toward your gun, I'm going to shoot you."

"I think you're lyin'," Vargas said.

Matt's smile broadened. "Try me."

"Strawn, can you see him? Does he have a gun under the table?"

"I don't know," Strawn said. "I can't see."

"I don't think he does," Vargas said.

"Well, like the man says, try him."

Vargas stood without moving and without speaking until a twitch began in his face. For a moment, Matt thought Vargas was going to make a try for his gun, but finally Vargas lifted both hands, palms facing Matt.

"All right, all right," he said. "You win . . . this time."

"Do you have any money, Vargas?" Matt asked.

"What? What do you care whether or not I have any money?"

"You are the one who was responsible for spilling the drinks that the young lady was bringing to my friends and me. I intend for you to buy three more drinks."

"The hell you say. I ain't buyin' drinks for nobody."

"Then I'll kill you, and take what money you do have."

"That's the same as robbery."

"No, it isn't. It is recompense for value lost. Bartender, how much did those drinks cost?" Matt asked.

"Fifteen cents," the bartender replied.

"It's going to cost you half a dollar," Matt said. "Fifteen cents for the drinks, a ten-cent tip for the barkeep, and a quarter tip for the young lady."

"The hell it is."

"Then you are going to have to ask yourself, Vargas," Matt said. "Is your life worth half a dollar?"

With an angry yell of rage, Vargas slapped half a dollar onto the bar. "Here!" he shouted. "Here's the damn money! Come on, Strawn, let's get out of here."

"Huh-uh," the scar-faced man replied. "I'm not the one who tripped the girl."

"You're not comin' with me?"

"I don't think so," Strawn said. "You got yourself into this mess."

With a snarl of disgust, Vargas turned and stomped out of the saloon. Matt stood up. It was obvious then, that he had not been holding a pistol in his hand.

"I'll be damn! You was runnin' a bluff!" Crabtree said.

Matthews and Crabtree started back to the table, as did the young woman with the drinks.

"No!" Matt said. He didn't shout the word, but he did say it resolutely. He held his hands out toward the two men from one side, and the girl from the other, to keep them from advancing any farther. "You'd best stay where you are."

Suddenly Vargas burst through the batwing doors, his pistol in his hand.

"You son of a bitch!" he shouted, pulling the trigger. Matt had stepped to one side a split second before Vargas fired, or the bullet would have hit him between the eyes. Instead, it punched through the stove piping, sending up a black cloud of soot and dust.

Matt pulled his pistol then, his draw so fast that he was able to fire before Vargas could correct his mistake. Those in the saloon saw a little spray of blood come from the wound in the middle of Vargas's chest. Shocked by the sudden and unexpected turn of events, Vargas dropped his pistol, and slapped his hand over the bleeding hole.

"How did you . . . ?" he said, but that was as far as he got before he fell, face first on the floor.

Matt sensed that the scar-faced man might be

going for his gun, and he swung his pistol around bringing it to bear.

"No, no!" Strawn said, holding out his hands. "This here ain't my fight, and it ain't been from the beginnin'."

Matt looked at him for a long moment, then, with a nod of acceptance, put his pistol back in his holster.

"What's your name?" Strawn asked.

"Jensen. Matt Jensen."

"I'll be damn," he said. "You shoulda told ol' Vargas who you was. I don't think he woulda ever tried you iffen he had know'd who you was."

"I think he would have."

"Yeah, you're probably right. All right, I guess I'll just be on my way now."

"I'd rather you not leave just yet."

"What do you mean? Why not?"

"I don't want to take a chance on you being out in the street, waiting for me. I'd feel a lot better if you would just stick around until after I leave." Matt smiled. "I'll even buy you a drink."

Now the scar-faced man smiled as well.

"Mister, you've got yourself a deal."

Matt went over and put a quarter on the bar. "Give the gentleman whatever he wants," he said.

"Yes, sir, Mr. Jensen," the bartender replied.

Lorenzo, New Mexico

Rufus Draco stood at the end of the bar in the Bent Creek Saloon, nursing his whiskey. He had to nurse them because the small amount of money he had taken from the Lewis ranch was nearly gone.

"Hey, pretty girl, are you goin' to the dance Saturday?" someone asked, and looking toward the speaker, Draco saw that he was talking to one of the young women who was working the room, hustling drinks.

"You know better than that, Al," the girl answered. "Girls like me aren't welcome at the town dances."

"You could go on my arm," the cowboy named Al replied. "Nobody would dare say anything to you if you were with me."

"Ha!" one of the other patrons said. "What about that, Michelle? Al is going to be your . . . what is it in them fairy tales now, one of them fellers that's all dressed up in a metal suit?"

Michelle laughed. "You mean Al is going to be my knight in shining armor?"

"Yeah!" Al said. He stood up. "That's me, Michelle. I'll be your knight in shining armor." Al held his arms up and flexed his muscles to the laughter of Michelle and everyone else in the saloon.

"Hey," Draco said a moment later as Michelle walked past him.

"Yes, sir, do you want another drink?" Michelle asked.

"I ain't interested in another drink," Draco said. "You know what I'm interested in."

The smile left Michelle's face.

"You might find what you are looking for down the street," Michelle said. "The only thing the girls do here is serve drinks. That's all that we do," she added pointedly.

"Don't give me that. You're a whore—otherwise you wouldn't be dressed like that."

Michelle started to walk away from Draco, but he reached out and grabbed her, squeezing her arm so hard that it hurt.

"Ooww! Quit, you are hurting me!"

Al and three other cowboys, hearing Michelle call out, stood up.

"Michelle, darlin', are you all right?" Al asked.

Draco let go of her arm, then, returning the glare of the others in the saloon, started toward the door.

"Mister, don't bother to come back!" Al called out, angrily.

After Michelle got off at midnight, she went upstairs to her room, where, for a few minutes, she examined herself in the mirror. She was wearing the same thing she had worn all day, a dress that displayed so much cleavage, and so much of her legs, that she couldn't possibly wear it outside the Bent Creek Saloon. She put her fingers on a locket she was wearing around her neck; then, opening it, she looked at the picture of her three-year-old daughter.

Wanda was back in Memphis, with Michelle's parents. Michelle's parents thought that she was working as a seamstress, and because she sent them money on a regular basis, they had told her how proud they were of her.

They had no idea that she was working as a bar

girl, and though she wasn't a prostitute, she was only one step above it, having from time to time actually entertained a man. She couldn't help but feel a sense of depression when she realized that the life she had expected, the life of wife and mother, was never to be.

She was a mother, but she wasn't, nor had she ever been, a wife. It was the disgrace of being an unwed mother that had caused her to leave Memphis. With a sigh, she removed the dress with the daringly low-cut neckline and put it on her bed. This was who she was now.

Rufus Draco had gone to a saloon across the street from the Bent Creek Saloon. There, he bought a couple of whiskeys, then sat by the window and stared across the street at the Bent Creek. He watched as the last customer left, and the lights went dark.

"Mister?"

It wasn't until then that he realized the bartender had come over to his table to speak to him.

"We're closin' up now, mister. You're goin' to have to leave," the bartender said.

Draco nodded, then left the saloon. He walked down to the corner before he crossed the street, then walked in between two buildings until he reached the alley. Once he reached the alley he followed it back down to back of the Bent Creek Saloon.

As he had been sure he would, he found an open window and he climbed through it to gain entry to the saloon. Once inside, he moved cautiously and quietly through the dark, navigating by the dim patches of street-lamp light that fell in through the windows. He walked up the stairs, taking them very slowly to avoid any creaking. There were four doors off the upstairs hallway, but only one of them showed any light from inside. Draco stepped up to that door, then bent down and looked through the keyhole. He saw her take off her dress. Trying the door, he was surprised to find that it wasn't locked. He pushed it open, quietly, closed it behind him just as quietly, then stepped up behind her before she even knew he was there.

Sensing someone was behind her, Michelle turned.

"Who are you? What are you doing in—?"

That was as far as Michelle got. She suddenly felt strong hands around her neck. She tried to scream, but the crushed larynx prevented that. It also stopped her from breathing.

Half an hour later, Draco mounted his horse and rode out of town, into the dark. It had been good. It had been so good. It had also been profitable. He had taken one hundred dollars in gold coins from Michelle's room.

Chapter Four

Still following Rufus south, Matt rode into Lorenzo, New Mexico, three days after Draco had departed the town. He tied Spirit to the hitching rail in front of the Bent Creek Saloon, then stepped up onto the porch. He was surprised to see a black bow tied to the batwing doors as he pushed through.

To be in such a small town, the Bent Creek Saloon was a fairly nice-looking establishment. It sported a real mahogany bar. A mirror behind the bar was bracketed by a shelf that was filled with scores of bottles of various kinds of liquor and spirits. A sign on the wall read: GENTLEMEN, KINDLY USE THE SPITTOONS.

"What'll it be?" the bartender asked, sliding down the bar with a towel tossed across his shoulder. The fact that the towel was relatively clean spoke volumes about the class of the establishment.

"Beer," Matt replied. "Maybe something to eat?"

"We baked a ham today, and bread," the bartender replied. "You can have a ham sandwich."

"I'll take it," Matt said. "And one of these." Scooping a peeled and pickled boiled egg from the large jar that sat on the end of the bar, Matt took it, and his beer, over to a nearby table. It didn't take long for one of the bar girls to approach him.

"Hello," she said. "My name is Julie."

Julie was tall and raw-boned, and full-breasted. She had wide-set, blue-gray eyes, high cheekbones, and a mouth that was almost too full. She was wearing a black armband. Looking back toward the bartender, Matt noticed that he was wearing one as well. He either hadn't noticed it, or hadn't paid attention to it when he ordered his food and drink, but now he thought again of the black bow on the batwing doors.

"I don't think I've seen you in here before," Julie said.

"I just got into town," Matt answered. He kicked a chair out by way of invitation, then nodded at the bartender. The bartender brought him a second beer, as well as a drink for the girl, even though the girl hadn't ordered.

"He must know your brand," Matt said.

"One glass of tea is pretty much like any other glass of tea," Julie said with unusual candidness. She picked it up and held it toward Matt in a toast.

"I can't argue with that." He touched his beer to her glass.

"Did somebody die?" Matt asked.

Julie was silent for a moment.

"The reason I ask is I see that you and the bartender are both wearing black armbands. And there is a black bow on the door."

"Yes, somebody died. Well, she didn't exactly die. She was killed."

"Was it someone who worked here?"

"Yes."

"I'm sorry."

"She was a mother. She has a three-year-old daughter—that is, she had a three-year-old daughter back in Memphis."

"Do they have the person who did it in custody?"

"Nobody even knows who did it," Julie said. "Let's talk about something else, if you don't mind."

"No, I don't mind at all. I'm sorry I brought the subject up."

"It isn't your fault. We've got black bunting all over the place. It's bound to make someone curious if they just come in here for the first time. So, what brings you to Lorenzo?" Julie asked.

"I'm looking for someone."

"Aren't we all?" Julie replied. "Everyone I know is looking for someone or something. Who are you looking for?"

"I'm looking for a man named Rufus Draco."

"Rufus Draco?" Julie shook her head. "I don't think I've ever heard of him. Does he live here?"

"No, he doesn't live here, but he may have been here. He may have been passing through."

"What does he look like?"

"He's a big man, not much of a neck, bald headed with a bushy red beard."

"Did he have an ugly nose?" Julie asked.

"Yes!" Matt replied, excitedly. He often left that part out, knowing that if someone else supplied the information about the nose it would validate any claim to have seen him. "Is he here?"

"I don't know if he is still in town, but he was here," Julie said.

"Thank you, Julie."

Julie frowned. "I don't want to say anything bad about your friend, but he isn't a very nice man."

"You are quite right, he isn't a very nice man. And he is also not my friend," Matt said. "But I'm curious, why do you say that? What did he do or say to you?"

"He didn't say or do anything to me. It was the way he treated Michelle. He wanted Michelle to go to bed with him, and evidently he didn't believe her when she said that she . . . *we*," she added pointedly, "aren't whores. We are bar girls, and there is a difference."

"Where is Michelle now? Is she here? Could I talk to her?"

A look that Matt could only describe as sadness came across Julie's face.

"Michelle is the girl I was talking about. The one who was killed."

"How did it happen?"

"The story was written up in the newspaper," Julie said. "Just a minute and I'll get it for you."

Julie walked around behind the bar, leaned down to get a newspaper from underneath, then she brought it back to the table.

"Maybe you should read this," she said, handing the paper to Matt. She pointed to one of the stories on the front page.

WOMAN FOUND STRANGLED

Michelle Loomis Killed in Her Room
At the Bent Creek Saloon

Michelle Loomis, a popular and attractive young woman who plied her avocation as bar hostess at the Bent Creek Saloon, was found dead in her room Sunday morning. She had been strangled and her body brutally abused and mutilated, the details so shameless that decorum and regard for the sensitivities of our readers preclude their description here.

Miss Loomis was last seen at midnight on Saturday, the 13th instant, as she bade good-bye to her friends and coworkers before ascending the stairs to her room. She was found on Sunday morning by Miss Julie Collier, who had gone to Miss Loomis's room to check on why she had not made an appearance.

Sheriff Billings has no suspects, though he believes robbery may have been the motive since the five twenty-dollar gold pieces Miss Loomis was known to have in her possession are missing.

"It says here that there are no suspects," Matt said as he finished the article. "Has the sheriff come up with anyone since the article was written?"

Julie shook her head no. "And I don't think he is even looking."

"Why do you say that?"

"Women like us, like Michelle and me, aren't a part of what you might call decent society. If something happens to one of us, it really doesn't matter much to the 'real' people."

"That's not true," Matt replied. "I care about her, and I never even met her."

"Why would you care?" Julie asked, the expression on her face one of challenge and disbelief.

"Because of a woman named Tamara."

Julie's features softened. "You were in love with a . . . uh . . . a woman like one of us?"

"Yes," Matt said. "And like Michelle, she was killed."

Julie shook her head. "I doubt that she was killed like Michelle was. She was . . . as the paper said, mutilated."

"The paper said you were the one who found her."

"Yes."

"How was she mutilated?"

Julie looked to one side and squeezed her eyes tightly shut, then shook her head. "I don't want to talk about it."

Matt took her hand and held it. "Julie, I know it is difficult for you. But believe me, I have my own reasons for asking. I tell you what, let me ask a few questions. All you have to do is nod yes, or shake your head, no. Can you do that?"

Julie nodded.

"Were her breasts cut off?"

"Yes!" Julie said, the word exploding from her mouth in an emotional outburst that was so intense that she forgot all about nodding a response.

"I know who killed her."

"What do you mean you know who killed her?" Sheriff Billings asked.

Matt had gone to the sheriff's office to make the declaration, which was being received with skepticism.

"I have been in pursuit of a man by the name of Rufus Draco. He murdered an entire family, father, mother, and their fourteen-year-old daughter, up in Colorado," Matt said. "And like with Michelle Loomis, the killer had cut off the breasts of the mother and daughter."

Sheriff Billings squinted at Matt. "How did you know Michelle Loomis had both her titties cut off? There wasn't nothin' in the paper about it."

"I spoke with Julie Collier. She was most helpful."

"Yeah, all right, well, she would know seein' as she was the one who discovered the body. What did you say the name of the man you think done it is?"

"His name is Draco. Rufus Draco. And I know he was here, because Julie saw him."

"Wait a minute. You mean Julie knows this man?"

"No, but apparently there was a man who tried to get rough with Michelle before he was chased out by some of the other customers. They and Julie described, perfectly, the man I'm looking for."

"Rufus Draco, you say." Sheriff Billings shook his head. "Well, I'll tell you the truth, that ain't a name that rings a bell with me. As far as I know, I ain't seen no dodgers on him. This family he killed, they was up in Colorado, was they?"

"Yes."

"Well, what are you doin' down here in New Mexico? If you are Colorado lawman, you ain't got no authority down here."

"I'm not a lawman."

"A bounty hunter?"

"You might say that."

"Well, even if you find this Rufus Draco feller, and you capture him, or kill him, there ain't likely to be any reward for him down here. You'd have to take him back to Colorado to collect anything."

"My reward will be in finding him," Matt said.

"Oh?"

"Jim, Martha, and Claire Lewis, the people he murdered up in Colorado, were friends of mine."

"I see. So what you're tellin' me is, you're sort of on the vendetta trail."

"Yes."

"What is your name, mister?"

"The name is Jensen. Matt Jensen."

Now the expression on the sheriff's face turned to one of surprise. "Matt Jensen?"

"Yes."

Sheriff Billings smiled, then shook Matt's hand. "Mr. Jensen, I've heard about you, and I want you to know that it's a pleasure meetin' you. And from what I've heard about you, I wouldn't want to be in Rufus Draco's boots right now. Say, what does this Draco feller look like?"

Matt described him, leaving out one of the elements as usual.

"Does this feller have a head that sort of sits right down on his shoulders so's that you don't hardly see no neck at all?"

"Yes."

Sheriff Billings nodded. "Yes, sir, I seen that feller around. I seen him a couple of times."

"Have you seen him since Michelle was killed?"

Sheriff Billings looked surprised by the question.

"No! No, I haven't. I'll be damn! If he done it, he would be wantin' to get out of town right away, wouldn't he?"

"Yes, sir, I expect he would," Matt said.

"You know what I'm goin' to do? I'm goin' to put some paper out on that son of a bitch right now. And more 'n likely, I'll be able to get the governor to put up some money. That means if you get him down here, you'll get a reward."

"As I said, Sheriff, just finding Rufus Draco and making certain that he is brought to justice is all the reward that I need."

* * *

Matt left town, continuing his ride south. He had no real trail to follow, other than one of instinct, and now the absolute certainty that Rufus Draco had been in Lorenzo.

He had been riding for two hours, and behind him, like a line drawn across the desert floor, the darker color of hoof-churned earth stood out against the lighter, sunbaked ground. Before him, the desert stretched out in motionless waves, one right after another. As each wave was crested, another was exposed, and beyond that another still.

The ride was a symphony of sound: the jangle of the horse's bit and harness, the squeaking leather as he shifted his weight on the saddle, and the dull thud of hoofbeats.

He had filled the canteen before leaving Lorenzo, and was heading for Espanola. The distance between the two points was twenty miles, all of it through rugged New Mexico desert.

The canteen was down by a third, and he had been told that there were no dependable water holes between Lorenzo and Espanola. Already, his tongue was swollen with thirst, but he was controlling his water consumption.

Squinting at the sun, he guessed that an hour had passed, and calculated that he had about two hours to go. His canteen should last him until he got there, if he continued to maintain water discipline. He stopped his horse, mopped his brow, then reached for the canteen. He had just pulled the cork when a bullet passed so close to his ear that he heard the pop, and felt the shock. That was followed by the sound of a rifle shot.

Matt urged Spirit into an immediate gallop, heading for the nearest elevation. On the other side of the rise, he pulled his rifle, dismounted, then, on his stomach, slithered up to the crest to look back in the direction from which the shot had come.

He saw nobody.

"Damn it! I missed!" Draco said aloud. He debated the idea of trying to get off a second shot but thought better of it. Jensen was now aware that he was here. Draco's best move would be to get away while he still had the opportunity to do so.

Mounting his horse, he galloped away, still heading south.

Chapter Five

Geseta, New Mexico

Although Matt never saw who fired at him, he was absolutely certain that it was Rufus Draco. He was able to trail the shooter's horse to Geseta, but once he reached town he lost the trail because the hoofprints were mixed up with all the others on the main street of the town, which was Juarez Street.

Matt stopped in front of the Red Rose Saloon.

The piano player in the Red Rose Saloon was bad. The only thing that was worse was the piano he was playing. Though in a way, Matt thought, the fact that the piano was so badly out of tune might be a blessing in disguise. That made it difficult to be able to differentiate from a discordant note badly played, and the harsh dissonance of the sound-board.

Matt stepped up to the bar and ordered a beer.

"Ain't seen you around," the bartender said as he held a mug under the beer spigot.

"I haven't been around."

"Well, welcome to the Red Rose." The bartender set the beer in front of Matt. "My name is Earl."

"Good to meet you, Earl. My name is Matt." Matt put a nickel on the bar. "Lot of roses grown in this town?"

"Roses? No, I don't think so. Why do you ask?"

Matt started to reference his question to the name of the saloon, but with smile and a shrug of his shoulders, he just said, "No reason."

In the mirror behind the bar, Matt saw someone come into the saloon. The man moved quickly away from the door, then backed up against the wall, standing there for a long moment while he surveyed the room. The man's face was white as chalk, and his eyes were pink.

Matt had never met Emmett Shardeen, but he had heard a description of the man, and from the way this man looked and acted, he would bet that this was the gunfighter. Even as he was thinking about it, Earl bore out his musings.

"Donnie," Earl said to a young man who was sweeping the floor. "Mr. Shardeen is here. Go into the back room and get his special bottle."

"All right," Donnie said. He bent down to pick up the little pile of trash he had swept up.

"Leave the trash, go get the bottle," Earl said.

Shardeen walked over and sat at an empty table. By the time he sat down, Donnie had returned with the special bottle and handed it to Earl. Earl poured a glass, then took it and the bottle to Shardeen.

"Here you go, Mr. Shardeen," he said obsequiously.

Shardeen said nothing. He just nodded and took the glass as Earl set the bottle on the table in front of him.

"Now, Mr. Shardeen, you know that if there is anything you need, anything at all, why, you just ask me," Earl said, wiping his hands on his apron.

Again, Shardeen just nodded.

Earl returned to the bar, then, seeing that Matt's beer was nearly empty, slid down the bar to talk to him.

"Do you know who that is?"

"I heard you say his name was Shardeen."

"I reckon you have heard of him, haven't you?"

"I've heard of him."

"They say he's kilt more 'n fourteen men," Earl said, not to be denied the opportunity to continue imparting the information.

"Fourteen, huh?" Matt replied.

"Yes, sir, at least that many. And truth to tell, they don't nobody really know just how many he's kilt. He might 'a kilt a lot more 'n that."

"You don't say," Matt said. "That's quite a reputation to be carrying around."

"Yes, sir, I reckon it is," Earl said.

For the next few minutes, Matt just stared at Shardeen's reflection in the mirror. Not only had he heard of Shardeen, he had also heard that Shardeen and Rufus Draco often rode together. He wondered if Draco had met Shardeen here.

After a moment or two, Shardeen seemed to sense that he was being stared at, and he glanced up. That's when Matt's and Shardeen's eyes caught and locked in the mirror.

Shardeen stared back at the man in the mirror and was surprised to see that whoever it was returned his stare with an unblinking gaze of his own. He wasn't used to that. There were very few men who could meet his gaze without turning away, whether in revulsion from his looks, or from fear of his reputation.

Shardeen glared at the image in the mirror, giving him his "killing" expression. That glare had made men soil their pants, but it looked to him as if the man at the bar actually found the moment amusing.

"Hey, you! I'm talking to you, the son of a bitch at the bar," Shardeen shouted. His challenging words brought all conversation in the saloon to a stop and everyone looked first at Shardeen, and then at Matt.

Matt did not look around.

"You, at the bar," Shardeen said. "Quit looking at me in that mirror."

This time Matt did turn, still with a bemused expression on his face.

"Do you know who I am?" Shardeen asked.

"I heard the bartender say your name was Shardeen," Matt replied.

"Does that name mean anything to you?"

"I've heard of you," Matt said easily.

"If you've heard of me, then you know I'm not a man to be riled."

Matt smiled, and lifted his beer. "I'll try to remember not to rile you," he said.

This wasn't going the way it should, and Shardeen found the situation somewhat disquieting. Clearly, this man knew who he was . . . and clearly, he wasn't frightened. Shardeen wasn't used to that kind of reaction from people.

"Maybe you can help me," Matt said.

"Help you with what?"

"I understand that you know Rufus Draco. Is that correct?"

"Yeah, I know him. What about him?"

"I'm looking for him. I was hoping you might be able to tell me where he is."

"What do you want with Rufus Draco?" Shardeen asked.

Matt took a swallow of his beer before he responded.

"I'm going to kill him," Matt said, easily.

Shardeen laughed. "You want to kill Rufus Draco?"

"Oh, did you misunderstand what I said?" Matt

questioned. "I didn't say I wanted to kill him, I said I am *going* to kill him."

"I see. Trying to make a reputation are you?" Shardeen asked derisively. "Because if that's all you want, you could try killin' me. That would give you a reputation." He smiled disparagingly.

"Thank you for the offer," Matt said. "But I don't kill unless I have a reason for it, and so far, you haven't given me a reason to kill you. And the truth is, I've already got a reputation of sorts, and sometimes reputations just get in your way."

Shardeen snorted what might have been a laugh. "You have a reputation, do you? Who are you?"

"The name is Jensen. Matt Jensen."

The challenging, mocking expression on Shardeen's face fell away.

"Any . . ." Shardeen started. Then he cleared his throat and started again. "Anyone could say they are Matt Jensen."

"Now that you mention it, I suppose they could," Matt said. "But, since it appears that you and I aren't going to dance, let's get back to my original question. Do you have any idea where I might find Rufus Draco?"

"You're the one who has been after him, aren't you?"

"He told you that, did he?"

"No, that's just what I heard. I haven't seen him."

"I don't believe you, Shardeen. I believe you have seen him, and I think you have seen him recently."

"Are you calling me a liar?" Shardeen asked.

"Well, if you put it that way, I reckon I am," Matt said. "So, just to make certain that you, and everyone else within the sound of my voice understands, I will make it clear. You are a liar, Shardeen."

Tendons stood out on Shardeen's neck, pulsing visibly, and beads of sweat broke out on his upper lip and forehead, easily seen because of his lack of color.

"I ain't seen him, and I ain't a liar," Shardeen said after a long pause. "I, uh, wish I could continue this little conversation, but I have to go."

Shardeen left the saloon then, and looking through the window, Matt watched as the albino gunman mounted his horse and rode away.

"Well, I'll be damn," Earl said, shaking his head. "I never thought I would see anything like that. Shardeen actually ran from you."

"I wouldn't say that he ran from me."

"Then, what would you call it?"

"If we had pushed it any further, one of us would be dead now," Matt said. "And it could have been me, as easily as it could have been him. I'll be honest with you, Earl, I'm just as glad he left when he did."

Leaving Geseta, Matt continued to ride south, now following the Denver and Rio Grande Railroad tracks, as well as the Rio Grande River. The river flowed out across the scrub-covered prairie before him, shining gold in the bright afternoon sun, sometimes white where it broke over rocks, other times shimmering a deep blue-green in the swirling eddies and trapped pools.

The Rocky Mountains were a purple shadow far to the northeast of him, while the Jemez Mountains, a wild and ragged range, lay to his immediate west, dotted with aspen, pine, cottonwood, and willow. There were bare spots on the mountains in between the trees. These bare spots of rock and dirt were sometimes gray and sometimes red, but always distant and foreboding.

Late in the afternoon, a rabbit hopped up in front of Matt and bounded down the trail ahead of him. Matt stopped his horse, pulled his rifle from the saddle scabbard, looped his leg around the pommel, raised the rifle to his shoulder, rested his elbow on his knee, and squeezed the trigger. He saw a puff of fur and spray of blood fly up from the rabbit. The rabbit made a head-first somersault, then lay perfectly still.

Matt stopped for the day, and making camp under a growth of cottonwoods on the bank of the Rio Grande, he started a fire, skinned and cleaned the rabbit, then skewered it on a green willow branch and suspended it over the fire between two forked limbs. When it was golden brown he seasoned it with his dwindling supply of salt and began eating, pulling the meat away with his teeth even when it was almost too hot to hold.

After his supper, Matt stirred the fire, then lay down alongside it, using his saddle as a pillow. He stared into the coals, watching while the red sparks rode a heated column of air high up into the night sky. There, the still-glowing red and orange sparks joined the jewel-like scattering of stars.

In the distance he could hear the sound of a train whistle, a long, lonesome howl. Lying on his bed-roll, he heard the chugging sound gradually build until it was rolling out across the plains in loud, rhythmic puffs. Then he saw the beam of the headlamp, and finally the locomotive itself, rushing through the night, the escaping white steam almost luminescent, a dull orange from the cab window, then the brightly lighted windows of the passenger cars as they hurried by like a string of shining beads.

He watched the train go by, separated from it only by the river itself. Then, he saw green marker light as the caboose approached, and the red rear light as the train proceeded on its way.

Matt had a full belly, a good fire, a good horse, and a nearby supply of water. Ordinarily, such a condition would leave him content. But as long as Rufus Draco was free, Matt could not be content.

Nambe, New Mexico

Draco needed money and the only way he knew how to get money was to steal it. He rode into the town of Nambe slowly, sizing it up as he did so. The north end of the town was the American side. It was made up of no more than a dozen whipsawed lumber shacks with unpainted, splitting wood turning gray. The south end of town was the Mexican side, and it was dominated by sand-colored, adobe buildings.

Draco was thinking about robbing a store, when he saw a building with a sign over the door that identified it as the Bank of Nambe. Draco didn't think the bank had much money, but then, since he didn't have anything except for the twenty-dollar gold pieces he had stolen from the whore's room, it didn't really matter how much the bank had. Anything would have to be an improvement over his current economic status. Besides, he was certain that in a town this small, the bank would be an easy target.

Draco dismounted, then looked up and down the street. Except for a few Mexicans at the far end of the street, he saw nobody outside, everyone tending to stay inside, out of the hot sun. Walking around to the side of the bank, he looked out beyond the town. As he stood there looking around, he worked out his escape. When he left, instead of following the road out of town, he would strike due east toward an arroyo, which would give him cover from anyone who might shoot at him.

He walked his horse between the bank building and the apothecary that was next door, then tied his horse to a low scrub bush out back. This would give him a head start when he made his getaway.

Pulling his pistol and checking the loads, he walked back to the front of the bank, stood there for a moment looking toward each end of the street, and seeing that it was still clear, stepped inside.

There were only two people in the bank, the teller and a young woman were standing at the teller window. Making a quick perusal of the bank, he saw that there was a back door, which was locked by means of a cross bar.

Unobserved by the teller and the woman customer, Draco locked the door behind him, then turned the sign around in the door window so that it read CLOSED.

This was going to be easier than he'd thought. Instead of drawing his pistol, he took out his knife, the same knife that had so recently done a carving job on the whore back in Lorenzo. Stepping up behind the woman, he grabbed her, then held his knife to her throat.

The woman gasped in shock and fear.

"If you scream, I'll cut your throat," Draco said in a low, guttural growl.

"Who are you? What do you want?" the teller asked in a quivering voice.

"I want all the money this bank has," Draco said.

"What? You're robbing the bank?"

"No, I'm just making a withdrawal," Draco said sarcastically. "Now, if you don't want to see this woman's blood all over, you'll hand over the money like I said."

"We're a small bank. We don't have very much money."

"How much do you have?"

"As of this morning, we have one thousand, six hundred, and fifty-seven dollars," the teller said.

Draco smiled. "Then I'll take one thousand, six hundred, and fifty-seven dollars."

Draco watched as, with shaking hands, the teller put the money in a cloth bag.

Then, Draco, still holding on to the woman, moved to the back door.

"Bring me the money," Draco said.

The teller brought the bag, then held it out toward Draco.

In a quick, slashing motion, Draco drew the knife across the woman's throat and, as blood gushed from her wound, she fell to the floor without a sound.

"No!" the teller said, but before he could make another sound, Draco thrust his knife into the teller's heart and he, too, fell to the floor, dead.

Now, with a cloth bag full of money, Draco opened the back door, walked, unobserved, to his horse, mounted, and rode off.

It was another hour before the robbery and the two dead bodies in the bank were discovered.

Chapter Six

Tesuque, New Mexico

When Draco stepped into Max's Barbershop, he saw that the barber chair was tipped all the way back and someone was in it, his face covered by the barber cape. Whoever was under the cape was asleep, as Draco could hear him snoring.

"Where's the barber?" Draco asked loudly.

The sleeping man snorted once, jerked the cape off, sat up, and stroked his chin.

"I'm Max. I'm the barber."

"I need your services."

"What for? You ain't got a hair on your head."

"I want my beard shaved."

"Trimmed, or shaved?"

"Shaved. I want it taken completely off."

"Are you sure? That's a damn fine-looking beard, if you ask me."

"I'm not askin'."

"All right." Max stood up. "Get in the chair."

Draco got into the chair and the barber began stropping his straight razor.

"I don't know why you are wantin' to get rid of your beard," Max said. "Seeing as you have no hair on top of your head, you'd think you'd at least want some on the bottom." The barber laughed at his own joke.

"Just do it," Draco said with a growl.

"Yes, sir, whatever you say."

The barber worked up a lather in the shaving cup, then began laying it onto the beard.

"Have me 'n' you ever met before?" Max asked.

"No."

"Are you sure? There's somethin' awful familiar about you. I'm sure we've met somewhere."

"Do you always talk this much?"

"Sorry."

Max began drawing his razor across Draco's cheeks and chin as clumps of red beard fell to the floor. After a few minutes he finished, then he wiped Draco's now bare chin with a warm, damp towel.

"How's that look for you?" the barber asked with a broad smile. "Yes, sir, you don't look nothin' at all like you did when you first come in." Max chuckled. "Except for the nose, and you've had that ever since . . . uh, that is, I can't do nothin' about that you're just goin' to have to . . ." The barber stopped in midsentence, and the smile left his face, to be replaced by a look of fear.

"Uh, that'll be a quarter," he said.

"You remember now, where we met, don't you?" Draco said.

"No, no, I was mistaken. I ain't never seen you nowhere before."

"You're lying, Max. You know who I am, don't you?"

"No, I . . . I don't have any idea."

"Then why are you so nervous?"

A few minutes later, a clean-shaven Draco shut the door behind him, untied his horse, mounted, and rode out of town at a leisurely pace, even exchanging waves with a wagon driver who was just coming into town. In the barbershop he had just left, Max was once again lying in the supine position, in his chair, under the barber's cape. But this time he wasn't sleeping. He was dead, from a stab wound to the chest.

Draco knew that it would likely be an hour or more before anyone grew curious enough to check on Max, and if he rode hard, he could be ten miles south of there by then.

Thirty Four Corners

Jimmy Patterson had just carried a load of wet clothes out into the backyard, where his mother was hanging out the wash.

"Here's the next load, Ma," Jimmy said, setting the basket down. The laundry wasn't just the family wash—it was the wash for a dozen or more people. Jimmy's father had been killed in a wagon accident six months earlier, and Jimmy's mother had taken in wash in order to bring in enough money to support herself and Jimmy.

"I'm goin' to go get a job," Jimmy said.

"Jimmy, no, you have to finish school."

"Why do I need any more schoolin', Ma?" Jimmy said. "I can read, and I can cipher. What else do I need?"

"But your pa wanted you to have more of an education than he had."

"I've already got more schoolin' than Pa had," Jimmy said. "And for me to sit around and let you do all the work . . . it just isn't right, Ma. It isn't right at all."

"Where you are going to go to work?"

"I'm goin' to the Tumbling P. I know some of their cowboys, and they're all good guys."

"Oh, Jimmy . . ."

"Ma, I'm goin' to do it whether you approve or not," Jimmy said, resolutely. "But I'd feel a lot better about it if I thought I had your blessing."

Jimmy's mother stared at him for a moment, then tears came to her eyes. She opened her arms and he came to her embrace.

"Of course you have my blessing," she said. "You are a wonderful son, Jimmy, and I am so proud of you."

Tumbling P Ranch

"How old are you, boy?" Gabe Mathis asked a couple of hours later, after Jimmy showed up to ask for work.

"I'm eighteen."

"Eighteen?" The expression on Gabe's face indicated that he didn't believe Jimmy.

"Sixteen."

"I don't know, boy. That's still awfully young," Gabe said.

"I can ride and rope. I can string barbed wire. What is it you think I can't do? Mr. Mathis, you know my pa died. My ma is takin' in washin', but that don't hardly pay enough to keep us both fed. I've got to make some money."

Gabe chuckled. "All right, boy, if you're that determined, I'll give you some work."

"Thanks!" Jimmy said with a big smile.

"You can start now," Gabe said, pointing to a corral. "We're branding calves today. Go over there and make yourself useful."

"Yes, sir!" Jimmy said happily.

Santa Domingo, New Mexico

The Horse Shoe Saloon had never seen a drop of paint, and the exterior was gray, weathered wood. It looked as if a good puff of wind could blow it down and was clearly the most rundown saloon, if not the most decrepit building, in the entire town. Because Draco was flush with money he had

stolen from the bank in Nambe, he could have
gone to the finest saloon, and eaten in the finest
restaurant, but he was here, in the Horse Shoe
Saloon, for a specific purpose.

Rufus Draco bought a beer and a plate of beans
and tortillas, and sat in the corner reading a newspaper.

Barber Murdered in Tesuque

Max Dawson, the only barber in Tesuque, was
found murdered in his barber chair, having
been stabbed in the heart. Fourteen dollars
was found in his cash box, so robbery has
been ruled out. Why he was murdered is still
a mystery, and the mystery as to who
murdered him is an even greater mystery.

Max Dawson had, at one time, been a barber for
the Colorado prison system at Cannon City, Colorado. Draco had recognized him the moment
he'd seen him, though he'd thought, for a while,
that Dawson had not recognized him. When he'd
realized that Dawson had recognized him, Draco
had known that he couldn't leave him alive, for to
do so would leave him in jeopardy.

Draco turned to the next story.

Feud Continues
Now Over Twenty Years Old

The town of Thirty Four Corners in Rio
Arriba County is as divided as was this nation

during the Civil War. The adversaries in this feud are Benjamin Ross and Morgan Poindexter. Once very good friends, the two men are now bitter enemies, each with their following.

Ross owns the BR Ranch, and Poindexter owns the Tumbling P. The ranches are very successful, and Ross and Poindexter are two of the wealthiest men in the entire territory of New Mexico. It has long been hoped that there would be a reconciliation between the two men, because if these two capable men would work in concert, Thirty Four Corners could not help but benefit.

"Draco?"

Looking up, Rufus Draco saw Norman Fox.

"Hello, Fox."

"I damn near didn't recognize you. I don't know as I've ever seen you without your beard before. What are you doin' in Santa Domingo?"

"I was lookin' for you, and I thought I might find you here," Draco said. "And, as you can see, I did."

"What? You mean you were lookin' for me?"

"Yes."

Fox got a puzzled look on his face. "What are you lookin' for me for? I ain't done nothin' to you."

"I'm puttin' together a plan that can make a lot of money, and you can be a part of it."

"How much money?"

"A lot of money," Draco said without being specific. "And some money for you, right away, if you are interested."

"How soon is right away?"

"Is right now soon enough for you?"

Fox smiled. "Yeah, it is. What do you need me to do?"

"There's someone on my trail that I need you to get rid of. Until he's gone, I can't put my plan into effect."

"What do you mean by 'get rid of'?"

"I mean I want you to kill him. It ain't like you've never kilt anyone before."

"I've kilt before. What's in for me?"

"I told you, money."

"Who is on your trail?"

"A man by the name of Matt Jensen. You ever heard of him?"

"Yes, I've heard of him."

"He's the one I want you to kill," Draco said, easily.

"Like I told you, I've heard of him," Fox said. "And from what I've heard, killin' him ain't goin' to be that easy."

"Look, I ain't expectin' you to face the son of a bitch down," Draco said. "All I'm askin' you to do is kill 'im."

"If you want him dead, how come you won't do it yourself?"

"He knows me, which means I can't get close to him. You've heard of him, but like as not, he's never heard of you, so you'll have the advantage over him. He won't be on the lookout for you. It shouldn't be that hard."

"What is this plan you're talkin' about, that will make a lot of money?" Fox asked.

"Huh-uh," Draco said, shaking his head. "It's not somethin' I want to tell anyone until I'm ready."

"You want me to kill Matt Jensen for you, but you won't tell me what it's for? What about the money that you said you'd give me right away?"

"I'll give you a hunnert dollars now, and another four hunnert after you take care of him," Draco said. "And the money you make now won't come off your share of the money when I divide it up with the others."

"What others?"

"There are no others, yet, but I'll soon be putting them together for the plan."

"A hunnert dollars now, and another four hunnert dollars after I kill Jensen? That's your offer?"

"Yes."

"I want an IOU for the four hunnert."

"What? That would lead him right back to me. Why would I do that?"

"I thought you said he was after you, anyway."

"Yes, he is."

"Then, how would an IOU lead him back to you? I mean if he is already after you. And if it's goin' to be as easy for me to kill him as you say, he ain't ever goin' to see the IOU in the first place, because he'll be dead."

"Why do you want one, anyway?"

"It doesn't make any difference why I want it,"

that he wanted a refill. He pushed a coin along with it, and this time Clyde took the money.

"For the time being."

"I know what you're doin' now. You're lookin' for him."

"Yes. Tell me, Clyde, do you know Rufus Draco? Would you recognize him if you saw him?"

"I can't rightly say as I would, Matt," Clyde said. "I've sure heard of him, but I don't think I've ever seen him. What does he look like?"

"He's a big man, no neck, a nose that's been mashed flat against his face, and a bald head that looks like a cannon ball with red whiskers."

Clyde shook his head. "I can't say as I've seen anyone like that. You think maybe he come this way?"

"I think he has."

"You think he's in town?"

"I don't know, but I'm going to hang around town for a few days just to make sure. I noticed there were two hotels. Which one would you suggest?"

"Oh, I'd say the Carson Hotel," Clyde said. "It's the closest, it has a dining room, and they change the sheets on the beds at least once a week."

Matt finished his drink, wiped his mouth with the back of his hand, and started toward the door. "Thanks, Clyde," he called back.

"I hope you find the son of a bitch, Matt," Clyde replied.

"I'll find him," Matt replied confidently.

Fox said. "If you want me to do this job for you, I want an IOU from you."

"All right, all right," Draco agreed. "Get me a piece of paper and a pen."

Fox held up his finger as if signaling Draco to stay in place, and he walked over to the bar. A moment later he brought a piece of paper and a pen back to Draco.

"You make damn sure that nobody ever sees this," Draco said as he began writing.

"You got 'ny idea how to find him?"

"It won't be hard," Draco said. "Like as not, he'll be comin' through here, lookin' for me. I would suggest you just wait for him." Draco handed Fox the IOU.

"Where's my hunnert dollars?"

Draco stuck his hand in his pocket and pulled out five twenty-dollar gold coins. "Will this do?" he asked.

Fox grinned broadly. "Damn, I ain't seen this much money in more 'n a year. Yeah, this'll do. This'll do just real good."

"After it's done, I'll look you up," Draco said.

"No need, I'll look you up," Fox said.

Draco shook his head. "If things are goin' as I plan, you won't be able to find me. I'll have to find you."

When Matt Jensen arrived in Santa Domingo the next day, he kept a close watch on the corners and rooftops of buildings, checking doorways and kiosks . . . anyplace that might provide concealment for a would-be shooter. On the one hand, he was considerably south of his normal wandering, so it was less likely that anyone down here would have heard of him and be anxious to make a name for themselves. On the other hand, he was after Rufus Draco, and the fact that someone had taken a shot at him a couple of weeks ago indicated to him that Draco was well aware of him . . . and would kill him if he had the opportunity.

There were two saloons in town, the Horse Shoe, which looked as if a good puff of wind could blow it down, and the Double Down, which was considerably more substantial looking. Matt pulled up in front of the Double Down Saloon, dismounted, and went inside. He slapped a silver coin down on the bar.

The sound of the coin made the saloon keeper look around.

"Damn, if it ain't Matt Jensen," the bartender said, smiling at him.

Matt was startled to hear his name spoken, especially since he had just been thinking that he could travel around down here in relative anonymity.

"I haven't see you since . . . when? Colorado Springs, two years ago?" the bartender asked. "What are you doin' down in this neck of the woods?"

"Hello, Clyde," Matt said, dredging up the barkeep's name from somewhere deep in the recesses

of his mind. The reference to Colorado Springs helped. "I'm just wandering around."

The broadening smile on the bartender's face showed how pleased he was to be remembered by this man. Clyde poured the drink, then shoved the coin back to Jensen. "First one is on me, Matt. Old friends who drop by always get the first one free."

"Thanks," Matt said.

"I was up in Colorado visiting family a couple of weeks ago, and I heard what happened to Jim Lewis and his wife and daughter," Clyde said. "And I know that Jim was a good friend of yours."

"Yes, he was," Matt replied without elaboration.

"They ain't caught up with the sons of bitches that killed them yet, have they? Who was it? Draco, Ferguson, and Hightower, I heard. They say all three of 'em got away."

"Not Ferguson and Hightower," Matt said.

"Yeah, I heard they got away too."

Matt tossed the drink down before he repeated, "Not Ferguson and Hightower."

For a second Clyde looked as if he might argue with him. Then he knew exactly what Matt was saying.

"I'll be damn. You got Ferguson and Highto didn't you?"

"Yeah."

"I shoulda knowed that. There ain't nobod to do somethin' like that to any of your frie get away with it. So, Draco is still on the loo

Matt pushed his glass across the bar,

Chapter Seven

Standing at the far end of the bar, but close enough to have heard every word that was exchanged, was a man named Norman Fox. Fox had correctly guessed that if Matt Jensen came through town, he was unlikely to stop at the Horse Shoe, but would choose the nicer of the two saloons.

Fox watched Jensen walk out the door; then he finished the rest of his drink and left the saloon as well. Standing out on the boardwalk in front of the saloon, he saw Jensen go into the Carson Hotel. Jensen had been less than ten feet away from him, but had given him no notice at all.

Fox smiled. Jensen didn't know him, and perceived no danger from him. Killing Jensen was going to be the easiest five hundred dollars Fox had ever earned.

Tumbling P Ranch

Somewhere in the predawn darkness a calf bawled anxiously and its mother answered. In the distance, a coyote sent up its long, lonesome wail, while out in the pond, frogs thrummed their night song. The moon was a thin sliver of silver, but the night was alive with stars . . . from the very bright, shining lights, all the way down to those stars that weren't visible as individual bodies at all, but whose glow added to the luminous powder that dusted the distant sky.

Around the milling shapes of shadows that made up the small herd rode three cowboys. One was much younger than the other two. Known as "nighthawks," their job was to keep watch over the herd during the night.

The night had been long, and in order to stay awake, the three young men were engaged in conversation.

"What do you mean? Are you trying to tell me you've never even *had* yourself a woman?" one of the older cowboys asked the youngest of the three.

Jimmy Patterson cleared his throat in embarrassment. "I told Mr. Mathis and Mr. Poindexter that I was sixteen, but truth is, I'm only fourteen. I ain't never give it that much thought."

"Why, boy, it's never too early to start. Don't you know you can never be a man until you go upstairs at Diamond Dina's Pleasure Palace?"'

"With Diamond Dina," the other added.

"With . . . with Diamond Dina?" Jimmy asked in

a plaintive voice that was decidedly devoid of any enthusiasm over the prospect.

"Hell yes, with Diamond Dina. Diamond Dina owns the place. That means ever'body who comes in there has to go with her first."

"I've seen Diamond Dina. She's a very big woman," Jimmy said. "She'd make two of me."

"Oh, don't let that worry you, Jimmy. Big women is the best. Ain't they, Jake?"

"Damn right they are," Jake said. "And here's the thing, Jimmy. First time with Diamond Dina is free. She loves breakin' 'em in. What's that she's always sayin', Roy?"

"She says, 'give me a boy, and I'll give you back a man,'" Roy said.

"Tell you what," Jake said. "Why don't we ride into Thirty Four Corners first thing after we get off work in the mornin'? It'll be daytime and there won't hardly be nobody else there, so we can have our pick."

"All except Jimmy," Roy insisted. "He don't get a pick. He has to go upstairs with Diamond Dina."

"Well, yeah, but then after that, he can go with anyone he wants to," Jake said.

"'Cept whoever me 'n' you has already took for our ownselves."

The calf's call for his mother came again, this time with more insistence. The mother's answer had a degree of anxiousness to it.

"Sounds like one of 'em's wandered off," Jimmy said. "Maybe I'd better go find it."

"Hell, why bother? It'll find its own way back."

"I don't mind," Jimmy said, slapping his legs against the side of his horse and riding off, disappearing in the darkness.

Roy laughed, a low, knowing, laugh. "If you ask me, Jimmy's just anxious to get away from us before we talk him into actually going upstairs with Dina."

"Who knows?" Jake teased. "Maybe we can convince him she is just what he needs."

"I'd hate to see the fella that really needs Diamond Dina," Roy said. Both cowboys laughed at their joke.

"Say, Roy, maybe we'd better ride out there with him," Jake suggested.

"Why is that?"

"What if it's some BR men?"

"BR men? What would they be doin' over here?"

"Well, there ain't nobody that don't know we've hired him on. I wouldn't put it past a bunch of those yahoos to come over here and pull something on him," Jake said.

"You mean like settin' him up with Diamond Dina?" Roy replied with a chuckle.

"Now, come on, you know we're just bringin' the boy on, makin' a man out of him," Jake said. "Come thirty or forty years from now, why, he'll be tellin' that story to anyone who will listen."

"I reckon he will, at that. And you're right, I don't feel all that good about Jimmy bein' out there all by hisself."

"Let's go find him," Jake said.

"Jimmy?" Roy called. "Jimmy, are you out there?"

"Yeah?" Jimmy answered, the sound of his voice coming back through the night. "What do you want?"

"Diamond Dina is here, Jimmy. She said she'd do you for free, right here, if you'll let us watch," Jake called.

"What?" Jimmy replied, his voice going up two octaves.

Jake and Roy laughed out loud.

Santa Domingo

When Matt reached his room, he lit a lantern, then had a look around. The room had one high-sprung, cast-iron bed, a chest, and a small table with a pitcher and basin. On the wall was a neatly lettered sign that read: DO NOT SPIT ON THE FLOOR. GENTLEMEN, PLEASE REMOVE SPURS WHILE IN BED.

Matt opened the window and saw that his room looked out over the street. He heard the train whistle blow and looked down toward the depot just in time to see a train pulling away.

It was a busy night. In addition to the clanging bell and puffing steam of the departing locomotive, there was a full cacophony of sound emanating from the street below. The voices of scores of animated conversations spilled out through the open windows and doors of the town's buildings and somewhere someone was singing. He heard a gunshot, but knew, instinctively, that it wasn't a shot fired in anger. That was borne out by the fact that the shot was followed by a woman's high-pitched scream, not of fear, but of excitement, then a man's deep-voiced laughter.

Matt blew out his lantern and went to bed.

"Where are you tonight, Rufus Draco?" Matt asked, saying the words aloud, but very quietly.

At one o'clock in the morning, Fox walked into the lobby of the Carson Hotel. As he'd expected, there was nobody sitting in the lobby at this hour. And as he had hoped, the night clerk at the front desk was sitting in a chair with his arms folded across his chest, and the chair tipped back against the wall. His eyes were closed and, though he wasn't snoring, he was breathing loudly, and rhythmically, with his lips flapping as he exhaled.

Fox turned the registration book around and ran his finger down the list of guests until he found the name he was looking for.

M. Jensen . . . . . Room 14

There was a board hanging on the wall just behind the desk. There were eighteen nails on the wall, commensurate with the number of rooms in the hotel, and just above each nail was a number. Keys were hanging from the nails, two keys from the rooms that were unoccupied, and one key, the house key, from those rooms that were occupied.

Stretching across the counter, Fox removed the house key from the nail that was numbered fourteen.

Taking one last look across the desk to make certain the clerk was still asleep, Fox started toward the stairs.

The second-floor corridor was long and narrow, and as he set foot on the red carpet runner, he could hear the quiet hiss of the gas lanterns, two on either side of the hallway. Room fourteen was the third room down, on the right. Pulling his pistol, he started toward it.

Matt was sound asleep, enjoying his second night in an actual bed in the last week. Then, in some way, an awareness that he was in danger cut through the layers of slumber as quickly as a knife through butter. If anyone had asked him how he knew he was in peril Matt would not be able to answer, but he knew, with every fiber of his being, that he was in jeopardy.

This preternatural cognizance caused the sleep to fall away and Matt, with reflexes born of years of living on the edge, rolled off the bed just as a gun boomed in the doorway of his room. The bullet slammed into the headboard of the bed where, but a second earlier, Matt had been sleeping.

Even as Matt was rolling off the bed, he was reaching for the pistol under his pillow. Now the advantage was his. The man who had attempted to kill him was temporarily blinded by the muzzle flash of his own shot and he could see nothing in the darkness of Matt's room. That same muzzle flash, however, had illuminated the assailant for Matt and he quickly aimed his pistol at the dark hulk in the doorway, closed his eyes against his own muzzle flash, and squeezed the trigger. The gun bucked in his hand as the roar filled the room.

In Santa Domingo, as in all the other Western towns of similar social structure, drunken patrons of the saloons often gave vent to high-spirited emotions with a celebratory and mostly harmless discharge of pistols. As a result of such a practice, the citizens of such towns had learned to recognize the difference in sound between shots fired in play and shots that were fired in anger.

The sound of these two shots, right on top of each other as they were, left no doubt in anyone's mind as to their character. Everyone within hearing distance knew that these were shots fired in anger. Some were curious, some were frightened, but all knew the likely outcome of the encounter, and a few of the more pious breathed little prayers as they realized that someone had just died.

Matt heard a groaning sound, then the heavy thump of a falling body.

"What is it? What's happening?" a voice called. All up and down the hallway of the hotel, doors opened as patrons, dressed in nightgowns and pajamas, peered out of their rooms in curiosity, their faces glowing in the greenish tint of the light of the hissing gas lamps.

Several of them, seeing a man lying on the floor, ventured toward him so that by the time Matt had pulled on his trousers and stepped into the door of his room, there were four of five gathered around the body.

"What were you two fighting about?" one of the hotel guests asked.

"Your guess is as good as mine," Matt said. "I've never seen him before."

"You've never seen him before, but you killed him?" another asked.

"What the hell, mister?" another guest said. "What was he supposed to do? This feller stepped up to his door and started shootin'."

"You saw it?" Matt asked.

"I did. I was just about to leave my room when I seen this feller standin' just outside your room with a gun in his hand. I stepped back into my room, but I kept the door open a crack so's I could see. I seen the whole thing."

"You'll be willing to tell the sheriff that?"

"Yes, sir, I'll tell him that," the man said.

"Does anyone know him?" Matt asked.

"You mean you don't?"

"I've never seen him before," Matt replied, but even as he responded to the question, he had a sudden memory of where he had seen him. He had seen him standing at the other end of the bar in the Double Down Saloon,

"His name is Fox," someone said. "Norman Fox. Does that ring a bell with you?"

Matt shook his head. "Nope."

"Well then, what for did he come for you like he done?"

"I don't have the slightest idea."

"What are you going to do about him now?" the hotel patron asked.

"What do you mean what am I going to do about him?" Matt asked. "I don't plan to do anything about him."

"Well, good lord, man, you don't plan to just leave him lying out here in the hall, do you?"

"I don't see as how his lying out here in the hall can be a problem to anyone. He's dead," Matt said.

"That's just it. He's dead. Nobody is goin' to be able to sleep with a dead man lyin' out here in the hall."

"If you want him out of here, take him out of here," Matt suggested.

"The hell you say. I didn't kill him."

"He's got a point there, mister," one of the others said. "You killed him. The least you can do is get rid of him."

"I didn't invite him up here."

"Nevertheless, he's here, and he's dead. And since you are the one who killed him, it would seem to me that's also your responsibility to get rid of him."

"All right, if it means that much to you," Matt

said. Leaning down, he picked the body up, and threw it over his shoulder.

"That's more like it," the complaining man said. "I think we will all appreciate that."

"No problem," Matt replied. Matt started toward the back of the hall, at the end opposite the stairway.

"Wait a minute, where are you goin'?" someone asked.

"What are you doing with him? Where are you going?" another called. "The stairway is at the other end."

When Matt reached the end of the hall, he raised the window that opened out onto the alley.

"Hey! What are you . . . ?"

That was as far as the questioner got, because, without any further hesitation, Matt pushed Norman Fox's body through the window. It fell with a crash to the alley below. That done, he lowered the window, then, brushing his hands as if having just completed an onerous task, returned to his own room.

"That should take care of it," Matt said. "Sleep well, everyone."

"That was no way to handle that!" the complaining man said. "I've a good mind to . . ."

"Go back to bed," Matt said.

"What?" the man sputtered. "See here, you can't . . ."

"I said go to bed."

"I will not be ordered around like some . . ."

"You can go to bed now, or you can join Mr. Fox down in the alley," Matt said. "Which will it be?"

Matt's response was not spoken in the form of a threat. His voice was quiet and well modulated, the words as devoid of anger as if he were inquiring of the time. And yet it was that cold calmness of his response, a declaration of intent, rather than a threat, that caused his antagonist to rethink his complaint.

The man opened his mouth as if to speak, but he said nothing. Then, defeated, and obviously frightened of Matt Jensen, he turned and moved quickly and quietly back to his room.

"I would suggest that all of you go back to bed," Matt said. "The show is over."

Chapter Eight

Thirty Four Corners—Diamond Dina's Pleasure Palace

In keeping with the plans they had made the night before, Jake, Roy, and Jimmy rode into town the next morning after their nighthawk duty.

"Here it is," Jake said, as they approached a white frame, two-story house. "Diamond Dina's Pleasure Palace." This was enemy territory but, they reasoned, worth the risk.

"You all go on," Jimmy said. "I've got some things to buy at the store."

"No, you don't," Roy said. "You are goin' to get broke in today."

"Look at 'im," Jake said with a little laugh. "Why, he's as skittish as an unbroken colt."

"You're goin' to have to do it sometime," Roy said. "Now is as good a time as any."

Reluctantly, Jimmy dismounted and tied his horse off with the others. Jake trumped up the front steps and banged on the door.

"Dina!" he called. "Dina, you got some horny cowboys standin' out here on the front porch!"

A moment later the front door opened and a large woman, wearing a bright red sequined dress that exposed the creamy white tops of melon-sized breasts opened the door. She was holding a long-stemmed cigarette holder in her hand, and smoke was curling up from the factory-rolled cigarette inside.

"Well, you boys come on in here then," she said. "We can't be leaving horny cowboys out in the heat now, can we?"

"Let's go, boys!" Jake said happily.

"My, oh my, who is this young man?" Dina asked, smiling broadly at Jimmy.

"He's someone we brung for you to break in," Roy said.

"Like you say, we're goin' to give you a boy, we want you to give us back a man."

"Oh? Are you a virgin, honey?" Dina asked.

"Yes, ma'am," Jimmy said.

"Then you come on upstairs with me."

"That's all right. I'll just wait down here," Jimmy said, nervously.

"No, you ain't," Jake said. "It's our duty to get you broke in, and it's your duty to get broke in. Now you go on upstairs with Dina, like she said."

With a look of despair, Jimmy followed her upstairs.

* * *

"How old are you, boy?" Diamond Dina asked, once they reached her room. Leaning back against the wall she studied him through a long stream of just-exhaled cigarette smoke.

Jimmy was sitting in a wooden chair on the opposite side of the room. He had gone directly to the chair as soon as they came up, and he hadn't moved.

"I'm eighteen," Jimmy said, hesitantly.

"Don't lie to me, boy," Dina said. "How old are you?"

"Sixt . . . uh," Jimmy started. Then, with a sigh, he corrected himself to tell the truth. "I'm fourteen."

"Fourteen," Dina said. She flicked the ash from the end of her cigarette into a fruit jar lid that was filled with the crushed residue of earlier cigarettes. The jar lid lay on the windowsill.

"Yes, ma'am," Jimmy said.

"Jake and Roy put you up to this, didn't they?"

"Yes, ma'am," Jimmy repeated.

Dina sighed, then walked over and ran her hand through Jimmy's hair. Jimmy cringed, and Dina laughed.

"Don't be frightened, honey. I don't seduce fourteen-year-old boys," she said.

"I . . . I'm not frightened."

"Good. Come back five or six years from now."

"Miss Dina?"

"Yes?"

"Don't tell Jake and Roy we didn't do nothin'. They might make me go somewhere else."

Dina laughed. "Tell you what, hon, you just hang around here for half an hour or so. We'll take good care of Jake and Roy. Do you play chess?"

"I ain't never played it before."

"Would you like to learn? I can teach you."

Jimmy smiled. "Yes, ma'am, I'd like that."

"The object is to take the king," she said as she started laying out the chessboard.

Half an hour later Dina and Jimmy started down the stairs. "Remember," she whispered to him, "you just follow my lead."

"Yes, ma'am."

Jake and Roy were sitting in the parlor, talking to a couple of the girls who weren't engaged at the moment. They looked up when they saw Jimmy and Dina come in.

"Well," Jake said, "how was it?"

"It was . . . ," Jimmy started to say, but Jake interrupted him.

"Don't be 'shamed if nothin' . . . uh . . . happened," Jake said. "It's near 'bout always like that for your first time in the saddle. You got to be broke in, you see and . . ."

"What do you mean if nothing happened?" Dina asked. "This young man has nothing to be ashamed of."

Jake and Roy looked at Dina with an expression of confusion on their faces.

"Wait a minute," Roy said. "Are you telling me that something did happen?"

"Whoowee, honey, that's exactly what I'm telling you." Dina fanned her face. "Don't let this young man's age fool you. Why, he's much more of man than either of you are, and I should know."

The other women in the parlor laughed.

"Honey, you come back anytime," Dina said, putting her hand on Jimmy's cheek.

"I will, and thank you, ma'am," Jimmy said. Smiling, Jimmy looked at the two cowboys who had brought him into town. "What do we do now?" he asked.

"We need to get back to the ranch," Roy said. "We can't be lollygagging around here all day."

Santa Domingo

Matt was awakened the next morning by a series of loud popping noises, which intruded into what had been a sound sleep. Startled, he sat straight up in bed, slipped his pistol from the holster that hung from the bedpost, then got to his feet, ready for any intrusion.

Moving over to the window, he pulled the curtain to one side and cautiously looked down on the street. He laughed when he saw the source of the popping sounds. Two young boys were running up and down the street, setting off strings of firecrackers.

Fifteen minutes later Matt was eating a sandwich of bacon and biscuit when the sheriff came into the dining room.

"My deputy tells me you had a busy night," the sheriff said.

"Busier than I planned," Matt replied.

"Let me ask you something, Mr. Jensen. Are you in a habit of throwing people out of upstairs windows?"

"I don't make a habit of it," Matt said. "But the others on my floor seemed to be uncomfortable with the intruder spending the rest of the night on the floor, so under the circumstances, it seemed like the logical thing to do. I didn't think he would mind. Since you didn't come to arrest me in the middle of the night, I take it that you are all right with what happened."

"Oh, I am indeed," the sheriff said. "There were enough witnesses to the circumstances that the judge had no difficulty in declaring it a justifiable homicide. Besides, I don't think anyone is going to particularly miss Mr. Fox. He wasn't exactly what you would call a leading citizen of our community."

"Good," Matt said. "I wouldn't want that getting in the way of what I have to do."

"By 'have to do,' you are talking about your search for Rufus Draco?"

"Yes! You know about that do you?"

"I know what he did to that family up in Colorado. And Sheriff Billings sent me a telegram about him. He's wanted in New Mexico now, too, for killing that whore back in Lorenzo."

"She wasn't a whore," Matt said.

"You knew her?" the sheriff asked in surprise.

"No, but I met her friends. She wasn't a whore."

"I'm sorry, I didn't mean anything by it. But I wish you luck in your search, and I hope you find him."

"I will find him," Matt said, resolutely.

"This might help," the sheriff said, pulling an envelope from his pocket.

"What is that?"

"If you had taken the time to look through Fox's pockets before you threw him through the window last night, you would have found this yourself."

The sheriff handed Matt a folded piece of paper. Opening it, Matt read the note.

I will pay you $400 dollars more when Matt Jensen is kilt.

Rufus Draco

"I'll be damn, Fox didn't just happen to choose my room, did he?" Matt asked.

"It doesn't appear so."

"It says four hundred dollars more," Matt said.

"Yes. We found ninety dollars in his pocket. Eighty dollars of it is in twenty-dollar gold pieces."

"Twenty-dollar gold pieces?"

"Which, according to the information I got from the sheriff back in Lorenzo, is what was stolen from the whor . . . uh, the young woman who was murdered. That makes me wonder if Fox might not have been the one who killed her."

"No, Fox didn't do it," Matt said, resolutely. "Not the way Michelle's body was left."

"But the gold twenty-dollar pieces," the sheriff said.

Matt thumped the note. "It says here that Draco was going to pay four hundred dollars *more.* I think Draco gave Fox the gold coins as part of the payment, the gold coins that he took from Michelle's room after he killed her. No, he didn't just kill her—the son of a bitch butchered her."

"You may be right," the sheriff said. "Fox didn't just happen to drop in on you, last night. He was trying to earn another four hundred dollars."

"Even without the note, I figured it had to be something like that," Matt said. "I had never met him before, so there was no other reason for him to come after me as he did."

"Too bad you had to kill him. He might have been able to give you a little information."

"It would have been helpful, that is true. But it doesn't matter. I'm going to find the son of a bitch."

"I believe you will."

"By the way, I haven't been keeping up with the date, is it the Fourth of July, or something?"

"The Fourth of July? No, that's nearly a month away. Why would you ask a thing like that?"

"I saw a couple of boys setting of firecrackers this morning."

The sheriff chuckled. "Oh, that would be Bryan James and Wes Pollard. I've already talked to them about disturbing the citizens with their shenanigans. It turns out that they have the same birthday, so they decided to make a little noise so that everyone would know it."

"Harmless enough, I guess."

"By the way, before you leave town, you might want to go down and take a look at the display that is in front of the hardware store," the sheriff said.

"What display? What are you talking about?"

"You'll see it as soon as you get there," the sheriff promised as he left Matt's table.

Finishing his biscuit, Matt left the hotel dining room and walked down toward the hardware store. There were several people there, men, women, and children, standing around the front porch looking at whatever it was the sheriff had said was on display.

When Matt got closer, he saw what it was. It was a dead man in a coffin, the coffin standing up in front of a hardware store. His arm was crossed in front of him, and a pistol was clutched in his hand. There was a sign posted above the coffin.

NORMAN FOX
shot dead while attempting to murder
Matt Jensen

Matt had not gotten that close of a look at him last night, so he studied him more closely this morning, just to make certain that he hadn't ever run across him under some other name.

Matt was pretty good at remembering faces, even a face that was now drawn of features and drained of blood by death.

"Hey!" someone said. "You're Matt Jensen, aren't you?"

Matt didn't answer.

"You are, I seen you when you was in the saloon last night. Clyde said that's who you was."

"Yes, I'm Jensen."

"Hey, Arnie!" the man shouted to someone was setting up a camera on a tripod, preparing to taking a photograph of the body of Norman Fox. "This here is Matt Jensen! He's the one that kilt Fox last night. Why don't you get his picture?"

"Mr. Jensen, would you consent to having your picture taken?" Arnie asked.

"I'd rather not," Matt replied.

"Come on, Jensen," the man who had spotted him first said. "Get up here and stand alongside ol' Norm's body, and have your picture took with him." The man chuckled. "I knew Norm. I think he'd actually get a kick out of that."

Matt had turned to walk away, but when he heard the man say that he knew Fox, he stopped.

"You knew Fox?"

"Yeah, I knew 'im."

"How well did you know him?"

"Well, we wasn't what you would actual call friends," the man said, growing a little unsure now, under Matt's more intense questioning. "I mean I just know'd 'im is all."

"Do you also know a man by the name of Rufus Draco?"

"I've heard of him, but I ain't never met him.

What about havin' your picture took? If you won't have it took with Norm, maybe you'd have it took with me."

"Hell, Lenny, if Matt Jensen does get his picture took, I might want to buy a copy of it from Arnie. But I sure as hell don't want your ugly mug standin' alongside him," someone from the crowd said, and the others laughed.

Matt had no desire to have his picture taken, certainly not standing beside the corpse of the man he had killed last night. On the other hand, he did want to spend a little more time in town, asking a few questions and he was afraid that if he came across as too aloof even to have his picture taken, he would get very little cooperation from anyone.

Then he saw Bryan James and Wes Pollard, the two boys who were celebrating their birthday, standing out toward the edge of the gathering. Matt smiled.

"I'll have my picture taken if those two young men will have theirs taken with me."

"What? You mean you want our picture took with you?" one of the boys asked. Although Matt knew their names, he didn't know which was which.

"Why not?" Matt said. "I understand today is Bryan James's and Wes Pollard's birthday. I'm not wrong, am I?"

"Whoa, Bryan! He knows who we are!" Wes said.

"Come on," Bryan said. "Let's get our picture took with him!"

The two boys hurried to stand beside Matt, one

on either side of him, and Arnie, who had been setting his camera up to photograph the corpse of Norman Fox, now repositioned it so he could get a picture of Matt, posing with the two boys.

Matt stood until the photograph was taken.

"Now, Mr. Jensen, if you don't mind, could I have a photograph of you, alone?"

"I want one, Arnie!" someone shouted.

"You're going to sell them, aren't you?"

"Yes, sir, but I would be glad to share any money I might make with you," Arnie said.

"That's not necessary. But what I do want you to do is to make certain that each of the two boys get a copy of the photograph you just took."

"Yes, sir," Arnie said with a broad smile. "I'll be glad to do that."

Chapter Nine

Springfield, Illinois

On what had been the last day of school two weeks earlier, Sylvia Poindexter's students all came up to her desk to tell her good-bye. Some brought her an apple; others brought her letters they had written to her. One such letter read:

> *Dear Miss Poindexter,*
>   *You are my favorite teacher. I'm sorry you won't be here next year.*
>
> > *Your friend,*
> > *Tony*

All the other letters were similar, all of them in response to her earlier announcement that this would be her last year. The reason this would be her last year was because a few weeks ago she had received a letter from her father.

Sylvia,

I know that you didn't want to leave home ten years ago when I sent you away after your mother died. I thought I was doing the right thing by you then, and I hope that is the case. Your brother and I have missed you terribly, and now that you are a grown woman, I think it is time for you to come back home.

Of course, the very fact that you are grown now means that I can only ask you to come back. I can't order you. The decision is yours, and while I have no right to hope that you will return, please know that, with all my heart, I want you to do so.

Your loving father

Sylvia had thought about writing her father and telling him that she had no intention of returning. After all these years, she was still upset with him for insisting that she leave the only home she had ever known.

But now, she knew another home. Her aunt and uncle had made a welcome and loving home for her. She had met friends, and had a good job teaching. What tilted her decision, though, was something that had happened just before school was out. H. M. Hood, the man that she was in love with, the man she had thought she was going to marry, had suddenly and unexpectedly married another woman.

Sylvia was aware of the circumstances surrounding the marriage of her mother and father, and she could not help but believe that this was karma coming to claim, if not her father, then at least her father's daughter. She bore the pain and humiliation of what Hood had done, and decided that she would respond to her father's request. She would go to New Mexico.

Sylvia hired a surrey to move her and her luggage from the apartment she had lived in for the last two years. The surrey rolled past the Abraham Lincoln home at Eighth and Jackson, recently deeded to the state of Illinois by Robert Lincoln, and already a popular destination for visitors. Sylvia had visited the home and, though she was looking forward to returning to New Mexico, she knew there was much about Springfield that she would miss.

Rio Grande River, New Mexico

That night, on the bank of the Rio Grande, several miles south of Espanola, a man calling himself Lucien Bodine walked over to the flickering campfire and, using his hat as a heat pad, picked up the blue-steel coffeepot and poured a black stream into his tin cup. Setting the pot back down, he blew on the coffee for a moment, then sucked a swallow in between extended lips, before turning to the others. There were five men gathered around him.

"All right now, here's our operation," Bodine began. "The BR and the Tumblin' P have been feudin' with one another for over twenty years now. Thirty Four Corners is split right down the middle, with half the town supportin' the BR Ranch, and half the town supportin' the Tumblin' P. And because of that, it's been pretty much kept under control, but make no mistake, they hate each other. And it won't take too much to get 'em into an actual shootin' war. And that's what we want."

"We want a shootin' war between the two ranches?" a man named Meeker asked.

"Yes. Once a shootin' war starts, they're goin' to be so concerned with each other that they won't be payin' any attention to us. That'll leave us free to take advantage of the situation. All we have to do is get 'em started. Then, when they're busy killin' off one another, we'll start stealin' 'em blind."

"How do we get 'em started?" one of the men asked.

The questioner was Sam Strawn. Strawn had killed at least twelve men in face-to-face gunfights, and though he had managed in every case to convince the law that it was a matter of self-defense, he had, in more than one case, bullied his victims into drawing on him.

"I'll be sending two men into town tomorrow to get things stirred up."

"Which ones of us are you going to send?" a man named Dooley asked.

"I'm not sending any of you. I've got two other men for that. And, once they take care of their business, we'll be ready to put the rest of the plan into operation. Sam, you'll take Meeker and Wallace with you, and go to work for Poindexter at the

Tumbling P. I'll take Massey and Dooley with me to join up with Ross at the BR Ranch."

"What about the two men you were just talkin' about? I mean the two that's goin' to stir things up?" Strawn asked. "Are you goin' to divide them up? Or will they both go to the same ranch?"

"No, they won't go to either ranch. For the time being I'm goin' to keep them separated from the rest of us," Bodine explained. "We are the only ones who will actually join up with the two ranches."

"Wait a minute," Dooley asked. "Didn't you just say that you plan to start a shootin' war between the BR and the Tumblin' P?"

"Yes, that is exactly what I plan."

"But, we're goin' to split up with half of us goin' to the BR and half goin' to the Tumblin' P?"

"Yes."

"Well now, that don't make no sense at all, Bodine. If we are goin' to be on opposite sides when the shootin' starts, why, we'll be fightin' agin' each other."

Bodine ran his hand back over the top of his head and sighed. "Will somebody explain this to Dooley? I thought I had already explained it, but evidently I didn't get through to him."

"It's like this," Strawn started, but Bodine stopped him.

"No, Sam, I know you understand, 'cause you 'n' me have talked about this. I want one of the others to explain it to him. If Dooley don't understand what we're a-doin', maybe someone else don't neither."

"I'll explain it," Wallace said. "It's like this,

Dooley. We ain't actually goin' to be a-fightin' agin' each other. Like Bodine says, the whole plan is to keep the two ranches feudin' agin' each other. And, one way we'll be doin' that is by stealin' cattle. Strawn, and me 'n' Meeker 'n' Bodine will be stealin' cattle from the Tumbling P. Massey will be stealin' cattle from the BR.

"Both ranchers will think it's the other rancher that's stealin' from 'em. That'll keep the feud goin', and we'll be buildin' up a pretty good size herd for ourselves."

"We can more'n likely gather us up a herd of a thousand head or more before anyone catches on to what we're doin'," Bodine said, finishing the explanation. "And by that time, we'll be well out of here."

"How much money would that be?" Meeker asked.

"Well, cattle is bringin' twenty-five dollars a head, right now. So that would be twenty-five thousand dollars."

"Damn!" Meeker said. "That's a lot of money!"

"Yes, it is, and all we got to do is keep this here feud a-goin'," Bodine said.

Somewhere in Kansas

The west-bound Southern Pacific train, on which Sylvia Poindexter was a passenger, made a midnight stop for water. Sylvia was in the top berth of the Pullman car, and only vaguely aware that the stop had been made. She was too comfortable and too tired from all the packing and preparation for her trip out west to pay too much attention to it. Tired as she was, though, she had been unable to sleep.

Rolling over in bed, she pulled the covers up and listened to the bumping sounds from outside as the fireman lowered the spout from the track-side water tower and began squirting water down into the tank. Sylvia thought of him standing out there in the middle of the night. By contrast it made her own condition, snuggled down in her berth, seem all the more comfortable, but not even that helped sleep come.

She thought of the last night before she'd left Springfield. Her erstwhile fiancé, H. M. Hood, had come to call on her.

"It isn't necessary for you to run away," Hood had told her. *"There is no need for that. Nothing has to change between us."*

"Nothing has to change? What are you talking about? Everything has changed! You are married!" Sylvia said.

"Yes, to the daughter of the head of the firm," Hood replied. *"Don't you see? It was a business decision. This way, I will soon become a partner. Love had nothing to do with it. You are the one I love, and nothing has changed."*

"You expect me to be what? Your mistress?"

"Mistress is such a harsh word," Hood said. *"Couldn't we have some sort of loving arrangement, without using the term mistress?"*

"No, H.M.," Sylvia said, resolutely. *"No, we cannot."*

The very idea that Hood had come to her with such a proposal still irritated her to no end. But, there was a positive side to it. She was so incensed by his thoughtless and selfish offer, that she no longer felt a sense of loss over his departure. On the contrary, she felt an enormous sense of relief, and knew now, more than ever, that coming to New Mexico was a good thing.

"Thank you, Papa, for sending for me," she murmured, and, as the train got under way again, she finally drifted off to sleep.

Chapter Ten

It was late afternoon of the next day when Matt Jensen approached the little town. From this perspective, and at this distance, the settlement looked little more inviting than any other group of the brown hummocks and hills common to this country. Matt stopped on a ridge and looked down at the town as he removed his canteen from the saddle pommel. He took a swallow, recorked the canteen, then put it back.

"Well now, Spirit, I do believe that this is a town we haven't seen before," Matt said. "What do you say we go have a look?"

Matt often talked to his horse, because on his long and lonely rides he sometimes needed to hear a human voice, even if it was his own. And, he reasoned, talking to his horse was better than talking to himself.

Slapping his legs against Spirit's sides, he headed the animal down the long slope of the ridge, wondering what town this was.

A small sign just on the edge of town answered the question for him.

SANTA ANA
Population 316
Come grow with us.

The weathered board and faded letters of the sign indicated that it had been there for some time, erected when there had still been some hope for the town's future. Matt doubted that there were a hundred and sixteen residents in the town today, and, despite the optimistic tone of the sign, he doubted if the town was still growing.

There were no more than three or four buildings of wooden construction; all the others were sod buildings, rising from a ground of the same color. The buildings straggled along for not much more than one hundred yards. Then, just as abruptly as the town started, it quit, and the prairie began again.

Matt knew about such towns—he had been in hundreds of them over the last several years. He knew that in the spring the street would be a muddy mire, worked by the horses' hooves and mixed with their droppings to become a stinking, sucking pool of ooze. In the winter it would be frozen solid, while in the summer it would bake as hard as rock.

It was summer now, and the sun was yellow and hot.

The buildings were weathered and the painted

signs on the front of the edifices were worn and hard to read. A wagon was backed up to the general store and a couple of men were listlessly unloading it. They looked over at Matt, curious as to who he was and what brought him to town, though neither of them was ambitious enough to speak to him.

Matt dismounted in front of a saloon that, according to the sign in front, called itself simply: SALOON. He stepped up onto the boardwalk in front of the establishment, where he made use of a brush shoe-scraper that had been nailed to the boardwalk just for that purpose. He stood for a moment outside the batwing doors, looking into the shadowed interior of the saloon.

Four or five rough-looking and unkempt men were standing at the bar when Matt went in. There was not a breath of air inside, and the men at the bar were sweating in their drinks and wiping their faces with bandanas.

Matt was not surprised to see that the bar was made of unpainted, rip-sawed lumber. Its only concession to decorum was to place towels in rings spaced about five feet apart on the customer side of the bar. But the towels looked as if they had not been changed in months, if ever, so their very filth negated the effect of having them there.

The bartender was washing glasses. Seeing Matt step up to the bar, he set down cloth and glass, and moved toward him.

"What'll you have?"

"Whiskey," Matt replied.

Reaching behind him, the bartender took down a bottle, pulled the cork, and poured the amber liquid into one of the glasses he had just washed.

"You're new in town," the bartender said. It wasn't a question; it was a declaration.

"I'm not in town," Matt said. "I'm just passing through. Thought I'd have a couple of drinks, eat some food that isn't trail-cooked, and maybe get a room for the night before moving on."

"What brings you to this neck of the woods?" the barkeep asked as he poured the whiskey.

Matt hesitated for a moment. Should he ask outright if Rufus Draco had come through here?

He decided against it. He had learned, long ago, that it was often easier to acquire information indirectly than by outright questioning.

"Nothing in particular," Matt said. "I'm just wandering around."

Matt paid for his drink, then lifted it to his lips. Taking a swallow, he wiped his mouth with the back of his hand.

"Is there a place to eat in this town?"

"Mollie's is just down the street. Nothin' fancy, but the food is good," the bartender said.

"Thanks, I'll give it a try," Matt said. He tossed his whiskey down, then set the glass back on the bar.

"Another whiskey?" the bartender asked.

"No, I think I'll have a beer this time," Matt said.

The bartender smiled. "Whiskey, with a beer chaser," he said. "Sounds like Matt Jensen."

"What?" Matt asked, surprised to hear his name

spoken here, in this place where he had never been before.

The bartender chuckled. "I know, I know, I got no business reading Ned Buntline's accounts of Smoke and Matt Jensen. My friends tell me such stories are for kids. Maybe I'm just a kid at heart."

"What's wrong with that?" Matt asked with a smile, knowing now that the bartender hadn't actually recognized him.

Matt listened in as best he could to the other conversations going on in the saloon, but nobody seemed to be talking about anything that might be helpful to him. Because of that, Matt's only chance of gathering any information here would be to just come right out and ask.

"Bartender, I'm trying to catch up with someone, and I've been following his trail south. I don't know if he came through here or not, but I'm thinking that he might have."

"Headin' south, you say?"

"Yes."

"Where'd he start from?"

"The last place that I saw him was the Brothers of Mercy Monastery up in Taos County."

"Yes, I know that place, an old Spanish monastery, ain't it? Been around for a couple hundred years or more. But that's a long way up from here."

"I'm pretty sure he was also in the town of Lorenzo. I didn't see him there, but some folks I spoke to there did."

"Well, if he was comin' south from there, like as

not he did come through here, 'cause there ain't a hell of a lot of other places he can go. What's the fella's name?"

"Draco. Rufus Draco."

The bartender scratched his head. "Ain't a name I recollect hearin'. Just a minute, let me yell at Belle, she keeps up on all the strangers that come through. Belle!" he yelled. "Belle, come out here for a minute, will you?"

A moment later, a woman came through a door at the back of the room. She had obviously been a very pretty woman at one time, but now she was heavily painted in an attempt to cover the dissipation of her profession. There was very little humor or life left to her eyes, but perceiving Matt as a potential customer, and realizing that he was a large step up from the clientele she normally serviced, she allowed a broad smile to play across her face.

"Well now, cowboy, what can I do for you?" she asked.

"He don't want to go to your room, Belle, all he wants is . . . ," the bartender started to say, but Matt interrupted him.

"Who said I don't want to go to her room? Of course I want to go to her room. Unless you are too busy," he added, looking at her with a friendly smile.

"Cowboy, even if I did have someone, I would send them away," she said. She curled her finger. "Come with me."

When they reached the woman's room, she started to get undressed.

"That won't be necessary," Matt said.

"What? What do you mean it won't be necessary?"

"I mean we won't be . . . uh . . ." Matt didn't finish his comment, but he made a motion toward the bed with his hand.

"Then what did we come into my room for?"

"How much do you get for a visit?" Matt asked.

"Two dollars. Five dollars for all night."

Matt took out a bill and handed it to her. "Here is five dollars."

"Five dollars? If we aren't going to lay together, what do you want me to do for five dollars?"

"Talk."

"Talk? Oh, I get it. You want to know what would make a woman become a whore, is that it?"

Matt didn't respond to Belle's question. He was silent for a long moment as he thought about Tamara, the girl he had spoken about to Julie. He recalled the girl he had known when he was a young orphan in the Home for Wayward Boys and Girls, back in Soda Creek, Colorado. The girl's name was Tamara, and, like him, she had been an orphan resident of the home. When Matt had decided that he could take no more mistreatment from Emanuel Mumford, the director of the home, he'd planned his escape, and Tamara had helped him.

Several years later, Matt had encountered Tamara again, only this time she had been working as a prostitute. She had come to nurse him when he had been badly wounded in a knife fight with two men who had attacked him.

"Tamara!" he gasped in surprise. "What are you doing here?"

"You're awake!" she said happily.

"Well, yes. It's morning. I normally wake up in the morning," Matt replied. "But you didn't answer my question. What are you doing here?"

"Why, I'm here to take care of you, of course," Tamara answered. "I came as soon as I heard you were hurt. As I recall, I did this once before, when we both lived in the home, remember? It was right after you had been horse-whipped by Connor."

"I remember." The expression on Matt's face reflected his confusion. "Wait a minute, you came as soon as you heard I was hurt? How is that possible? I was just wounded last night."

"Last night?" Tamara said. She laughed. "Silly goose. Do you actually think you were wounded last night?"

"Yes, of course. I had just come out of the saloon when a couple of . . ." Matt stopped in midsentence.

Suddenly a jumbled series of scenes began tumbling through Matt's mind.

He recalled the fight.

He remembered going into the saloon.

A worried-looking doctor had cleaned his wound and sewed it shut.

Some men had carried him to the hotel room.

Sometime during all this, Tamara had shown up and

now, as he thought back on it, he could recall seeing her face many times, worried as she sat on the edge of the bed, looking down at him, sometimes washing his face with a damp cloth, other times stroking his cheek. Sometimes she kissed him.

He looked up at her, and saw that she had been watching him go through the thought process.

"You're right," he said. "How long have I been here?"

"Ten days."

"Ten days?" Matt gasped. "Have I been out all that time?"

"Not entirely," Tamara said. "You've been in and out of it, and a few times you have even recognized me."

"Really? Have we—uh—have we been together?" Matt asked.

Tamara laughed. "You haven't exactly been in the mood," she said. "Why do you ask? Are you in the mood now?"

"I might be," Matt said.

"Oh my," Tamara said. "Then I would say you are just about fully recovered."

Tamara walked over to her door, opened it, looked outside, then closed and locked it. When she returned to the bed, she began removing her dress. She lay it neatly on a chair, then stepped out of her petticoat. Next came the camisole, exposing her rather small but well-formed breasts.

"You know, when I first started in this business, the way I was able to get through it was to imagine that the man I was with was you," she said.

"How did that help?" Matt asked. "You remembered me as a twelve-year-old boy."

"Maybe it was my fantasy of what you would become," Tamara said. "And I was right, because look at you now."

Smiling, Tamara started to step out of her bloomers.

Suddenly there was the tinkling sound of broken glass as something whizzed through the window, followed by a solid "thock," like the sound of a hammer hitting a nail.

Tamara pitched forward, even as a mist of blood was spraying out from the back of her head.

*"No!" Matt shouted in a loud, grief-stricken voice.**

"Where did you go?" Belle asked.

"What?"

"Why did you grow so quiet?"

"I'm sorry," Matt said. "I was just thinking about something. So, how about it? Will you talk to me?"

Belle held up the five-dollar bill and smiled. "Well, honey, you've bought my time, so if all you want to do is talk, why you just go right ahead. What do you want to talk about?"

"It's not what I want to talk about, it's who I want to talk about. I want to talk about Rufus Draco."

The expression on Belle's face twisted into one of confusion.

"Honey, that ain't a name I've ever heard before. Does that mean I don't get to keep the money?"

"No, you can keep the money. Maybe he isn't using that name."

"What does he look like?"

*Matt Jensen: The Last Mountain Man

"He's a big man, with a bald head that sits so low on his shoulders that he practically has no neck, a broken nose that's mashed flat, and a bushy red beard."

This time Matt violated his rule of leaving one of the elements out of the description because he wanted to provide the maximum opportunity for Belle to remember.

"Oh!" Belle said. "Well, except for the bushy red beard, there was a man that looked like that came through here last week. Only his name wasn't Rufus Draco, though."

"What was his name?"

Belle squinted her eyes as if trying to remember. Then, she realized why she couldn't remember. "He didn't give his name," she said.

Chapter Eleven

Thirty Four Corners

Two days after Bodine held his strategy meeting with Strawn and the other four men, two of the cowboys who worked for the BR Ranch, Seth Miller and Lou Turner, rode into town. Leaving their horses tied up at the edge of town, the two men started up the boardwalk, making certain to stay on their side of the wide, sunbaked street as they hurried from the shade of one adobe building to the next, taking every opportunity to get out of the sun.

A sign posted outside Black Bull Saloon promised cold beer, and they thought nothing could be better than that, so they pushed their way through the batwing doors and went inside. A bartender with pomaded black hair and a waxed handlebar mustache stood behind the bar industriously polishing glasses. He looked up as the two cowboys approached the bar. There were two men standing together at the bar, but as Seth and Lou approached, the two men at the bar separated, one moving to either side, opening up a space for Seth and Lou in between them.

"Hello, Seth, Lou," the bartender said. "How are you two boys getting along?"

"We got us a thirst that's somethin' awful," Seth said. "How cold is your beer today, Hodge?"

"Oh, I'd say it's maybe a little colder 'n horse piss," he said.

Seth laughed. "That's cold enough." Seth glanced into the mirror to check out the two men who had moved out of the way. He didn't recognize either of them, and he leaned over the bar and spoke very quietly.

"Who are them two?"

"I don't know," Hodge replied just as quietly. "They come in a few minutes ago, and that was the first time I ever saw them."

Seth and Lou put down a nickel apiece, and the bartender drew two mugs, then set them before the two cowboys.

At that moment, the two men who had separated to give Seth and Lou room to approach the bar now moved back so that they flanked the two BR riders.

"You boys are gettin' a little close there, ain't you?" Seth said, clearly irritated by the invasion of his space.

"We'll take those," one of the two men said and, in a coordinated move, he and the other man reached down to pick up the beers that had just been set in front of Seth and Lou.

"Here! What the hell do you think you're doin'?" Seth demanded, angrily.

"What's it look like we're doin'? We're drinkin' beer."

"We paid for that beer, mister," Seth said.

"Let's just say it's a peace offering," the man said.

"A peace offering?"

"Yeah. We just came into town. We've hired on to work for Mr. Poindexter and the Tumbling P."

"You just hired on to the Tumbling P? Well, you bein' new 'n all, maybe you don't know. But this side of Central Street is all for the men who work for the BR," Seth explained. "Tumbling P cowboys are supposed stay on the north side of the street. You don't come over on this side, and we don't go over on the other side. That way, we stay out of each other's way, and there don't no one get into trouble. I figure, since you two is new, you more 'n like ain't aware of that."

"What do you mean, we're supposed to stay on the north side of the street?"

"It shouldn't be that hard for you to understand," Lou said. "Like my pard just told you, the north side of the street is for the Tumblin' P. The south side of the street, this side, is for the BR riders. That means you're on the wrong side."

"Yeah? Is there a law that says we can't be on this side of the street?"

"Well, no, there ain't no law against it," Seth said.

"But like I said, we learned a long time ago that if we both stay on our side of the street, there's not as much trouble."

"Trouble don't bother me none at all," the belligerent cowboy said. He smiled at his friend. "Does trouble bother you, Tully?"

"No, Poke," Tully replied. "Trouble don't bother me none at all, neither."

"Well, there you have it, cowboy," Poke said. "Me 'n' my friend, Tully, here will go anywhere in town we want to."

"You aren't going to like it on this side. As soon as ever'one finds out that you are riders for the Tumblin' P, they're goin' to make it pretty uncomfortable for you," Seth insisted.

"Is that a fact?" Poke asked. "Why don't we just see how uncomfortable we can make it?" Poke pulled his gun.

"Wait a minute, what are you doing?" Seth asked, his voice betraying his fear.

"What's it look like I'm doin'? I'm holdin' a gun on you, that's what I'm doin'. Now, you want to explain to me again that rule about I can't come on this side of the street?"

"Put that gun away, mister, or I'll spill your guts all over the floor," Hodge said coldly. The bartender had pulled a double-barrel twelve gauge from under the bar and he had his finger on the trigger, with the shotgun pointed toward Poke.

Poke put the pistol away.

"I expect you two men had better get on back across the street where you belong," Hodge said.

"Oh, we're goin' over on the other side of the street," Poke said. "But you'll be gettin' a message from us."

"What kind of message?" Seth asked.

"You'll see."

Poke and Tully finished the beers, then walked out. Seth put his hand on his gun and took a step toward the door.

"I wouldn't do that if I was you, Seth," the bartender said. "I've seen their kind before. Those two aren't regular cowboys. It's clear as the nose on your face that they're out to make trouble."

"They drank our beer," Seth said, angrily.

"Have another one, on the house," the bartender said, setting two more beers in front of them. "Let it go."

Seth smiled. "Well, if you're goin' to put it that way, maybe I will let it go. Thank you, Hodge. That's real kind of you."

"I don't want any trouble in my saloon."

"Well, you won't be gettin' any trouble from us. We're just goin' to have us a beer, and maybe get us somethin' to eat, then shop around a bit. I aim to get me a silver hatband. Women like a man with a silver hat band."

"Do they now?" Hodge asked with a smile. "You know that for a fact do you?"

"Oh, yeah, I know it."

"Well that's just where you're wrong," Lou said,

knowledgably. "I happen to know for a fact that the ladies like a turquoise hat band, with a red feather stickin' out of it."

"What about that, Lucy?" Hodge called. "Which do women like the best? A silver hat band, or a turquoise hat band?"

"With a red feather stickin' out of it," Lou added. "Don't forget the red feather."

"Ha! Like a red feather is going to do you any good," Seth said. "Maybe if you replace the red feather with a ten dollar bill you might get some lady to . . ."

That was as far Seth got. There was the sound of breaking glass as a bullet came through the window and hit Seth in the back of the head. He went down, dead before he hit the floor.

"Seth!" Lou shouted in distress. Lou looked around the saloon. "Where the hell did that bullet come from?"

"From outside," one of the other saloon customers said. "It come through the window."

With his pistol drawn, Lou ran to the batwing doors of the saloon and looked over them, out into the street.

"Do you see anyone out there, Lou?" the bartender asked. Once more he was holding his double-barrel shotgun.

"No," Lou answered. "I don't see nothin' a'tall."

"Where the hell did that shot come from?"

* * *

Directly across the street from the Black Bull Saloon, Poke and Tully were on the roof of the Hog Waller Saloon, crouched down behind the false front. Poke was holding a rifle in his hand, and he moved the lever down then back up, jerking a spent shell casing from the chamber and replacing it with a live load.

"Did you get 'im?" Tully asked.

"Yeah, I got the son of a bitch," Poke replied. "Come on, let's get the hell out of here."

"Wait, the other'n is standin' at the door," Tully said. "Maybe we should take him out too."

"No need. One's enough to get things started."

Rex Ross was down the street from the Black Bull Saloon, in Sal's Saddle Shop, when Lou came running in.

"Rex! Seth's been shot!"

"What? Where? How? What happened?"

"We was in the Black Bull, just standin' at the bar drinkin' and talkin', when a bullet come crashin' through the window and kilt him."

"Where is he now?"

"He's still lyin' out on the floor back at the saloon," Lou said. "Hodge said maybe I'd better come get you."

"Sal, I'll be back to talk about that saddle," Rex promised. "I need to look into this."

"Do whatever you have to do, Rex," Sal said.

"Damn, you mean a bullet just happened to

Lou who said those two men were bedeviling Seth and him just before the shooting. Hodge says it too, and so does everyone else who was in the saloon at the time. And everyone heard them say that they were riding for the Tumbling P."

"Give me those two names again," Marshal Hunter said. "I'm talking about the names of the two men who were arguing with Seth and Lou."

"Hodge said they called themselves Poke and Tully."

"Poke and Tully. No last names?"

Rex shook his head. "No last names that anyone heard."

"Uh-huh. They called themselves Poke and Tully, and they said they were working for Poindexter, but I don't believe it. Now, here's the thing, Rex. I know ever'one who works for the Tumbling P, and I don't know anyone named Poke or Tully. Hell, you know most of 'em yourself. Have you ever heard either of those names before this?"

"No, I haven't heard of them, but what does that matter? It's probably someone he just hired."

"Hodge also said that they didn't look like cowboys."

"All the more reason to be suspicious. What if the Poindexters have hired themselves a couple of gunmen?"

"Why would they do something like that now? I mean, think about it, Rex. Your pa and Mr. Poindexter have been at war for more than twenty years, and all that time there's never been any blood spilt.

come through the window and hit Seth?" Rex asked as he and Lou hurried down the boardwalk toward the Black Bull. The shooting was already drawing a crowd; ahead of them, many other citizens of the town were hurrying to the saloon.

"No, sir, I don't think it just happened," Rex said. "This wasn't no accident. There ain't no doubt about it in my mind."

"Are you saying that someone intended to shoot Seth, and he did it from outside?"

"Yes, sir, that's exactly what I'm sayin'," Lou said.

Lou told Rex about the altercation he and Seth had had with the two men who'd said they were working for the Tumbling P.

By now, they had reached the saloon. When Rex and Lou went inside, those who had already arrived, recognizing Rex, moved out of the way to allow him access to the body. Hodge was standing nearby.

"Where's the undertaker?"

"I've sent for Tom Nunnlee," Hodge said.

"Thanks, Hodge," Rex said. "What about the marshal?"

"I sent for him too. He's—there he is now."

Marshal Jeb Hunter was in his early sixties, a heavyset man with very full white mustache that completely covered his mouth.

"What have we here?"

"Tell him what you told me," Rex said.

Lou repeated his story.

"And so, what I think happened," Lou said in

conclusion, "is after the little fracas we was havin' with those two men, well, they went outside and one of them shot Seth through the window."

"How am I supposed to arrest anyone?" Marshal Hunter asked, later that same day after two hours of investigating. "Nobody saw the shooter, which they would have done if he had been standin' out in the street. Besides which, Miller was in the saloon standing at the bar, and the shot came from somewhere outside. It isn't like someone was aiming at him. Hell, that shot coulda come from a mile away, someone maybe shootin' in this direction and didn't have no idea that the bullet would wind up killin' someone. I think it was just an accident."

"An accident?" Rex Ross said, angrily. "How can you call it an accident? It had to be intentional."

"Who would intentionally shoot into a saloon?"

"That's an easy enough question to answer," Rex said. "Which side of the street is the Black Bull on? It's on the south side, that's which side. And the bullet come from the north, which means it was shot by someone who is from the Tumbling P."

"Morgan Poindexter has more than twenty men workin' for him. You expect me to arrest all of 'em?"

"You aren't going to arrest anyone, are you?" Rex challenged.

"How can I arrest someone if I don't know who to arrest? For crying out loud, be reasonable, Rex."

"Reasonable," Rex replied. "Yes, I'll be reasonable. You just let Poindexter know that we don't intend to put up with this."

"You don't intend to put up with this? What do you mean by that?"

"I just mean we aren't going to put up with it," Rex said, without being more specific.

"Don't go starting any trouble now, Rex," Marshal Hunter warned.

"The trouble has already begun, and we didn't start it," Rex replied. "Besides, if it happens out of town, it won't be any of your concern anyway. Your authority doesn't go beyond the city limits. Not that happening in town makes any difference, seeing as how you're just letting this go."

Hunter sighed. "You got no call to be talkin' to me like that, Rex. Me 'n' your pa has been friends ever since he came here."

"You've also been friends with Morgan Poindexter ever since he came here."

"That's right, I'm friends with both of them," Hunter said. "That's how come I'm the marshal this town. The town decided that they need someone who ain't goin' to be takin' up sides."

Rex was silent for moment; then he put his on Marshal Hunter's shoulder.

"I know it, Marshal. I'm sorry I was ridin' y that. It's just that I know damn well someor the Tumbling P did this, and I know they purpose. You're right, though, without any there's nothing we can do about it. But i

Yeah, there's been some fights, some bloody noses, even a few broke bones, but there ain't never been no killin'. Now, you tell me why, after all this time, would Morgan Poindexter suddenly decide that's it's time to hire a couple of men like that?"

"I don't know," Rex said. "But I don't like it. And I'd appreciate it if you would sort of keep a closer eye on things for a while."

"I'll do what I can," Hunter said with a resigned sigh.

Chapter Twelve

"I'm not even sure Seth Miller is his real name," Ben Ross said. "He came here to work for us about ten years ago, and he never talked much about where he came from."

"Some of the men say that the reason he never talked much was because he took part in a stage coach robbery up in Wyoming several years ago," Dean Kelly replied.

"Do you believe that?" Ben asked his foreman.

"To be honest with you, Ben, I don't know whether I believe it or not," Dean replied. "You know how it is out here—we never pry too deep into a man's past. We figure if he wants us to know, he'll tell us."

"You're right, what's done is done," Ben replied.

Ben figured that his foreman had his own reason for not prying. There were rumors that Dean Kelly had ridden with Quantrill during the war, but he had never spoken about it, and Ben had never pressed him about it.

"All I know is that Seth was a good man. He never gave me any guff about any job I ever gave him. He'd ride fence, or pull a cow out of the mud, always doin' it without complainin' about it."

"Yes, he was a good man," Ben agreed. "And, since we really don't know anything about him—I mean, his family 'n' all—looks to me like 'bout the only thing we can do is be his family and bury him ourselves."

"Yeah, that's what I'm thinkin' as well," Dean said.

"What do the men think about Seth getting killed?" Ben asked. "Do they think that Tumbling P riders were responsible for it?"

"Most of them do think that, yes," Dean said. "Especially after what they heard about the two men who were puttin' the spurs to Seth and Lou."

"But nobody has ever heard of these two men before now," Ben said. "And nobody has seen them since the killing. I don't know, Dean, I've known Morgan Poindexter since we were boys together. Yes, I know, we've had our differences for well over twenty years now. But there is no one who is going to make me believe that Morgan Poindexter would have his men go so far as to actually kill one of our riders."

"Maybe he didn't order them to do it, Ben. But over the years the men of both ranches have sort of become more and more enemies," Dean said. "And that's like building steam pressure in a boiler. It's bound to blow some time."

"I guess you're right. All right, I may as well go into town and make arrangements for getting Seth buried."

A simple, unpainted pine box lay on the edge of the already opened grave, the box recognizable as a coffin only by its shape, flared at the top end of but tapering down toward the bottom.

The mourners were composed of men from the BR, as well as several citizens from the town, those who did their business on the south side of Central Street, and those who had establishments on the cross streets and who did business with both the BR and the Tumbling P ranches.

There had not been a church service, but the Reverend Charles Landers, who had taken the church one year earlier, volunteered to say a few words at the committal. Attendance at the church had dropped off sharply after Reverend E. D. Owen died, because Landers's "fire and brimstone" style of preaching wasn't all that well received. Still, Ben thought that there should be some clergy present, so he welcomed Landers's offer to conduct the graveside service.

"As I look out over those gathered here, I am reminded that I have seen so few of you in church, and that means that your souls are in peril. It is a sad thing when your only contact with the word of God"—he said the word as gawd-uh—"is when you come to put one of your own into the ground. And notice, I said into the ground, not at rest. Because you see, for Seth Miller, there will be no rest. For him, it is too late. Never once did I see him in church, never once did he hear the salvation that is promised to all who believe. And now, even as we put his mortal remains in the ground, his soul is writhing in eternal damnation and torment as he burns in hell. Amen."

"Damn, Preacher, was that supposed to be comforting?" Ben asked in annoyance.

"My obligation, Mr. Ross, is to the living, not to the dead," Landers replied. "As I said, it is too late for poor Mr. Miller."

"Suppose you just go on back to the church," Ben said. "We'll finish burying our friend."

Tumbling P Ranch

"I don't have the slightest idea who killed him," Gabe Mathis said. He and Nate Poindexter were currying horses and discussing the recent funeral for Seth Miller, one of the BR cowboys. "Truth to tell, most think it was an accident, what with the bullet just coming through the window like that."

"Yes, but there are witnesses who said that Miller and Lou Turner had gotten into an argument with two men who claimed to be Tumbling P cowboys," Nate replied. "So my question is, what were a couple of our men doing on the south side of Central

Street in the first place? Everybody knows that's just asking for trouble."

"I don't believe it was any of our men," Gabe replied. "I've asked ever'body on the place, and they all swear that there wasn't none of 'em who was on the other side of the street. None of 'em was arguin' with Miller and Turner. And what's more, when the marshal investigated, why, he didn't find anyone who could actually identify whoever the two men was, other than to say that said their names was Poke and Tully. And we sure as hell don't have nobody workin' for us named Poke and Tully."

"No, we definitely don't have a Poke and Tully," Nate said.

About an hour after that conversation, Gabe Mathis was inside the equipment room off the barn, taking an inventory of the tack. Looking through the window, he saw three riders coming toward him. They weren't approaching in any sort of threatening mode, but under the circumstances, Gabe figured he couldn't be too careful. He walked to the open door, but reached back beside him to wrap his hand around the double-barrel Greener twelve-gauge shotgun that was leaning against the wall.

"What can I do for you fellas?" Gabe asked.

"It's more like what we can do for you," one of the men replied. The man who spoke had a disfiguring scar that came down through his left eye and across his cheek. "But I reckon we'd better speak to the boss hisself."

"I'm the foreman," Gabe said.

"Yes, sir, and I'm sure that's an important job but what I got to say out rightly be said to Mr. Poindexter. And I'm sure he'll be thankful to us for bringing him the information."

Gabe paused for a second; then he nodded. "All right, wait here. I'll get him."

"Mind if we water our horses?"

"No, go ahead."

As the three riders dismounted and led their horses over to a watering trough, Gabe left the shotgun where it was, and went into big house to summon Morgan Poindexter.

"Morgan, they's some men outside want to talk to you. They say they got somethin' to tell you, and that you'll be wantin' to hear what it is."

"Do you know them?"

Gabe shook his head. "Ain't never seen hide nor hair of nary a one of 'em. I'll say this for the one that's doin' the talkin', though. He might well be 'bout the ugliest man I ever seen."

Morgan followed Gabe outside and saw the men gathered around the huge, circular watering tank. He chuckled, quietly.

"I see what you mean," Morgan said under his breath. "He's an ugly one, all right."

Morgan walked up to the men. "Gentlemen, I'm Morgan Poindexter. My foreman tells me you've got something to tell me."

"I'm Sam Strawn," the ugly one said. "And yes, sir, I do have somethin' to tell you."

"Sam Strawn?" Morgan replied. It was obvious that he recognized the name.

"I see you've heard of me," Strawn said.

"I have."

"Well, sir, it's good that you've heard of me, 'cause that means that when I make the offer, you know I'm someone that can back up what I promise."

Morgan was a little apprehensive, and when he responded, his suspicion was reflected in the tone of his voice.

"What . . . exactly is your offer?"

"I'm offerin' me 'n' my two men as protection for you and your ranch," Strawn said. "You might call us detectives."

"Detectives?"

"Yes, sir, cattle detectives. Like I said, cattle detectives for your protection."

"Protection from what?"

"It looks like Mr. Poindexter don't know," Strawn said to one of the other men. "I told you that like as not, he wouldn't have no idea about it."

"Mr. Strawn, what are you talking about?" Morgan asked. "What is it that I have no idea about?"

"Tell 'im, Wallace," Strawn said.

Wallace had a narrow, pockmarked face and a big, bushy mustache that filled his upper lip.

"Yes, sir, well, I was over to the BR Ranch, offerin' to cowboy for Ben Ross. He said he didn't need no more cowboys, but that he might could use me for somethin' else. Then he called out to a feller he's got workin' for him, Bodine, the feller's name was. 'Bodine,' Ross says. "'Take this feller with you next time you go out.'"

"'Go out where?' I says. 'Why to make mischief for the Tumbling P,' Bodine says.

"Then, Mr. Ross, he says, 'We're goin' to teach Morgan Poindexter and the Tumbling P that they can't kill one of our'n and get away with it."

"And you heard all that?" Morgan asked.

"Yes, sir, I heard all that. Only, that wasn't what I thought I was signin' on for, so I rode off. Then, when I run across Strawn, who's an old friend of mine, I told him what I heard, and he figured we might better come to see you, to tell you what's goin' on," Wallace said.

"What I figure, Mr. Poindexter," Strawn said, interrupting Wallace, "is that Ross plans to use Bodine to maybe make a few raids agin' your ranch. Do you know Bodine?"

"No, I don't think I have ever heard the name before."

"Well, maybe his name ain't all that well known down here, seein' as he is most known up in Colorado 'n' Montana. But let me tell you from some knowledge that I know personal, firsthand, you might say. Bodine is a bad one. From what I've heard, they was some strikin' miners up in Montana once and the mine owners hired Bodine to come in and bust up the strike. Bodine brung in some men and he 'n' his men busted up the strike. And you know how he done that?"

"Since I've never heard of anyone named Bodine, I don't have the slightest idea how he might have done it."

"Well, sir, what he done was, he kilt seven of the strikin' miners, that's how he done it. And his killin' them miners like he done made the rest of 'em go back to work."

"None of my men are striking," Morgan said.

"Yes, sir, 'n' that's just the point," Strawn said. "But I figure that what Bodine has in mind is to maybe kill three or four of your cowboys, 'n' that would more 'n likely make the rest of your cowboys run off."

"I don't believe Ben Ross would do a thing like that," Morgan said.

"When is the last time you talked to Ross?" Strawn asked.

Morgan shook his head. "We don't talk. We haven't talked in well over twenty years."

"Then you don't really know him all that well, do you? Thing is, ever since one of his cowboys was kilt, he wants revenge."

"I heard about Seth Miller getting shot, but neither I, nor anyone else on the Tumbling P, had anything to do with it," Morgan said.

"It don't matter whether you had anything to do with it or not," Strawn said. "Ross thinks you did, and that's all that matters. But, maybe you're right, maybe Ross will just let it pass and do nothin'. If that's the case, if he don't do nothin' at all, then you won't need anyone to protect your cowboys, will you? But what if he does do somethin'? Iffen he was to do somethin', and maybe one or two of your cowboys was to get kilt, then you're more 'n likely goin' to feel awful bad about not bein' ready for 'im, ain't you?" Strawn concluded.

"Ben wouldn't do anything like that."

"Morgan, Ben Ross might not do it himself," Gabe said. "But half the county thinks it was some of our men that killed Seth Miller, so it's damn sure that Ben thinks that as well," Gabe said.

"So, what are you saying, Gabe?"

"I'm saying that it might not be a bad idea to hire these fellers, at least for a little while 'til we see whether or not Ben Ross has anything planned."

"I'd be willing to say yes, but I'm not sure I can afford them," Morgan said.

"If you can afford to pay cowboys, you can afford us," Strawn said. "You don't have to pay us no more 'n you pay any of your other cowboys."

"Wait a minute," Morgan said. "Are you telling me you'd be willing to be—what was it you called yourself, cattle detectives? You'd be willing to do that kind of work for no more than cowboy wages?"

Strawn may have smiled, though the movement of his mouth did little to soften the image on his face.

"We'll work for cowboy wages so long as we don't

have to do no actual cowboy work," Strawn said. "We don't want to be pullin' no cows out of mud holes, or runnin' 'em down for brandin', or ridin' fence line, or anythin' like that."

Morgan chuckled. "All right, Strawn, you've got yourself a deal."

Chapter Thirteen

The BR Ranch

"You aren't going to convince me that Morgan Poindexter has hired some gun hands for no purpose other than to make trouble," Ben Ross said.

"I don't know, Pop, seems to me like the men that work for Mr. Poindexter have all gotten more contrary lately. It wouldn't surprise me at all to hear that he had hired some ne'er-do-wells for just such a purpose."

"This ain't somethin' I just heard about, Mr. Ross," Bodine said. "Massey here was goin' to hire on over at the Tumbling P with the other men, thinkin' they was goin' to be nothin' but cowboys. When he heard what they was plannin', he changed his mind."

"And just what are they planning?" Ben Ross asked.

"From what I've heard, they're plannin' on makin' things uncomfortable enough for the men that work for you that they'll up and leave. As I understand it, he figures that if you can't keep men workin' for you, why, then you won't be able to keep your ranch."

"And don't forget, Ben Ross, it was someone from the Tumbling P that kilt Seth Miller," Bill Lewis said. Lewis had been with the BR ever since the BR and the Tumbling P had split into two ranches.

Dean Kelly, foreman of the BR, shook his head. "We've looked into that, Bill. Marshal Hunter says there's no proof of that. Nobody saw the shooter."

"No, but they were in the saloon arguing with a couple of men who said they was with the Tumbling P."

"That's just it. They said they were with the Tumbling P, but nobody has ever heard of them before. Poke and Tully. Do you know who they were?"

"No," Lewis admitted.

"It may be that these two fellas are a couple of the new men Poindexter has hired," Bodine said. "Which is all the more reason you need to hire me 'n' my men."

"And what, exactly, are you offering?" Ben Ross asked.

"It's real simple. Me 'n' my men will just ride around, keepin' an eye on things for you."

"What about at night? If Morgan Poindexter really did have such an idea in mind, there's no doubt in my mind but that he would do things at night."

"Yes, sir, and I expect you're right about that. That's why I intend to have someone watchin' out at night, too."

"And you don't intend to charge any more than any of my cowboys?"

"No, sir, not one cent more," Bodine said.

Ben nodded. "All right, we'll give it a try for a little while. I hate it that what started out as a misunderstanding between Morgan and me has now gone on to involve the whole county. Or at least, this part of the county. We were good friends once, did you know that?"

"Yes, sir, I've heard that," Bodine said. "But I've also heard that there ain't nobody can be more contrary and more dangerous than old friends who have become enemies."

Ben nodded. "You may have something there," he said. "But Bodine?" Ben held his finger up.

"Yes, sir?"

"The only thing I'm going to want from you is that you keep your eyes open for any trouble or danger. I have no wish to be the instigator of any further problems between Morgan Poindexter and me. I'll not have you starting anything."

"No, sir, we won't be startin' nothin'," Bodine said. "But, if they start somethin', I hope you ain't sayin' that we can't hit back. Lettin' 'em get away with causin' trouble is the biggest way to just have more trouble."

"If they start something, you can hit back," Ben said. "But I hope having you here is all it will take to keep them from starting anything."

* * *

Less than two hours after Ben Ross hired Bodine, Dooley, and Massey, Bodine and two of his riders were at the extreme north end of the ranch, some distance from any of the other riders of the BR.

"The Tumbling P is running about five hundred head down just over the rise," Bodine said. "We can cut through the fence and pull off about fifty head or so with no difficulty at all."

"What are we going to do with them?" Massey asked.

"Ten of 'em, we're goin' to turn loose into the BR herd," Bodine said. "But I've got a dead-end canyon picked out about two miles west of either ranch. We'll put the other forty cows in there."

"I get it," Massey said. "If we put ten head in with the BR cows, when the Tumblin' P gets to missin' 'em, well, they'll show up here."

"That's right. And in a couple of days, Strawn will cut about fifty head away from the BR ranch, run some of 'em in with the Tumblin' P herd, and put the others into the dead-end canyon."

"It's goin' to take a long time buildin' up a herd just by taking forty head at a time," Dooley said.

"What we're doing now is just testing it out," Bodine said. "Once we get the hang of it, we'll start takin' 'em a hunnert to two hunnert at a time."

"What about the cows we're mixin' in with the BR herd. We ain't goin' to just leave 'em there, are we?"

"Yes, we are. They're seed cattle."

"They're what?"

"You ever been around a farm, Dooley?"

"No."

"I didn't think so. When you're growin' corn, ever' year when you take in the harvest, you have to hold some of it back for seed to put in the next crop. What we're doin' with the cattle we're mixin' in with the BR herd is feedin' the feud. 'Cause, without the feud, we couldn't be doin' none of what we're a-doin' now."

"Yeah," Dooley said. "Yeah, I understand that."

"Good. Now, let's go get us fifty cows."

Tumbling P Ranch

Jimmy Patterson was riding fence when he saw that some of the fence was down and a couple of men were herding about several cows through the cut fence. He urged his horse into a gallop to catch up with them.

"Here, you men!" Jimmy called to them. "What are you doing with them cows?"

"What does it look like we're doin', boy? These cows wandered over there when the fence went down. We're bringin' 'em back onto BR land where they belong."

Jimmy might have taken their word for it, but he recognized a distinctive scar on the side of one of the steers.

"Well, you need to be more careful with the ones you're takin'. I know for a fact that that one don't belong to you, 'cause I know that cow," he said, riding toward the animals to point out the one with the scar. That was when he saw the brand, the letter P, which was lying a quarter of the way on its side. That same brand was on all of the cows. "Wait a minute!" he said. "There don't none of these cows belong to you!"

"Are you sayin' we're stealin' cows, boy?"

"I'm just sayin' these here cows don't belong to you. Look at the brands. Go on, look at 'em."

"What I see is fifty cows eatin' BR grass. Any cow that comes onto BR land and starts eatin' BR grass, belongs to Mr. Ross."

"No, sir, these cows don't," Jimmy said. "These cows wouldn't be eatin' BR grass if you didn't cut the fence and bring 'em through. They belong to Mr. Poindexter, and I'm takin' 'em back."

Jimmy turned toward the cattle, but one of the BR Ranch cowboys threw a rope around him, and jerked him out of his saddle and off his horse. Then, urging his horse to a gallop, he dragged Jimmy behind him back through the open spot in the fence. Jimmy's horse followed.

Once they got Jimmy back onto the Tumbling P side of the fence, they cut out a long strand of barbed wire and began wrapping it around him, making certain that the points of the barbs penetrated his skin.

"Now," the two men said to him. "Don't let us catch you over on BR Ranch land again. If we do, we won't be so gentle with you."

Jimmy didn't hear anything they said, because he was unconscious.

"Is he dead?" Bodine asked.

"No," Dooley answered. "Do you want him to be?"

"No, it's better to leave him like this. We want him to tell Poindexter that the BR is stealing their cattle. Remember, the whole idea is to get this feud to heat up."

Nate and Gabe were working on the windmill that supplied the watering trough for the horses that were kept in the corral.

"That's the problem right there," Gabe said, pointing to the pump shaft. "That bearing is bone dry. All we have to do is get some grease on it."

"Yeah, I think you're right," Nate said. "There's some grease in the machine shed—I'll go get it."

"Nate, wait a minute, look there," Gabe said. "Ain't that the horse Jimmy Patterson's been ridin'?"

Nate, who had already started toward the machine shed for grease, looked back around to see a saddled but rider-less horse come trotting in.

"Yes, I believe it is," Nate said. "But where's Jimmy?"

"I don't know, but he's a good kid. He wouldn't just let his horse go like that unless something happened."

"Where did you have him working today?" Nate asked.

"I've got 'im ridin' the north fence."

"That's right next to BR Ranch property. I expect we had better go check it out," Nate said.

Nate and Gabe saddled their horses, then rode, quickly, toward the area where Gabe said he had sent Jimmy to work today. They saw buzzards making lazy circles in the sky.

"Whatever happened to him must be pretty bad," Gabe said. "He's got buzzards circlin' around him."

"Yeah, but they haven't gone down yet. I hope that means he's still alive," Nate said.

"More 'n likely he just got hisself throwed," Gabe suggested.

"I don't know. I've seen him ride. Jimmy is too good a rider just to get thrown from a horse for no reason," Nate said.

"You're right, now that I think about it. But if he didn't get throwed, what did happen to him? I don't know what we're ridin' into, but I don't think I'm goin' to like it all that much, especially us ridin' in alone."

"If he's still alive, and we take the time to go get help, he's likely to be dead by the time we get back," Nate said. He pulled his pistol. "Looks to me like we got no choice."

"Yeah," Gabe said. He, too, pulled his pistol. "All right, let's go check it out."

They found the young cowboy a few minutes later, all bound up in barbed wire, lying in a gulley. His clothes were soaked with blood from the penetrations of the barbs.

"Jimmy!" Nate said, dismounting and hurrying to him. "Jimmy, what happened?"

Jimmy opened his eyes, and the lids fluttered as he tried to make a connection with Gabe and Nate. His lips moved, but neither Nate nor Gabe could hear what he was trying to say.

"We've got to get this wire off him," Gabe said.

"I'll take care of that," Nate said. "Go back as fast as you can, get a buckboard. We need to get him into town. And bring something to use as bandages. Better bring some iodine too."

"Right!" Gabe shouted as he leaped onto his horse and started back at a gallop.

After Gabe left, Jimmy opened his eyes again, and he saw Nate.

"Some of the fence is down, Mr. Poindexter. And I seen some of our cows over on the other side. I went to bring them back when I seen some men takin' 'em. I tried to tell 'em, Mr. Poindexter. I tried to tell 'em them was our cows, but they wouldn't listen."

"They knew they were our cattle," Nate said. "They were stealing them."

"Yes, sir, that's what I was thinkin'." Jimmy looked around. "You seen my horse? I don't know where my horse got to, but if you see it aroun', well, I'll get mounted 'n' get back to work."

"You aren't going anywhere but to the doctor," Nate said.

"What for am I goin' to a doctor?" Jimmy asked, just before he passed out again.

It was a good half hour before Gabe came back,

driving the team at a gallop, with dust streaming up in a huge rooster tail behind the buckboard. Sliding to a stop, Gabe jumped down and the two men lifted Jimmy into the back of the buckboard. Gabe had put hay in the back, and spread cloth to make a soft bed. Nate poured iodine over the wounds, then bandaged them. He was bothered by the fact that Jimmy didn't even wince from the application of the iodine.

"Come on, help me get Jimmy into the back of the buckboard."

It was another half hour before Nate and Gabe, driving the buckboard as fast as the team would pull them, reached the doctor's office at Thirty Four Corners. Dr. V. Scott Taylor's office was on First Avenue, which formed a T at the end of Central Street and, as such, it was neither north nor south of the street. That was important because by being in the middle of the street the doctor—through a truce arranged between Ross and Poindexter—could tend to all. There was only one bank, one leather-goods store, one feed store, and one livery in town, also on First Avenue. There was one church and one blacksmith shop on Second Avenue, and one school, on Third Avenue. The town consisted only of Central Street, and the three crossing avenues, First Avenue being at the extreme west end, Second Avenue in the middle, and Third Avenue at the east end of Central.

All the other businesses in town were separated by Central Street. There were four saloons, two hotels, two apothecaries, two grocery stores, and two mercantile stores, evenly divided by the town's main street, which was the debarkation line between both parties of the feud. There were also two bawdy houses, Diamond Dina's Pleasure Palace, on the south side, whose ladies serviced the men who rode with, or supported, the BR Ranch, and Sunset Lil's Parlor of Delight on the north side, servicing the Tumbling P and its supporters.

"Is he goin' to make it, Doc?" Nate asked when they brought Jimmy into the doctor's office.

"It's too early to tell. You did well applying the iodine and putting on the bandages," Dr. Taylor answered. "We'll just have to see if he comes through it."

"Can you wake him up so we can talk to him?"

Dr. Taylor held a solution of sal volatile under Jimmy's nose, and he regained consciousness.

"Where am I?" he asked.

"You're in the doctor's office, Jimmy."

"How'd I get here?"

"We brought you, when we found you injured."

"What happened to me?"

"You mean you don't remember?"

"Last thing I remember is talkin' to you 'bout where my horse was."

"Do you remember anything before that?" Nate asked.

"Yeah," Jimmy said, recalling now. "Yeah, I do

remember something. I remember some of the BR men drivin' off some of our cows."

"Did you confront them?"

"What does that mean?"

"Did you talk to them?"

"Yes, sir, I told 'em that them cows was our'n. Only, I don't mean our'n like I own any of 'em or anythin'. I hope you don't think that."

"I know exactly what you mean, Jimmy," Nate said. "After you confronted—that is, after you talked to them—what happened then?"

"I don't rightly know," Jimmy replied. "Truth is, I don't remember nothin' after that. I figure I must've fell off my horse though, 'cause I'm hurtin' all over."

"You know a lot of the BR riders, don't you, Jimmy?"

"Yes, sir, I know quite a few of 'em. Some of 'em I went to school with."

"Did you recognize any of the men who were driving off the cattle?" Nate asked.

"No sir, now that you mention it, I don't reckon I ever seen any one of 'em before. They weren't any of the BR cowboys I know, that's for sure."

"I didn't think they would be," Nate said.

"You know what I'm a-thinkin', Mr. Poindexter?" Jimmie asked. "I'm a-beginnin' to think that maybe I didn't fall off my horse a'tall. I'm thinkin' maybe them men I seen done somethin' to me."

"That is exactly what happened to you," Nate said.

"Let the boy get some rest now," Dr. Taylor said. "And I'd feel better if you would let me keep him here for a couple of days."

"No problem, Doc. Keep him as long as you need."

"I can't miss work," Jimmy said.

Nate smiled, and ruffled Jimmy's hair. "Don't worry about it, Jimmy. You won't lose any pay."

"Thanks, Mr. Poindexter. I'm sorry I put you to all this trouble."

"No trouble. We'll come get you day after tomorrow."

"How's the boy?" Morgan Poindexter asked when Nate and Gabe returned to the big house.

"He's hurt pretty bad," Nate said. "He's got holes poked all in him from the barbed wire."

"That's a hell of a thing to do to anyone, especially to someone who's no more than a boy," Morgan said.

Gabe chuckled. "Don't let Jimmy hear you call him a boy."

"I know. He does a man's work, and he does it well," Morgan said. "But say what you want, he is still just a boy. And I don't know what kind of men Ben Ross has working for him now, that he would let them do something like that. Truth is, I know a lot of his riders. I never thought any of them would do anything like that, either."

"I don't think it was any of Ross's regular riders.

Jimmy said he didn't recognize any of them," Nate said.

"Then who was it?"

"I think it was some of those men that Strawn was talking about. You remember, he said that Ross had hired some riders who were supposed to cause trouble for us. Well, I think we've just run into some of them."

"You may be right. I was hoping that hiring Strawn would prevent anything like this from happening."

There was a knock at the door and Gabe went over to open it. It was Dr. Taylor, and there was a troubled expression on his face.

"Doc, what is it?" Nate asked.

"I'm sorry," Dr. Taylor said.

"Sorry? Sorry about what? Jimmy? Is it the boy?"

"Terrible infection set in," Dr. Taylor said. "And once that started, there was nothing I could do. There's no way to fight it. The boy died about an hour ago."

Morgan lowered his head and pinched the bridge of his nose. "Have you told the boy's mother?"

"Yes, I went to see her before I came out here."

"Damn, how did all this get started?" Morgan asked, shaking his head.

"What do you mean, how did this all get started? Pop, you and Ben Ross have been going at it with each other from before I was born. You've never spoken of the reason, but I've known about it since I was twelve years old. Did you think that neither Sylvia nor I would ever find out? The whole town knew what happened, and they couldn't wait to tell us. Mom was supposed to marry Mr. Ross, but you and she ran off on the day of the wedding. How did you expect him to react?"

"Boy, I swear to you, if I had known then that all this was going to happen, I would never have done it. But even with all that, nothing like this has ever happened before. I almost wish that I hadn't sent for Sylvia. I hate to bring her here now, under the circumstances."

"It's a little late now, isn't it, Pop?"

"Yes, I've already sent the letter."

Chapter Fourteen

Thirty Four Corners

Once again, there was a funeral in Thirty Four Corners. The funeral cortege moved slowly down Central Street, headed toward the cemetery that was just north of town. The hearse, its black lacquer and brass fittings highly polished and flashing brilliantly in the sun, led the way, pulled by a team of matching black horses. Jimmy Patterson's coffin, made of polished mahogany and trimmed in glistening silver, could be seen through the glass.

Because the victim was a fourteen-year-old boy, and especially because of the brutal way he had been killed, practically the entire town had turned out for the funeral.

Mrs. Patterson, dressed all in black, and with her face covered by a long black veil, rode in Morgan Poindexter's elegant Victoria carriage, which was being driven by Jimmy's friend, Jake. Morgan, wearing a black suit, was sitting in the carriage beside Jimmy's mother, holding her hand.

Diamond Dina watched from Diamond Dina's Pleasure Palace. She wanted to go to the funeral but knew that she wouldn't be welcome. She knew, also, that even if she stood out on the balcony of her establishment to watch as the funeral cortege passed by, that it would be unwelcome, so she watched from behind the curtained windows of her bedroom, wiping tears from her eyes.

"What a sweet, sweet young boy he was," she said aloud.

As the hearse turned into the cemetery, it was followed by hundreds of people, some on horseback, some in carriages, surreys, buckboards, or wagons, but most on foot.

There were no more than half a dozen customers in the Black Bull Saloon. The Black Bull catered to BR, and none of the BR people took part in the funeral, but, almost by mutual agreement, today was a day of truce.

One person who was in the Black Bull was Rex Ross, and he stood at the bar, staring into a shot glass of unconsumed whiskey.

"Are you all right, Rex?" the bartender asked.

"What? What did you say, Hodge?"

"I asked if you were all right," Hodge repeated.

Rex tossed down his drink. "Yeah," he said. "Yeah, I'm all right."

"Want another?" Hodge asked.

Without answering, Rex pushed his empty glass

across the bar. "Who the hell would do such a thing, Hodge?" Rex asked.

"Well, half the town thinks that one or more of your boys did it," Hodge answered as he poured another drink.

"I know," Rex said, as he tossed down a second drink.

A loud burst of laughter erupted from the back of the room, and looking around in irritation, Rex saw three men sitting at a table. He had never seen any of the three before, and he did a sharp double take at the appearance of one of them. The man's face was white as chalk, and his eyes were pink.

"Quiet!" Rex shouted at the top of voice. The shout got the attention of everyone in the saloon, especially the three men toward whom his shout was directed.

"You shouting at us, mister?" the albino asked.

"Yes, I'm shouting at you. There is a funeral going on. Can't you men show a little respect? Have you no decency?"

"I notice you ain't at the funeral."

"I would be there," Rex said. He held his glass out for Hodge to refill. "I would be there if I could," he added, speaking quietly now. "But, under the circumstances, I'm afraid I wouldn't be welcome."

"You wouldn't be welcome, 'cause you're one of the ones that done it," the albino challenged.

"How dare you say that?" Rex responded sharply. "I had nothing to do with it."

"You're with the BR, ain't you?" the albino said.
"Yes."

"Then what do you care? As I understand it, the man who was killed worked for the Tumbling P. If you wasn't the one who done it, more 'n likely you know who it was. Ever'one knows that it was some BR cowboy that killed him, and he done it as payback for the BR rider that was killed."

"In the first place, it wasn't a man who was killed. It was a boy," Rex said. "A fourteen-year-old boy. And if I find out that any of my men did it, I will personally arrest them, and take them to jail."

"Any of your men? What do you mean, any of your men?"

"Don't you know him, Shardeen? That's Rex Ross," one of the other men said. "He's the son of the man that owns BR."

"Is he now?" Shardeen said.

Rex left the saloon, mounted his horse, and rode out of town, taking the long way around so that he didn't pass by the funeral. It wasn't that he was frightened of passing close to any of the Tumbling P riders. It was that he was ashamed.

Los Luna, New Mexico

Now, late in the afternoon of the forty-fifth day since Matt had made the personal commitment to bringing to justice the three men who had killed Jim, Martha, and Claire Lewis, he approached the town of Los Luna. Los Luna, which was on the junction of the

Denver and Rio Grande, and the Atchison, Topeka, and Santa Fe railroads, was the biggest town he had been in for quite a while.

He surveyed the town as he rode in, and though it was considerably larger than all the towns he had visited over the last two months, in construction it was no different from the others, made of houses of rip-sawed lumber, false-fronted businesses, and a few sod buildings.

It had rained earlier in the day, and now the street was a quagmire. The mud, worked into the consistency of quicksand by the horses' hooves, had mixed with the droppings to become one long, stinking, sucking pool of ooze. When the rain stopped the sun, yellow and hot in its late afternoon transit, it had begun the process of evaporation. The result was a foul miasma, rising from the offal of the street.

Matt rode up to the first saloon he saw, dismounted, and tied Spirit to the hitching rail. He entered the saloon the way he always did, surveying the place with such calmness that the average person would think it no more than a glance of idle curiosity. In reality it was a very thorough appraisal of the room as he checked out who was armed, what type of weapons they were carrying, and whether or not those who were armed were wearing their guns in such a way as to indicate that they knew how to use them.

He also checked to see if there was anyone he knew, or, more specifically, if there was anyone who reacted as if they might know him. It wasn't easy to pick out people who knew him, because his reputation was such that there were many more people who knew him than he knew. And, because he lived one of most violent lives of anyone in the West, there was nearly always someone gunning for him for one reason or another.

None of the drinkers seemed to pose a problem. From all he could tell, there were only cowboys and drifters here, and less than half of them were even wearing guns. A couple of the cowboys were wearing their guns low and kicked out, gunfighter style, but Matt could tell at a glance that it was all for show. He was certain they had never used them for anything but target practice, and probably were not very successful at that.

The bartender stood and moved down toward Matt.

"What'll it be, sir?"

"Whiskey," Matt said. The bartender started to turn away.

"With a beer chaser," he added.

Nodding, the bartender poured the whisky, then filled a beer mug from the barrel.

Matt listened in on the conversation for a bit, but heard nothing helpful. He finished his beer, then set the empty mug on the bar.

"Would you like another?"

"No, thanks. I believe I'll just get a room, a bath, and supper. Any suggestions?"

"The Mixon Hotel has a bathing room on every floor, with hot running water. And they have a hotel dining room."

"Thanks," Matt said.

The Mixon Hotel was one of only three buildings in town made of brick, the other two being the Bank of Los Luna and the railroad depot. It also had its own stable, which made it convenient for boarding Spirit. When he stepped up to the desk, the clerk was reading a newspaper, and the clerk began chuckling.

"What's so funny?" Matt asked.

"It's somethin' I'm readin' in the paper," the clerk said. "Mr. Vaughan, the editor, always puts in something he calls 'Quaints,' which are humorous stories. He has a real good one in this week. Listen to this." The desk clerk cleared his throat, and began to read. "A gentleman, with a woman at his side, approached the teller at the bank. 'If I give you forty, can I have two twenties?' the gentleman asked. 'But of course,' the bank teller replied. The gentleman produced the woman at his side. 'Here she is, she is forty years old. I would like two twenty-year-old women.'"

The teller laughed heartily. "Now, isn't that quite the funniest thing you have ever heard?"

"It is funny," Matt said, laughing courteously though he didn't find the joke that humorous.

"You shall be wanting a room?"

"Yes. And how is your stable? I would like to board my horse."

"Mr. Fitzhugh tends to our stable, sir, and he takes great pride in his task. Clean stalls with fresh hay and water, cooled by a pleasant cross breeze. By all accounts, our stable is much better than the city livery. I assure you, sir, that your horse will be very comfortable."

"Forget the horse," Matt said, "you make it sound comfortable enough that I'll just stay there."

"Oh, sir, but you can't do . . . ," the clerk started. Then he laughed. "I see, sir, you were teasing."

"Yes. I'll take the room."

"Very well, the rate is one dollar for the room, and fifteen cents for your horse. If you would just sign the registration book, please?" the clerk said, turning the book toward him.

Matt signed the book, then took out a dollar. The desk clerk took the dollar and handed Matt a key.

"You shall have room thirty-one. It is on the third floor, overlooking the street, mister . . ." The clerk looked at the signature, then with a start, looked a second time. "Jensen? You are Matt Jensen?"

"Yes," Matt said.

"Well, my goodness, Mr. Jensen, may I shake your hand? And welcome to the Mixon Hotel! My name is Bruce Tyson. If there is anything I can do for you while you are here, and I mean anything, why, you just let me know.

"My, my, to think that Matt Jensen stayed in my hotel. Yes, sir, this is quite an honor."

* * *

Matt went upstairs to take his bath. It had been a long time since he had been able to relax in a tub of warm water, so he lingered there for at least thirty minutes.

After the bath he returned to his room, found a pair of jeans and a shirt in his saddlebags that were somewhat cleaner than what he had been wearing. As he was getting dressed, he heard the whistle of an arriving train.

Onboard the train

"Los Luna!" the conductor was calling loudly, as he walked through all the cars. "This stop is Los Luna!"

Sylvia felt a sense of relief that was almost elation. She had been on the train for three nights and four days and now, at last, her long trip was over. It was dark outside, so though she was aware of the great, looming presence of the mountains, the gleaming lights of the approaching town were the only things she could actually see. She felt the brakes being applied as the train slowed, then, finally, came to a complete stop.

Once the train stopped, several others in the car stood and started reaching for items they had brought on board with them. A small boy started running up the aisle.

"Cephus, you come back here, right now!" his mother called, and sheepishly, the boy turned and started back. When he got even with Sylvia's seat he looked at her and smiled, and she returned his smile.

"Cephus?" the mother called again, and with a little wave, the boy returned to his mother.

For a moment, Sylvia found herself envying the woman with her young son. It was the kind of life that she'd thought she would have with H. M. Hood. But that was not to be. The comfortable future she had selected for herself—marriage, a home, and children—she knew now that none of that would ever be.

She had left Springfield, Illinois, to find a new life for herself. But the more she thought of it, the more she realized that she wasn't running to anything. She was running away from something.

Because she remained in her seat in such deep reflection, she was relatively surprised when she looked up to see that everyone else who was leaving the train had already exited. She had a sudden fear that the train might leave with her still aboard, so she got up and moved quickly to the door, then stepped outside.

Chapter Fifteen

Sylvia had arrived in Los Luna at eight forty-five in the evening, and as she stood on the platform of the Atchison, Topeka, and Santa Fe Railway depot, the train behind her, though temporarily still, wasn't quiet. The drive cylinder relieve valve was opening and closing, venting rhythmic puffs of steam. The water in the boiler of the locomotive boiled and hissed, and the journals and gearboxes of the cars popped and snapped as they cooled.

She looked around for her father, but he wasn't here. And it wasn't because she wouldn't recognize him. He had come to Springfield for Christmas three years ago. She knew exactly what he looked like. He just wasn't here.

Sylvia watched as her belongings were off loaded from the baggage car and loaded onto a luggage cart that was green, with red iron wheels.

"Where do you want your luggage, miss?" the baggage handler asked.

"I don't know," Sylvia said. "My father was supposed to meet me here, but I don't see him."

"You can check with the ticket agent," the baggage handler suggested.

"Thank you."

The depot waiting room, which was illuminated by gas lights, was empty. Those who had been waiting to board the southbound train were now doing so. Behind a half wall, a man, wearing a green felt visor, was writing something.

"Excuse me, sir," Sylvia said.

Her voice startled the ticket agent, and he jumped. "Oh, miss, if you've come to board the train, you may be too late, unless I can persuade the conductor to hold up the departure."

"No, I just arrived on the train," Sylvia said. "My father was supposed to meet me here, but I don't see him. I wonder if you know anything about it?"

"Who is your father?"

"Morgan Poindexter."

The ticket agent smiled. "As a matter of fact, miss, I do know something about it," he said. "Your father sent you a telegram."

"He sent me a telegram? I didn't receive it."

"No, I mean he sent it here, with instructions to hold it for you. Just a moment, and I'll get it for you."

"Thank you."

A moment later the ticket agent handed Sylvia a small envelope.

DELAYED. WILL PICK YOU UP
TOMORROW AFTERNOON. HAVE
ARRANGED ROOM FOR YOU AT MIXON
HOTEL. LOVE DAD

"Thank you," Sylvia said. "Could you tell me where the Mixon Hotel is?"

"Here's your luggage, miss," the baggage handler said, coming into the waiting room then with four grips and a trunk.

"It's down at the far end of the street," the ticket agent said. "But they have a courtesy country wagon for their guests. I'll call them and have them send it down here for you."

"Thank you," Sylvia said.

About fifteen minutes after the telephone call was placed from the depot to the hotel, a vehicle about the size of a buckboard, though a little fancier, arrived. The wagon was green. The writing on the side was in white letters, outlined with yellow.

COURTESY CONVEYANCE— MIXON HOTEL

As soon as it stopped, the driver and baggage handler loaded Sylvia's luggage aboard. Then, after helping her board, the driver headed back to the hotel.

The floor of the hotel lobby was made of wide, unvarnished planks of wood, though much of it was covered with a patterned carpet of rose and gray. There were several comfortable chairs and a leather sofa scattered about. There were at least three steam radiators, as well as a fireplace, though, as it was quite warm, there was no fire. Sylvia walked across the lobby to the front desk.

"My name is Sylvia Poindexter. I believe you may have a room for me."

"Yes, ma'am, Miss Poindexter, indeed we do," the clerk said.

Sylvia smiled. "You know without checking?"

"The hotel only has twenty-four," the desk clerk said. "It isn't hard to remember when someone makes a reservation. If you would just sign in, please?"

The registration book was turned toward her, and Sylvia signed in with a neat flourish, in what she called her "teacher hand," because she took the time to make her signature legible.

"How much is the room?"

"Oh, it's paid for," the hotel clerk said. "Your father wired the money."

"That was quite nice of him. I see that you have a dining room. How late will it be open?"

"The dining room will be open until ten." The clerk turned to look at the clock behind him. "You have forty-three minutes remaining," he said.

"Thank you."

"If you would like, I can have your luggage sent up to your room, and you can go right into the dining room."

"Oh, thank you, that's very nice of you."

When Sylvia stepped into the dining room a few minutes later, there was only one more diner in the room, a tall, broad-shouldered man with hair the color of ripened wheat, and bright blue eyes that contrasted with his suntanned face. Glancing toward Sylvia, he nodded a friendly greeting, and she returned the nod.

The other diner left before Sylvia finished her meal. After she finished and her bill was delivered, the waiter asked, "Do you know who that gentleman was, who was in here earlier? It was Matt Jensen, that's who it was. I suppose you've heard of him."

"No, I haven't. Should I have?"

"Yes, ma'am, I would certainly think so," the waiter said. "He's a right well-known man, what with books bein' written about him and all. And he's stayin' right here in our hotel. You can tell your family and friends that you stayed in the same hotel as the famous Matt Jensen."

Sylvia smiled. "I'll be sure to remember that," she said.

When Sylvia came downstairs for her breakfast that morning she saw that, unlike the night before, the dining room was quite crowded. Though she wasn't specifically looking for him, she did glance around the room to determine if Matt Jensen was having his breakfast. Or should that be "the famous Matt Jensen"? She smiled as she recalled the awe with which the waiter had spoken of him the night before.

Her perusal of the dining room produced no results, so she turned her attention to the menu that had been delivered to her a moment earlier.

"Order what you wish, madam," the waiter said when he returned to take her breakfast order. "There will be no charge."

"What? Why is that?"

"Your father is a frequent guest of our hotel, and we are always pleased to have him. When Mr. Mixon himself learned that you were a guest in his hotel, he left instructions that you were to be provided with breakfast, free of charge."

"Well, how nice of Mr. Mixon," Sylvia said. "Thank you." She began perusing the menu, pleased to see that, despite the seeming isolation of this place, the menu offered a bountiful choice.

Sylvia didn't expect her father until at least noon, so after breakfast she decided to take a walk around town. Although the elevation of Los Luna was four thousand and eight hundred feet, it was relatively flat. To the west, though, the Navajo

Mountains rose high into the sky, and Sylvia felt a twinge of nostalgia at seeing them again.

She had been here ten years earlier and she remembered, vividly, the day she had climbed onto the train to leave home and head east to live with an aunt she had only seen one time in her entire life. How frightening that trip east had been. She had wondered and worried about her aunt and uncle. How would they receive her? Would they treat her kindly, or would they consider her an imposition?

As it turned out, her aunt and uncle had been wonderful to her, treating her as if she were their own daughter. It had been a very good ten years, and she, and they, had cried when she'd left to come back west. Now, she was as apprehensive about coming back to New Mexico as she had been about leaving it.

Stepping into the Railroad Saloon, which was a different saloon from the one he had been in the night before, Matt made a careful scrutiny of the place. A card game was in progress near the back, and at one of the front tables, there was some earnest conversation. Three men stood at the bar, each complete within themselves, concentrating only on their drink and private thoughts. A heavily made-up soiled dove stood at the far end of the bar. She smiled at Matt, but getting no encouragement, stayed put.

"What'll it be, mister?" the bartender asked, making a swipe across the bar with a sour-smelling cloth.

"Whiskey," Matt said.

"You're Matt Jensen, aren't you? You're the one that killed Fox."

"With a beer chaser," Matt added, without a direct answer.

The whiskey was set before him and Matt raised it to his lips, then tossed it down. He could feel its raw burn all the way to his stomach. When the beer was served, he picked it up, then turned his back to the bar for a more leisurely survey of the room. He listened in on the conversation.

"From what I he'erd, they didn't nobody even suspect that the bank had been robbed. Nobody even went inside for a long time, 'cause there was a sign that said the bank was closed. Then, when they went inside, they found the teller 'n' a woman, dead, both of 'em pretty much carved up, they was."

"How much money was took?"

"Somethin' over a thousand dollars, is what I he'erd," the man who was telling the story said.

"And there didn't nobody see nothin' at all?"

"Nope, not a thing. It's a pure mystery who done it."

Matt walked over to the table and pointed to an empty chair. "I wonder if you folks would mind if I joined in with the jawboning?"

"No sir, we wouldn't mind at all," one of the men said. "I heard the bartender call you Matt Jensen. Is that who you are?"

"Yes."

"Well, Mr. Jensen, you are mighty welcome."

"Here, have a seat," one of the other men invited.

"Thanks," Matt said.

Oftentimes, a good talk session would break out in a saloon, and when it did, it could be more entertaining than a card game. And with the introduction of Matt Jensen, a name nearly everyone recognized, if few recognized him in person, the conversation could be even more interesting.

"What brings you to Los Luna, Mr. Jensen?"

"I'm looking for someone."

"Ha! From what I heard, you found him back in Santa Domingo. They left him standin' up in front of the hardware store for three days," someone said. "What was his name?"

"Fox, Norman Fox," one of the others said. "Is that who you were looking for?"

"Actually, it turns out that Fox was looking for me. The man I'm looking for paid Fox to kill me."

"How do you know that?"

"The sheriff found this note in his pocket." He showed the note to the others around the table.

"I know Rufus Draco," one of them said. "I just seen 'im not more 'n a couple of weeks ago."

"What? You saw him?"

"Yep. Right here in town," the man said. "He was standin' outside the livery, just as big as you please. I 'most didn't recognize him, seein' as he ain't wearing that big red beard of his'n. But that nose, being crushed up against his face like it is . . . well, you can't change that."

"How is that you know Draco?" Matt asked. "I'm only asking, because I want to make certain that the man you saw is him."

"It was him all right." The man looked around the table at the others.

"Tell 'im, Hank. A man like Matt Jensen ain't goin' to hold it agin' you. None of us do," one of the others said.

Hank nodded, and cleared his throat. "I ain't proud of it, Mr. Jensen, but the truth is, I spent some time in prison oncet . . . and Draco . . . he was in there too. And like I said, he had shaved his beard."

"Yes, I heard that he had shaved his beard," Matt said.

"Why are you looking for him?" one of the other men asked.

Matt told them about what had happened with the Lewis family, as well as with Michelle, back in Lorenzo.

"Yeah, I heard about that. They said whoever kilt her cut off her titties. What kind of lowlife son of a bitch would do somethin' like that?"

"A lowlife son of a bitch like Rufus Draco," Matt replied.

Chapter Sixteen

Tome, New Mexico

Bodine sat at a table in the back corner of the Vaquero Cantina talking with Tully Cates, Poke Gillespie, and Emmett Shardeen. The subject of their conversation was Morgan Poindexter.

"He's gone to pick up his daughter. He took a buckboard to Los Luna this morning, and will be coming back this afternoon," Bodine said. "The best place for you to intercept him would be at the Loter Mesa."

"All right," Shardeen said.

"Take the girl, but don't hurt Poindexter. We need to keep him and Ross both alive."

"What are we going to do with the girl, once we have her?" Tully asked.

Bodine smiled. "Once you get her away from him, you can do anything you want with her. She's not important. What is important is that Poindexter thinks that Ross is behind it. We need this feud to turn into a real shootin' war."

"I thought killin' one of someone from each ranch was supposed to do that," Poke said.

"Yeah, I thought so too," Bodine said. "But I guess that wasn't close enough. We're goin' to have to make 'em hurt, if we want this thing to work."

"We'll make 'em hurt," Shardeen said.

"Wear hoods," Bodine said. "I've purposely kept you three away from the others, because I don't want anyone to see you and attach you to one ranch or the other. This way we can use you where we need you."

"Anything we want, huh?" Poke said.

"What?"

"The girl," he said. "We can do anything with her that we want?"

"Yes, after you get her away from Poindexter. He needs to think that she is still alive, and he needs to think that Ross has her."

Los Luna

Sylvia saw her father step into the hotel lobby, and smiled as she watched him peruse the room, looking for her. Rising from the chair where she had been waiting for him, she started toward him.

"Papa, don't you recognize your own daughter?" she asked.

A huge smile spread across Morgan's face. "Sylvia,"

he said. "Yes, I recognized you at once. I was just thinking how much you look like your mother."

Morgan opened his arms and Sylvia stepped into them as they hugged. "Welcome home, daughter."

"It's good to be home. How is Nate?"

"Nate is doing well, and anxious to see you again."

Morgan and the hotel bellboy gathered up Sylvia's baggage and put it in the back of the buckboard.

"I guess I could have come to fetch you in somethin' a bit fancier," Morgan said. "But I figured you'd have a lot of luggage, so this was the best for that."

Sylvia laughed. "A buckboard is fine, Papa. It makes me feel like I'm really back home again."

"So, how did you enjoy your stay in Illinois?" Morgan asked as they started back.

"I hated it when I first got there," Sylvia said. "You might remember, Papa, I didn't want to leave."

"Oh, I remember, all right," Morgan said with a chuckle. "You really made me feel bad, but honey, I only did what I thought was best for you."

Sylvia reached over to put her hand on Morgan's arm. "I know you did, Papa, and it didn't take me too long to realize that. Aunt Emma and Uncle Wendell were wonderful to me. Aunt Emma cried when I left."

"Your Aunt Emma is a good woman," Morgan said. "She always has been."

"She sends her love to her little brother, by the way," Sylvia said with a smile.

"Ha! I guess I'll always be Emma's little brother," Morgan said with a chuckle.

"How long will it take us to get home?" Sylvia asked.

"No more than two hours. It'll be a nice, pleasant drive. And we'll be able to catch each other up on things," Morgan said.

As Morgan Poindexter and his daughter were just starting back to the ranch, Matt, now convinced that Rufus Draco was nowhere in town, was saddling Spirit. Hank came out to the stable to talk to him.

"Mr. Jensen?"

"Yes, Hank."

"Uh, I hope you don't think bad of me 'cause I was in prison oncet. But I was a lot younger then." Hank chuckled self-deprecatingly. "I was a lot dumber too. What I done was, I stoled a horse."

"You were lucky you went to prison," Matt said. "Sometimes people can be real harsh to someone who steals a horse."

"Yes, sir, don't think I don't know that. I was lucky in another way too, 'cause while I was there, I made up my mind never to do nothin' like that ever again."

"A good decision," Matt said as he tightened the girth strap.

"That's why I come out here to see you," Hank said. He looked around cautiously to make certain there was no one close enough to overhear him.

"The truth is, I done more than just seen Rufus Draco. I talked to him. He tried to get me to come with him. He said he had a plan to make a lot of money."

"Really?" Matt said, his interest now aroused. "What is the plan?"

"I don't know. He wouldn't tell me. But it might have something to do with Risco."

"Risco?"

"Yes, sir. It's a town about twenty miles west of here. You go like you're goin' to Thirty Four Corners, but just the other side of the Loter Mesa you turn south for about five miles."

"What about Risco?"

Hank shook his head. "I don't really know nothin' more 'n that," he said. "The only think I know is that Draco said that if I changed my mind and decided I wanted to come in with 'im, I could meet with him there."

"Thanks."

"I'm sorry I can't be no more help than that. Most especially after I heard what all Draco had done, I mean, what with your friends and all that."

Matt reached out to shake Hank's hand. "You've been a big help, Hank. Thank you, very much."

Mounting Spirit, Matt rode out of town, this time heading west. The information from Hank had given him a new direction. He would go to Risco. He knew, with absolute certainty, that he would find Draco one day. By heading toward Risco, Matt was riding in the same direction that had been taken a short time earlier by Morgan and Sylvia Poindexter, but of course, he didn't know that.

Morgan and Sylvia were about ten miles west of Los Luna, and approaching the Loter Mesa, when three masked men jumped out in front of the buckboard, pointing pistols at the two occupants.

"Hold it right there!" one of them shouted.

The team was startled by their sudden appearance and they reared up so that Morgan had to fight to get them under control.

"What is this? Are you crazy? What do you want?" Morgan asked.

"What do you think we want?" one of the men said. "We want money."

Morgan took out his billfold and removed ten dollars. "This is all the money I have," he said.

"Ha! We know who you are, Poindexter. You are a big ranch owner, and you expect to buy us off with ten dollars?"

"Good Lord, man, you don't expect me to travel with a lot of money, do you?"

"It isn't the money you have with you," the masked

man said. So far, he was the only one who had spoken. "It's the money you can raise."

"Why should I raise money for you?"

"You didn't let me finish my comment. It's the money you can raise to get your daughter back."

"What?"

The spokesman for the three masked men pointed his pistol toward Sylvia. "Get down from there."

"You leave my daughter alone. She has nothing to do with this."

"If you want your daughter back, it's goin' to cost you five thousand dollars," one of the men said.

"I'm not going anywhere," Sylvia said resolutely.

"Oh, I think you will," the spokesman said. He pointed his pistol toward Morgan. "If you don't step down from that rig right now, I'm going to shoot your old man . . . and get the money from your brother."

"Do you men work for Ben Ross?" Morgan asked, angrily.

"Well now, you ain't so dumb after all, are you?" He looked back at Sylvia. "I said get down! Now!"

Matt Jensen had just reached the top of a rise in the road when, looking ahead, he saw the three men and the buckboard. He saw, too, that the men were masked and armed. Dismounting, he walked Spirit back over the other side of the rise so that he couldn't be seen against the skyline. Then he pulled his rifle and, staying low, climbed back to the top of the rise. That was when he saw that they were forcing the girl down from the buckboard.

Jacking a shell into the chamber, he aimed at the man who was holding his pistol pointed toward the girl, and fired.

"Uhh!" the armed road agent grunted, as a little spray of blood squirted from the hole that appeared in the middle of his shirt. Dropping his pistol, he slapped his hand over the bullet wound, which pumped blood through his spread fingers.

"Where did that shot come from?" one of the two remaining outlaws asked.

"I don't know, but let's get the hell out of here!" the other outlaw shouted. They turned and ran up the hill on the opposite side of the road from Matt. Matt aimed at them, but he didn't shoot again.

Matt watched as the driver of the buckboard slapped the reins against the back of the team. The horses started forward at a gallop . . . moving quickly up the road, leaving behind a billowing rooster tail of dust. For a moment he thought about trying to catch up with it, but decided that the danger was over, so he let the driver and the woman go on alone.

* * *

Morgan kept the team at a gallop for at least two miles before he slowed them down. Turning in his seat, he studied the road behind him and saw that it was clear.

"I think they're gone," he said.

"Who were they, Papa? Did you know those men?"

"I didn't know them, but you heard what they said. They said they were Ben Ross's men."

"Why?"

"Why what?"

"Why this . . . this war between you and Mr. Ross? Aunt Emma told me that you and Mr. Ross were once very good friends. She said you grew up together, and that you saved his life during the war."

"That was my mistake," Morgan said.

"I know that Mama was supposed to marry Mr. Ross, but that you and she ran off together. But why has the feud lasted this long?"

Morgan put his arm around his daughter's shoulder and pulled her closer to him.

"Darlin', there are some things that are best not to talk about. Please accept that."

Sylvia kissed her father on the cheek.

"All right, Papa. I'll respect your wishes."

"What I'm wondering is, who is it that came to our rescue? And why?" Morgan asked.

Matt didn't follow the rapidly retreating buckboard because he figured that they would think he was after them, and might drive so recklessly as to have a wreck. Instead, he bent down to look at the body of the man he had shot. The man was dead; it didn't even take a second look to ascertain that.

"Who the hell are you?" he asked quietly.

The outlaw was still wearing his hood, and Matt reached down to pull it off. Exposing the man's face didn't help. . . . Matt still had no idea who it was.

He heard a sound behind him and, pulling his pistol, he spun around. The sound had been made by a saddled horse that had no rider. The horse came all the way up, then bent his head down toward the dead outlaw.

"Sorry, horse," Matt said, rubbing the horse behind his ears. "It's not your fault you had a rider who was about to take a young woman at gunpoint. I'm afraid he left me no choice."

Matt picked the body up and draped it, belly down, across the horse. The horse offered no resistance. Then, taking a coil of rope from the saddle of the outlaw's horse, Matt tied the body, hands and feet, so it wouldn't slide off.

"All right," he said. "Let's go on into town and see what we can find out."

Tumbling P Ranch

Night had fallen by the time Morgan and Sylvia turned onto the long, curving, gravel-covered drive at the ranch. The "big house" was glowing with light at nearly every window, and as Morgan pulled the team to a halt, Nate came out the front door and bounding down the porch steps.

"Well, well, little sister!" Nate said, greeting Sylvia, and helping her down from the buckboard. "I swear, I wouldn't recognize you. What happened to the ugly little tomboy that used to follow me around?"

"I left her in Springfield," Sylvia replied with a smile as she and her brother embraced.

"Hello, Sylvia. Though I guess, now that you are all grown up, it should be Miss Sylvia," Gabe said.

"Didn't you tell me years ago that you would always be my special friend?" Sylvia said.

"Yes, ma'am, I sure did."

"Am I still your special friend?"

"Yes, ma'am, you are."

"Then it's still Sylvia."

Gabe's smile spread, then he called some of the cowboys over. One of the men looked after the buckboard and the team, while the other two grabbed Sylvia's luggage.

"Your old room is ready for you, honey," Morgan said. "Show the men where to put your luggage."

"Sure," Sylvia said. "Come along."

Morgan watched his daughter lead the two cowboys toward the house. "I sure am happy to have her back," he said.

"Yeah, I've missed her too," Nate said.

"Nate, we need to tell your pa," Gabe said.

"Tell me? Tell me what?" Morgan asked, concerned by the tone in Gabe's voice. "What is it? What has happened?"

"There is nothing that has happened yet, but some of the men want to get revenge for what the BR folks did to Jimmy," Gabe said.

Morgan shook his head. "No. Keep them in check. I'm afraid this whole thing is on the verge of getting completely out of hand. A feud is one thing. A war is something else."

"I'll do what I can," Gabe said.

"And I may as well tell you, we got held up on the way back," Morgan said.

"Held up? What do you mean? You mean you were robbed? Well, how much money did you have?"

"It wasn't the money they were after," Morgan said. "They tried to take your sister. They were going to hold her for ransom."

"Damn! What happened?"

"Someone . . . and I don't have the slightest idea who it was . . . but someone who was close by saw what was going on and shot one of the men. The other two ran off, and I put the team to gallop."

"Well, thank heavens for whoever it was."

"Do you know who the road agents were?" Nate asked.

"They said they were working for the BR," Morgan said.

"You mean they just came out and told you that?"

"Not exactly, but when I accused them of being Ross men, they validated it."

"Do you believe them?"

"Why would they say they were riding for him if they weren't?" Ben asked.

"I don't know, could just be some outlaws who have heard what's going on here and figure to cash in on it some way," Gabe suggested.

Morgan stroked his chin, then nodded. "Yeah," he said. "Yeah, I suppose I could see someone doing that. But I hope that's not it. I hate to see this thing get any further out of hand."

Chapter Seventeen

Risco, New Mexico

It was dark by the time Matt reached the town of Risco and as Spirit and the horse he was leading plodded down the dirt street, the hollow clopping sound of their hoof falls echoing back from the darkened, false-fronted stores and houses. From the back of one of the houses a baby cried, and Matt heard the cooing sound of its mother comforting it.

Such sounds barely registered with Matt now. He was well aware that another world existed outside his own . . . a world of husbands and wives, children and homes, schools, churches and socials, but such things were so remote from his own experience that he was unable to dredge up even a twinge of envy, or regret, for his exclusion.

Someone saw that he was leading a horse, over which was draped a dead body, and he called out.

"Someone's bringin' in a body!"

His call was picked up by another, and then another, so that by the time Matt was one third of the way down the street he had picked up an entourage of curious men who were walking along the boardwalk, moving quickly enough to keep pace with him.

"Who you got there, mister?" someone called.

"Who is that?" another asked.

"Where's the marshal's office?" Matt replied.

"It's just in front of you."

Even as he was answered, he saw the words, dimly illuminated in a gas-burning street lamp, on the front of a small building. The sign read CITY MARSHAL so he headed there.

By the time he reached the marshal's office, at least a dozen of his impromptu followers were already there, and one of them opened the door and called inside.

"Marshal Kincaid! Marshal, you better get out here! We got a body for you!"

By the time Matt dismounted, Marshal Kincaid, a tall, slender man with white hair and dark eyes, was coming toward the horse with the body.

"Who killed 'im?" the marshal asked, lifting the head of the body for a closer examination.

"I killed him," Matt replied.

"Was it a needed killin'?"

"Doesn't seem likely I would've brought him back here if I didn't think the killing was justified, does it?" Matt asked.

The marshal expectorated a wad of tobacco, then wiped his mouth with the back of his hand.

"No," he agreed. "That don't seem likely a'tall. Who is this feller?"

"I don't have any idea."

"You don't know? You kill a man, and you don't even know who he is?"

"You aren't accusing me of anything, are you, Marshal?" Matt asked pointedly.

"Now, hold on there," the marshal said easily. "You ain't in no trouble. Leastwise, not with me, you ain't. Like you said, you brung 'im in your ownself. I don't reckon you woulda done that if you had somethin' you wanted to hide. How come you to kill 'im?"

"He was about to kill a man and a woman."

"Who was he about to kill?"

"I don't have any idea.

"You didn't ask 'em their names?"

"I didn't get the chance to talk to them. After I shot this man, they ran away before I could get to them."

"Get to them?"

"I shot this one with a rifle, from some distance away," Matt said. "There were two more road agents with them, all three of them wearing a hood. Like this one," he added, pulling a hood from his pocket and showing it to the marshal. But they ran off as well."

"You a bounty hunter? Because if you are, I can't

be authorizin' no bounty for somebody if I don't even know he who is."

"I've collected a few bounties from time to time, but I wasn't after one with this man."

"You've collected a few bounties? Damn, mister, a person doesn't just collect a bounty from time to time. Who are you, anyway?"

"The name is Jensen. Matt Jensen."

"Matt Jensen!" someone in the crowd said, speaking the name not only in awe, but also with a sense of pride in letting the others know that he recognized the name.

"Come on in," Marshal Kincaid invited. "I'll need to get a statement from you for the judge. And I've got some coffee."

"All right," Matt said, and he followed Kincaid into the office. There, another man inside, also wearing a badge, stood up as they entered.

"Boykin, there's a body draped over a horse outside. Take him down to Yancey's place, will you?"

"Marshal, the undertakin' office is more 'n likely closed at this hour," Boykin said.

"Well, knock on the door until he opens up, unless you plan to just let the body stay out front all night."

"All right," Boykin said.

Marshal Kincaid stepped over to a small stove, where sat a pot. He picked up the pot, poured some coffee into a cup, and handed it to Matt.

"Thanks," Matt said, reaching for the coffee.

"Matt Jensen, you say?"

"Yes."

"I've heard of you."

Matt didn't reply, but took a swallow of coffee.

"And, from what I've heard of you," the marshal continued, "You ain't the kind of man who kills someone without they need killin'. But I thought you mostly stayed in Colorado."

"I do, mostly," Matt said.

"What brings you to New Mexico."

"Rufus Draco."

The marshal looked up quickly, reacting to the name. "Rufus Draco?"

"You know him?"

"Oh, yeah, I know him. I've been knowing Draco for over twenty years. I was the first one to ever put him jail. He was only fourteen or fifteen then, and if I could have put him in prison, I would've done it."

"What did he do?"

"There was some girl he was tryin' to spark, but she didn't want to have anything to do with him, so he killed her pet dog. I know this will be hard for you to believe, but he didn't just kill the dog, he carved it up into pieces, and left it on the girl's front porch."

Matt thought of what Draco had done to the Lewis family, and to Michelle. "No, it's not at all hard to believe," he said.

"You said you was here, lookin' for 'im. You think he's back in New Mexico, do you?"

"I know he is in New Mexico, and I have reason to believe that he might be here."

"What?" Marshal Kincaid said in surprise. "Do you mean here in Risco?"

"I've heard that he might be."

Marshal Kincaid shook his head. "No, sir, he ain't here, and I can tell you that for a fact. If he was here, I woulda seen him."

"What if he is here, but he doesn't want to be seen? Is that possible?"

"Well, sir, I reckon it is possible," Kincaid said. "But it sure don't seem likely. What makes you think he might be here?"

"I've heard that he is trying to put together some sort of operation that is supposed to make a lot of money."

Marshal Kincaid laughed. "Well, hell, that right there ought to prove that he ain't here. There ain't no lot of money to be made in Risco, 'cause there ain't no lot of money in Risco."

"You said you wanted a statement about the body I brought in?"

"Yes. Can you write?"

"Yes, I can write."

"There's pen and paper on the desk. Just write in your own words what happened, then sign it. That's all I'll need for the judge."

"All right," Matt agreed.

Sitting at the desk, Matt wrote, in only one paragraph, what had happened.

*I saw three armed and masked men stop a
buckboard. A man and woman were in the
buckboard and, under gunpoint, one of the
three armed and masked men was forcing
the woman from the buckboard. I shot him,
and the other two ran away. I don't know
who the man and woman were, as they also
ran away.*

Matt signed the paper and handed it to the
marshal. "If you don't need me anymore, I'm going
down to the saloon to have a beer."

"Go ahead. You're finished here," Marshal Kincaid said.

Under the soft, golden light of three gleaming
chandeliers, the atmosphere in the Belly Up Saloon
was quite congenial. Half a dozen men stood at one
end of the bar, engaged in friendly conversation,
while at the other end, the barkeep stayed busy
cleaning glasses. Most of the tables were filled
with cowboys and storekeepers laughing over exchanged stories, or flirting with one of the several
bar girls whose presence added to the agreeable
atmosphere.

The saloon was nearly full, but it was relatively
quiet. The girls were moving from table to table,
smiling and flirting with the men, sometimes taking
off a customer's hat and running their fingers
through his hair.

At a table at the rear of the saloon, Kris Dagan sat with his back to the wall, playing a game of solitaire. Dagan was a little shorter than average, a particularly ugly man with stringy, brown hair, dark, beady eyes, a narrow mouth, and a nose that was shaped somewhat like a hawk's beak.

A few minutes earlier Dagan had been one of the many who had followed Matt up the street when he arrived with the dead body, belly down over a horse. What separated Dagan from the rest of the onlookers was that he knew who the dead man was. It was Poke Gillespie. Dagan knew Gillespie, and he knew that he was involved in something with Tully Cates over in Thirty Four Corners . . . something that Gillespie said was going to make him a lot of money. Well, Gillespie was dead now, and that meant that if whatever he was involved in with Cates was still going on, they might need someone to take Gillespie's place, especially if there was a lot of money to be made.

Dagan smiled, and dealt the cards out for a new game. He would have to go over to Thirty Four Corners and look up Cates. It could turn into a very profitable trip.

When Matt went downstairs from his hotel room the next morning, he saw Marshal Kincaid standing at the check-in desk.

"Mr. Jensen," Marshal Kincaid said with a touch of thumb and forefinger to the brim of his hat.

"Marshal. Are you here to see me? Something wrong with the statement I wrote out for you?"

"No, the statement is fine," Marshal Kincaid said. "Have you ever heard of a man named Poke Gillespie?"

"Poke Gillespie? No, I can't say as I have. Should I have?"

"The only reason I asked is because that's the name of the man that you killed."

"Like I said, I've never heard of him."

"Well, he's worth five hundred dollars, but if you want it, you're going to have to stay around for a couple of days until I get the authorization."

Matt smiled. "I can always stay a few more days for five hundred dollars," he said.

"I thought you might."

"Say, where's the best place to get breakfast?"

"Well, that depends," the marshal answered.

"Depends on what?"

"It depends on how hungry you are. If you are wantin' fancy food, you might try Delmonico's. But if you are really hungry, you can't beat Billy Frank's Eats."

"I'm really hungry."

"Then Billy Frank's is the place for you. Come outside, I'll show you where it is."

"Better yet, why don't you have breakfast with me, my treat?" Matt invited. He smiled. "I'm five hundred dollars richer this morning than I was when I went to bed last night."

Marshal Kincaid smiled. "I know the day is still young, but it's the best offer I've had so far."

"Hello, Marshal," someone called out to them as Matt and the marshal stepped inside the restaurant.

"Hello, Billy Frank."

"Brought me a new customer this morning, did you, Marshal?"

"Actually, he brought me," Marshal Kincaid said. "I'm his guest."

"Well, you know where your table is," Billy Frank said. "I'll be there in a minute."

By now, word had spread around town that the man who'd arrived with a body belly down on a horse the night before was none other than Matt Jensen, and his name was whispered from customer to customer as Matt and Marshal Kincaid moved to a table in the back corner. Because the table was in the corner, both Matt and Marshal Kincaid were able to have their backs against a wall.

"How did you find out who Gillespie was?" Matt asked.

"Someone in town recognized him," Marshal Kincaid said. "Then I started looking through all my dodgers and found one on him. The description matches perfectly."

"Well, I'm glad someone recognized him."

"Here is something else you might be interested in," Marshal Kincaid said. "When I went through everything I have on him, I saw that one of his known associates is Rufus Draco."

"Draco? I wonder if Draco was one of the other two men?"

"Could be."

"Damn. If he was, it's too bad I shot Gillespie instead of him."

"If you knew who the two people in the buckboard were, the man and woman, it might help in your search," Marshal Kincaid suggested.

"When the left, they were heading west," Matt said. "What is the next town west of Loter Mesa?"

"Thirty Four Corners."

"Then that is my next stop."

Billy Frank approached the table then, with a small tablet in his hand.

"All right, gents, what will it be?" he asked.

"Bacon, two eggs over easy, and biscuits," Marshal Kincaid said.

"And you, sir?"

"Do you have pancakes?"

Billy smiled, and nodded. "I have the best in New Mexico," he said, proudly.

"Good, I'll take half a dozen pancakes," Matt said.

"All right, coffee with that?" Billy asked as he started to leave the table.

"Yes, but wait, I'm not through. I'll also want three or four pieces of bacon, about the same number of sausage patties, and a large piece of fried ham."

"My, that's quite an appetite," Billy said.

"It's been a while. I haven't eaten since last night."

Billy chuckled. "You haven't eaten since last night," he said. "That's a good one." Again, he started to turn, but Matt still wasn't finished.

"Better bring me a couple of eggs, over easy, and some fried potatoes. Oh, and do you have any gravy?"

"Gravy? You want gravy over your pancakes?"

Matt chuckled. "No, I want gravy over biscuits."

"Yes, sir, of course, you'll be wanting biscuits."

Billy remained at the table for several more seconds.

"What is it?" Matt asked. "What are you waiting on?"

"I wasn't sure you were through with your order," Billy said.

"No, I think that'll do it," Matt said. "But you might check with me from time to time to see if I need anything else."

"Check with you, indeed," Billy said as he walked away.

Marshal Kincaid laughed. "Are you really going to eat all of that, or are you just putting Billy Frank on?"

"I think I can eat it all," Matt said with a chuckle. "But I confess that I was sort of enjoying laying it on for him."

"I could see that," Marshal Kincaid replied.

Chapter Eighteen

Tumbling P Ranch

One of the first things Sylvia did when she got back home was to reestablish a friendship she had with Linda Stallings. The two girls had been best friends when they were in school.

"I have missed you so much," Linda said. "There have been so many fun things to do that I just knew I would have enjoyed more if you had been here to do them with me."

"Well, we'll just have to make up for lost time, won't we?" Sylvia said.

"Oh, I know what we can do tonight! There is a dance over in San Jose. Do see if your father will let you go."

Nate was close enough to have overheard the conversation between his sister and her friend, and with a roguish smile on his lips, he came over to them.

"I know how to get Pop to give you permission to go," he said.

"How?"

"If Linda would agree to let me escort her to the dance, then you could come with us."

"Why, Nate, if you are wanting to court Linda, why don't you just say so? There is no need for such subterfuge," Sylvia teased. "But," she added hastily. "I think that is a wonderful idea."

San Jose, New Mexico

Rex Ross, of the BR Ranch, and the ranch foreman, Dean Kelly, stopped for a moment to read a sign that was posted at the edge of town.

FIREMAN'S BENEFIT DANCE TONIGHT
Come One! Come All!
Dunn Hotel Ballroom.
Fifty Cents.

"Hey, Dean, do you think there'll be any women at that dance?" Rex asked.

Dean laughed. "Have you ever been to a dance where there weren't any women?" he asked

"I know we're over here to book some railroad cars for Pa, but I don't see any reason why we couldn't go the dance tonight, do you?"

"No, I don't see any reason at all. Sounds like a good idea to me."

"Then, we'll go. Only, what do you say we get us a beer first?"

"Ha! That sounds like an even better idea," Dean agreed.

A few minutes later the two men dismounted in front of the Nippy Jones Saloon.

"Look," Rex said, pointing to a couple of the other horses that were tied up at the next hitching rail. "Those horses have the Tumbling P brand."

"Yeah, I noticed," Kelly said.

When they went inside, Kelly stuck his hand out to stop Rex.

"I'll be damn," he said. "Them wasn't just cowboy horses. There's Nate Poindexter himself."

Nate Poindexter was standing at the far end of the bar, nursing a drink. Gabe Mathis was with him, and both of them tensed when they saw Rex Ross and Dean Kelly come into the saloon.

The town of San Jose was ten miles northeast of Thirty Four Corners. It was the closest railhead, needed by both the BR and the Tumbling P, so by mutual understanding, the long-running feud between Ben Ross and Morgan Poindexter would recognize a truce in this town.

"It's all right," Rex said. "We've got a truce here. Hello, Nate."

Nate glared at Rex, but said nothing.

Rex and Kelly stopped at the opposite end of the bar from Nate and Gabe and ordered a beer.

The others in the saloon, well aware that the long-standing feud had recently turned violent, grew quiet and attentive at the sight of two of the principals in the disagreement.

* * *

"That son of a bitch has some nerve coming in here," Nate said.

"Easy, Nate," Gabe said. "You know what your pa says. We can't afford to get into trouble over here, we need the railhead."

"Yeah, well, that's not going to keep me from telling him what I think," Nate said. Tossing down the rest of his drink, Nate walked to the opposite end of the bar, then stopped just a few feet away.

"I wouldn't think you would have the guts to show your face after everything that you have been doing," Nate said, his voice low and menacing.

"Nate, if you are talking about the boy, I swear to you, I didn't have anything to do with that. And if any of my men did, and I find out about it, they will pay for it."

"It's not just Jimmy. It's what you did to my pa and my sister. Or at least, what you tried to do."

Rex gave a genuine look of surprise in response to Nate's challenge.

"Your pa and your sister? I don't have the slightest idea what you are talking about."

"Don't lie to me, Ross," Nate said. "You had your men waylay them on the road on the way back from Los Luna."

"Why the hell would I do something like that?"

"That's what I want to know. Why would you do such a thing?"

"Mr. Poindexter, we don't even know what you

are talking about," Dean said. "But I promise you, whatever happened to your pa and your sister, the BR had nothing to do with it."

"Nate," Gabe said, reaching out to put his hand on Nate's arm. "Come on, let's find us another place to drink."

"Why should we go somewhere else?" Nate asked. We were here first."

"You were, indeed, here first," Rex said. "We'll go somewhere else. I'm sorry about young Jimmy Patterson, and I'm sorry that someone accosted your father and sister. I wish you a good day, my friend."

"I am not your friend," Nate said between clenched teeth.

Rex nodded without responding; then he and Dean left the saloon.

"I thought that went rather well, didn't you?" Rex asked.

Dean laughed. "Where do you want to go now?"

"Tell the truth, if we are going to go to that dance, I'd like to get a hotel room and take a bath," Rex said.

"Since the dance is going to be at the Dunn Hotel, we may as well take a room there," Dean suggested.

"Good idea."

Rex took the key to his room upstairs. Before he went to his room he walked down to the end of the hall to one of the bathing rooms. He went into one and started a fire in the water heater. Then he walked down to check out his room while he gave the water time to warm up.

He had a front room so he walked over to look out the window. From here he had a good view of the main street. The street, scarred with wagon ruts and dotted with horse droppings, formed an X with the track. The railroad station was halfway down the street and from here he could see the cattle pens that made this town so important, not only to the BR and the Tumbling P, but to many other ranches in the county. Thirty Four Corners had started out as the largest town in San Jose County, but the railroads had made both Los Luna and San Jose larger.

Rex saw a train, heading west, just now pulling away. It would be in San Diego by this time tomorrow night.

On the far side of the track he saw a scattering of adobe buildings. On this side of the track the buildings were false-fronted and made of unpainted, rip-sawed lumber. Right across the street from the hotel was the livery stable. Below him and two doors down from the hotel, was the Nippy Jones Saloon, where he had just had his encounter with Nate Poindexter.

Because the saloon was under him, he couldn't actually see it from his window, but he could see the bright splash of light it threw into the street, and he could hear laughter and piano music. He wished he had not had that encounter with Nate. For a while, when they were in grade school, Rex and

Nate had been friends. It was only when they got old enough to realize the animosity that existed between their families that their own relationship changed.

He left the room and walked down to the end of the hall to take his bath.

Sylvia Poindexter and her friend Linda Stallings had taken a room at the Dunn Hotel.

"I'm looking forward to the dance tonight," Sylvia said. "It's a shame we have to come this far, though. How often do they have them in Thirty Four Corners?"

"Oh, Sylvia, you've been gone too long if you actually think that's ever going to happen," Linda said. "That isn't possible. Not as long as the feud is going on."

"Oh pooh. This feud is the dumbest thing. I wish it would stop."

"I think everybody wishes that, but now that people have been killed I think it's just going to get worse," Linda said.

"You know what Papa says. He says that he thinks a lot of people are just using the feud. They've got their own reasons for wanting to shoot someone, so they do it, and then they say it is because of the feud."

"Then why won't your papa and Mr. Ross shake hands, and call this thing over?" Linda asked.

"I don't know. I believe Papa would, if Mr. Ross would."

"It may have gone too far for that now," Linda said. "What with the killings that have happened."

"Yes," Sylvia said. "I heard about those, a man who worked at the BR and a boy who worked for Papa. It's awful, it's just awful."

Linda smiled. "Well, there's no feud here, at least. And we've got a dance to go to tonight."

"We must get dressed, because I don't want to miss any of it," Sylvia said.

Rex was just getting into the tub when a woman opened the door. He stood there for a moment, so surprised by her unexpected appearance that he made no effort to cover himself. He was totally nude and the woman gasped in shock at having walked in on him like this.

"Miss, as you can readily see, this room is occupied," Rex said calmly.

"Yes, I do see," the woman replied. "I'm sorry. I was told that if the bathing room was unlocked, that meant it was available for anyone who might want to use it." She stared pointedly at the man's nudity and, realizing he was coming under such intense scrutiny, Rex smiled audaciously, shamelessly, then slowly sat down in the water.

"I would invite you in, but I don't think there's room in the tub."

"I . . . the door was unlocked. I was sure that meant that the room was unoccupied."

"I'm sorry. I must have forgotten to lock the door."

The woman smiled self-consciously. "Yes, well, perhaps I should have knocked."

"No harm done," Rex said. "There's another bathing room next door."

"Yes, thank you, I'll use that one. Oh, and I'll knock first," she added.

"That might be a good idea," Rex said.

Sylvia stepped out of the room and closed the door behind her. Never in her life had she been so embarrassed, and now she looked up and down the hall to see if anyone had seen her make such a colossal mistake. She felt a heat that wasn't related to the ambient temperature, then, fanning herself, stepped into the bathing room next door to the one she had just entered. She made certain that the door was locked before she began to draw the water for her bath.

As she slipped down into the tub a few minutes later, she could hear the man in the room next to hers. He was singing. Had he forgotten that she was just next door to him? Or did he remember, and he was singing just for her?

Ta-ra-ra Boom-de-ay!
Ta-ra-ra Boom-de-ay
I'm not extravagantly shy
And when a nice young girl is nigh
For her heart I'll have a try

Sylvia smiled, and slipped farther down into the water.

"Oh, Linda," she said when she returned to the room she was sharing with Linda. "You'll never believe what just happened."

"What?"

A broad smile spread across her lips. "I suppose I should have knocked," she said, as she began the story.

When she finished the story, both she and Linda were laughing heartily.

"And what I like about the song he was singing was when he said he wasn't extravagantly shy," Sylvia said. "I'll say he wasn't extravagantly shy! He was anything *but* shy!"

They laughed again.

A short time later, just before it was time to go to the dance, Sylvia was standing in front of the mirror examining herself. The dress was green, with a narrow waist, and a deeply scooped neck. She was beginning to have second thoughts about wearing this dress, and she said as much to Linda.

"What? No, what are you talking about? That is a beautiful dress, and you look beautiful in it."

"But I don't think I realized how low it was cut in front. Why, it is practically scandalous."

"Nonsense. You'll be the belle of the ball."

Chapter Nineteen

Rex was standing by the wall when he saw the two women enter. He had a quick intake of breath when he saw the woman in the green dress. Had she come in totally naked, he did not think she could have presented a more provocative appearance. And yet, he could tell by the hesitant expression on her face that she was not used to wearing such a revealing dress. He also thought that he had never seen a more beautiful woman—then, suddenly, he realized that he had seen her before. This was the same woman who had walked in on him in his bath!

Someone walked to the platform and signaled for the band leader to play a trumpet fanfare that got everyone's attention. Once the fanfare was played, he held up his arms.

"Ladies and gentlemen, may I have your attention please? First of all, thank you all for coming. As you know, this dance is to be a benefit to raise money to buy a new pumper for the fire department. And to raise money, we are having a silent auction with dozens of donated items to bid on, so please stop by the table where Mrs. Kellogg and Mrs. Clayton are sitting. Make generous bids on whatever catches your fancy. Some of the ladies have knitted some nice scarves, and others have made cakes and cookies. It's all for a good cause, so don't be stingy."

At the conclusion of the announcement, there was generous applause.

"Now if you would, choose your partners for the grand march."

Rex walked over to the lady in green, smiled at her, and offered her his arm.

"I wonder, *ma dame en vert,* if you might be my partner in the grand march."

Sylvia returned his smile; then she gasped. "It's you!" she said.

Rex chuckled. "Yes, but as you can see, or in this case, not see, there isn't quite as much of me."

Sylvia couldn't repress her own laugh. "I must say, sir, you seem to have taken it in all good cheer."

"What would you have had me do? Scream and make an effort to cover myself?"

"No, on hindsight, I think your reaction was proper, bringing about the least amount of embarrassment for both of us. *Ma dame en vert?* What is that?"

"That's French for 'my lady in green,'" Rex said. "I was just showing off, trying to impress you."

"Impress me? Or confuse me?"

Rex laughed. "Good point," he said, keeping his arm out. Sylvia took it, and the music began.

As the procession began, they marched, two by two and arm in arm, to the far end of the floor. Curving around, they came back to where they had started. Then, as the music continued, the marchers weaved back and forth until their numbers increased to four. Then the numbers in the file increased again, until there was the grand finale.

On the following dances, Rex danced with the lady in green as often as he could, making a conscious decision to dance with nobody else except her. There were more men than women at the dance, which meant that sometimes he would have to stand against the wall and watch her dance with other men. Then, when he finally claimed her for one dance, he asked if she was tired.

"Why do you think I might be tired?"

"I would think that you might be, because you have danced every dance. Would you like to skip this one? Perhaps we could step outside for a breath of fresh air."

"Yes," she said. "Yes, thank you, that is a wonderful idea."

Rex took her by the arm and led her outside, where, in the dark, they walked over to stand under a tree.

"We can stand in the shade here," Rex said.

She laughed. "What do you mean shade, silly? It's nighttime."

"Perhaps I should have said that we could stand

in the shadows," Rex said. "As long as we are here, nobody can see us, even if they step outside."

"Why do you not want to be seen?"

"Because I want to kiss you. And I thought that you might not want to be seen."

"Oh."

Rex moved toward her, and when she offered no resistance, he did kiss her.

"I know that was very forward of me," Rex said. "I hope you aren't angry."

"Not at all. After all, I was forewarned that you would try."

"Forewarned?"

"Didn't you sing a song that said you were not extravagantly shy, and when a nice young girl was nigh, that for her heart you would have a try?"

"You were listening, to me from the next room, weren't you?"

Sylvia smiled, and even in the shadows Rex could see her white, even teeth. "Wasn't it your intention that I listen?"

"All right, you caught on to my secret. Yes, it was my intention for you to listen. I guess I must be a pretty good singer, huh?"

"Why do you say that?"

"It worked. I got you to kiss me."

"I wanted you to kiss me," Sylvia said, easily.

Rex laughed.

"What is it?"

"Here we are, kissing each other, and I don't

even know your name, other than Lady in Green. What is your name? My name is . . ."

"No!" Sylvia said, interrupting Rex in midsentence and putting her fingers to his lips. "Let's not share our names. At least, not yet."

"Why not?"

"Don't you think it is more romantic if we don't share names? This way we can be *Ships that pass in the night, and speak each other in passing, Only a signal shown and a distant voice in the darkness; So on the ocean of life we pass and speak one another, Only a look and a voice; then darkness again and a silence.*"

"Henry Wadsworth Longfellow," Rex said.

"I knew you would recognize it!"

"Since we have so much in common, don't you think we should know other's names?"

"Why?"

"Suppose I wanted to call on you again?"

"If it is meant to be, it will be," Sylvia said.

"But, should we tempt fate so?"

"Yes, for only by tempting fate, shall our true destiny be determined," Sylvia replied.

Rex chuckled quietly. "You have quite a way with words. But I particularly like what you just said, when you referred to it as *our* destiny."

In the ballroom behind them, they heard the music stop.

"I had better get back inside," she said.

"I'll walk you to the door."

Rex offered her arm, and Sylvia took it. Just as they stepped inside, though, they were met by Nate

Poindexter. Without so much as a word, Nate threw a punch that landed on Rex's chin. The punch was totally unexpected, and Rex went down like a sack of potatoes.

"Nate!" Sylvia gasped in anger and fear. "Are you insane? What are you doing?"

"Get back inside, now!" Nate ordered.

"What? What has gotten into you?"

"Sylvia, come with me," Linda said, taking Sylvia's arm.

"What is this? What is going on?"

"Please, come with me," Linda pleaded. "I'll explain everything."

"Why did Nate . . . good Lord! Nate is holding a gun!"

"Sylvia, don't you know who that was that you were with?"

"Yes, he is the man that I barged in on, while he was taking his bath. But, Linda, nothing happened! Absolutely nothing! Nate had no cause to attack him like that."

"Seeing him in the bath has nothing to do with it. Sylvia, that is Rex Ross."

"Ross?" Sylvie replied, putting her fingers to her lips, the same lips that could still feel his kiss. "That was Rex Ross?"

"Yes. Now do you see why your brother reacted as he did? He was just trying to protect you."

* * *

When Rex regained his feet, he was about to go after Nate in retaliation for the attack, but he stopped short when he saw that Nate was pointing a pistol at him.

"What were you two doing out there?" Nate asked.

"What do you mean, what were we doing? What the hell business is that of yours?" Rex asked angrily.

"You had better never let me catch you with her again. Leave her alone."

Rex smiled, a mocking smile.

"Oh, I get it now. Well, Nate, if you can't hang on to your girlfriend, that's not my problem."

"She isn't my girlfriend, you pretentious son of a bitch! She is my sister!"

"Your sister?"

"Sylvia is my sister."

Rex, shocked by the news, took a couple of steps back and stared at Nate. "That was Sylvia?" he asked in a quiet voice.

"Yes. And I'm telling you now, stay away from her," Nate ordered.

"Don't worry, I will. I don't want anything to do with anyone who is named Poindexter."

Wedge Hill Ranch

Although the BR and the Tumbling P were the two biggest ranches in the county, theirs weren't the only ranches. There were at least half-a-dozen others, including Wedge Hill, a small ranch owned by Kyle Stallings. At one time, Kyle Stallings had ridden for Ben Ross, but in doing some research he'd discovered that the land claims filed by both Ross and Poindexter had left a fifteen-thousand-acre pie-slice-shaped wedge at the eastern end of the two large ranches, so he'd filed on it. Not only did his ranch have some of the best grassland in the county, the "arc" of the pie was on the Rio Puerco, providing Stallings with a year-round source of water.

Although neither Ben Ross nor Morgan Poindexter was happy with the arrangement, their animosity toward each other was so great that, for the most part, they tended to leave Stallings alone. There were some who advised Stallings to ally himself with either Ross or Poindexter so that he would have their protection. But it was Stallings's belief that his best option would be, to the extent possible, to keep himself completely free of the feud, and that's what he did.

On the Stallings ranch, Kyle sat on a rock outcropping and leaned back against a boulder. His foreman had just brought him a skillet of beans and bacon. There were a couple of biscuits and an onion slice on the side.

"Uhmm, biscuits," Stallings said.

"They can't no one make biscuits like Andy," one of the drovers, said. "Boss, I tell you, Andy is gonna make some hard-drivin' woman a awful good husband," he teased.

Stallings and the others laughed, and Andy, who was emptying the last dregs of a cup of coffee, threw the rest toward the man who was teasing him. It was all in good fun though, with little chance of an actual fight erupting. There were four men sitting around the fire and two more out riding night-herd. Those six represented Stallings's entire outfit. The fire had just about burned down and was little more than glowing embers.

"Boss, when it comes time for you to bed down, well, I throw'd your roll down over here," Joe Canby said. Nearly sixty, Canby was by far the oldest of the drovers and was sort of the father figure to all of them. "It's on high ground 'n' 'bout as level as any-place I could find around here."

"Thanks, Mr. Canby," Stallings said as he raked his biscuit through the last of the bean juice. He dunked his kit in a bucket of water, cleaned it off with some sand, then folded it and put it away.

Stallings's riders had all ridden for other spreads before they came to work for him. He wasn't able to pay them the same wages as the other ranchers, but he offered them something more. He offered them a share in the herd. He would keep the land for his own, but he promised his cowboys that they would share in ownership of the herd. That arrangement had created binding loyalties and strengthened friendships. Stallings's ranch might be the smallest in the county, he reasoned, but everyone who worked there believed it was, by far, the best place to be.

When the men who worked for Stallings encoun-tered the hands from the other ranches in town, they sometimes teased them for being cowboys, while they, by virtue of their joint ownership of the herd, were cattlemen. It made for some lively discussions in the saloons in town.

"Boss, you know Ben Ross. Do you really think he hired someone to kill the Patterson boy?" Andy asked. Andy Warren was a former soldier who had been with General Crook in the chase for Geronimo.

"No, I don't believe Ben was any more behind that than Morgan Poindexter was behind Seth Miller gettin' killed," Kyle said.

"Well, if they ain't doin' it, who is a-doin' it?"

Stallings shook his head. "I don't have an idea in hell who it is that's a-doin' all this," Kyle replied. "But I just can't believe that either one of 'em would do anything like that. I've known both of 'em for a long time. Sure, Ben 'n' Morgan has got 'em a feud going, but it just isn't like either one of them to do something like what was done to the Patterson boy."

"Well, you know what they're sayin', don't you? They're sayin' that the Patterson boy was kilt for revenge for Seth Miller gettin' kilt," Andy said.

"I still don't believe Ross had anything to do with it."

"Maybe not, but I'm tellin' you the truth, boss, it's gettin' harder and harder to go into town with what's goin' on and all. You don't never know when bullets is goin' to start flyin'."

"The whole town is all divided up, half for Ross and half for Poindexter," another said.

"Hell, the town has been divided up for over twenty years," Kyle said.

"That's true, but always before the dividing up has been a show of support more 'n anythin' else. There never was no real shootin' before, and I've got a mind that what's been happenin' here lately is just the beginnin'," Canby said. "And it ain't just the town that's divided. Hell, all of Valencia country this side of the Rio Grande is divided."

"Except for us," one of the drovers said. "We ain't took no sides."

"You think we ought to take sides, do you, Marty?" Stallings asked.

"Seems like we ought to, else we'll wind up havin' ever'one against us," Marty replied.

"Whose side do you think we should take?"

"Well, I . . . I don't rightly know. I rode some for Ross for a while, but Tommy rode for Poindexter. And I reckon Tommy is about my best friend, and I sure wouldn't want to wind up on the other side from him."

Tommy was Tommy Murchison, who was, at the moment, one of the two riders now out with the herd.

"You just put your finger on it, Marty," Stallings said. "Which side do we take? It's not an easy decision to make, is it? Especially when we don't have a stake in this fight."

"What is it they are a-fightin' about, anyhow?" Andy asked. "Does anyone even know?"

"I heard oncet that they was fightin' over a

woman," Marty said. "It's said that they give the woman a choice between 'em, and she chose Ross."

"That ain't it at all," Canby said.

"Then what happened?"

Canby laughed. "Ross was goin' to marry him one of those mail-order brides. Poindexter was supposed to act as if he was the bride's papa, goin' to give her away. Only thing is, he didn't give her away. He run off with her . . . right while Ross was standin' up at the altar, waitin' for 'em to come walkin' down the aisle."

"I've always heard that as well," Stallings said. "But I wasn't sure if it was true or not."

"It's true all right," Canby said.

"How do you know it's true?" Andy asked.

"I know it's true 'cause I was right there when it happened. I was sittin' in the church along with near 'bout the rest of the town, waitin' on the weddin' to happen."

"I'll be damn," Andy said. "No wonder Ross 'n' Poindexter are fightin'."

Chapter Twenty

Thirty Four Corners

"Who did you say kilt Gillespie?" Shardeen asked. Shardeen and Cates were in the Hog Waller Saloon, talking to Dagan, who had made a special trip over to Thirty Four Corners from Risco, just to give Tully Cates the news that his friend had been killed.

"A man by the name of Matt Jensen," Dagan said. "Have you ever heard of him?"

"Yeah," Shardeen said. "I've heard of him."

"So that's who it was that was shootin' at us," Cates said.

"Wait a minute! You mean you was with Gillespie when he was kilt?" Dagan asked.

"Yes."

"I knew it!" Dagan said. "I knew it had to have somethin' to do with whatever it is Gillespie was workin' on. I want in on it."

"You want in on what?"

"I want in on whatever it was that Gillespie was doin'. He said there was goin' to be a lot of money in it."

"Are you sure you want to take Gillespie's place? It got him killed, you know," Cates said.

"Are you still a part of it?" Dagan asked.

"A part of what?"

"I don't know a part of what," Dagan replied in an exasperated voice. "But if it's somethin' that could get you kilt, and it did get Gillespie kilt, but you're still a-doin' it, then it must be worth a lot of money."

"There's no money yet, but yeah, we stand to make a lot of money," Cates said.

"Then, count me in."

"We'll have to talk to Bodine about it," Cates said.

Two days later, Matt Jensen, now five hundred dollars richer, rode into Thirty Four Corners. It was no different from any of the hundreds of other Western settlements Matt Jensen had come through in his long quest for Rufus Draco. Thirty Four Corners was fly-blown, with its main street lined on both sides by unpainted, rip-sawed, false-fronted buildings. As he passed by one of the buildings, a couple of half-naked women, their breasts spilling over the top of their chemises, called down to him from a balcony.

"Hey, darlin', which side of the street will you be goin' to?" one of them called down to him.

"Which side of the street? Does it matter?"

"You're new to town, ain't you?" the other asked.

"Yes."

"Well here's the thing, honey. In this town you choose a side of the street, and once you choose, that's the side you stay on."

"Choose this side, then come on up and keep us company. We'll give you a good welcome," the other woman said.

"You mean both of you will give me a good welcome?"

"Honey, if you can handle both of us, we'll do it for free," one of the women said, laughing.

Matt laughed with her, then rode on down to the far end of the street, where it ended on a cross street that made a T with this one. There, he saw a livery stable. He dismounted as someone came out to greet him. He was about forty, Matt guessed, and showed the signs of a life of hard work, weathered skin and calloused hands, but his eyes were bright and alert.

"The name is Gregory, Wes Gregory," the man greeted. "What can I do for you?"

"I'd like to put my horse up for a while."

"Yes, sir, that'll be a quarter a day," Gregory said. "Which side?"

"Which side what?"

"We've got stalls in the north and stalls on the south. Which side do you want your horse on?"

"Hell, Mr. Gregory, I don't care which side. Why would you ask me a question like that? All I want is for him to have a place to stay, and to be fed and watered. Does it matter which side he is on for that?"

"No, sir, we take very good care of all the horses here, no matter which side they are on. I don't reckon you've chose up your side yet, have you?" Gregory asked.

"Evidently not," Matt replied, and though he found this reference to sides curious, remembering that even the whores had spoken of choosing a side, his biggest interest at the moment was in getting a bath, then something to drink, and a meal, in that order. Because of that, he didn't pursue the issue any further, though he knew that the livery-man wanted to carry on the conversation.

"I'll put him on the south side, if you have no objections."

"Fine."

"How long will he be with us?"

"I don't know yet. Here's ten dollars—that should give us forty days, if my math is correct."

"Your math is absolutely correct," the hostler said, taking the money with a broad smile. "I'll take very good care of your horse for you."

"Oh, I know you will," Matt replied. "Because you don't want to see what would happen if you didn't."

Gregory laughed. "I like a man who is concerned about his horse. What's the horse's name?"

"Spirit."

"Come along, Spirit. I just know we are going to be good friends."

Leaving Spirit at the livery, Matt started back up the street toward the Homestead Hotel. He chose the Homestead for no other reason than that it was the closest to the livery. By coincidence, the Homestead was located on the north side of the street, which was the same side as the two women who had greeted him earlier.

He stepped into the lobby, looked around for a second, and, seeing that it was empty, moved over to the front desk.

"I need a room," Matt said as he signed the registry.

An hour later, with the trail dirt and the stink washed away, Matt stepped out onto the boardwalk in front of the hotel. Looking back toward where he had seen the women earlier, he saw that only one was still standing out there.

"Oh my, honey, you clean up just real pretty!" the woman called out to him.

Matt smiled, and touched the brim of his hat, then started in the opposite direction. After walking half a block, he came to the Circle Thirty Four Saloon. There was a drunk passed out on the steps in front of the place, and Matt had to step over him in order to go inside. Smoke-filled rays of outside light spilled in through the windows. The place smelled of cheap whiskey, stale beer, and strong tobacco. There was a long bar on the left, dirty towels hanging on hooks about every five feet along its front. A large mirror was behind the bar, but what images Matt could see were distorted by imperfections in the glass.

Over against the back wall, near the foot of the stairs, a cigar-scarred, beer-stained upright piano was being played by a bald-headed musician. Out on the floor of the saloon, nearly all the tables were filled. A few bar gals were flitting about, pushing drinks and promising more than they really intended to deliver. There was a card game in progress, but most of the patrons were just drinking and talking.

"You can't get much more evil than to wrap barbed wire around somebody that ain't much more'n a boy," Matt heard someone say. "The BR spread must have them some pretty low-down sons of bitches workin' for 'em, for someone to do somethin' like that."

"More 'n likely, they was just gettin' revenge," another said.

"Revenge for what?"

"Don't forget, Seth Miller was a cowboy ridin' for the BR, and he got hisself shot, and he wasn't doin' nothin' no more 'n standin' at the bar drinkin' a beer."

"He was shot accidental," the first speaker said.

"How do you know it was accidental?"

"The bullet come in from outside, didn't it? It had to be accidental."

"They's a lot of folks don't believe that. You might remember that just before it happened, they was two cowboys that was bedevilin' Seth and Lou."

"They wasn't cowboys."

"No, but they was from the Tumbling P."

"Did you know that one of them two fellers that was arguin' with Seth and Lou has done got hisself shot?" one of the other men asked.

"Got himself shot? Where?"

"Over in Risco."

"How do you know?"

"I know, 'cause Elmer Puckett had to be in Risco, and he seen the body. It was standin' up in front of the hardware store, just as pretty as you please, is what Elmer said. Anyhow, Elmer said that he went over to take a look at the body and when he did, he seen that it was one of the two men that kilt Seth Miller."

"You mean allegedly killed Seth Miller, don't you, Mr. Powell? There were no eyewitnesses, so we can never be sure."

"You can never be sure, Dempster, because you are a lawyer, and you'd argue which side the sun come up on this mornin', if you didn't see it personal."

The others laughed.

"A lawyer's stock in trade are truth and facts," Dempster replied.

"Truth and facts? Ain't that the same thing?"

"No, no, not at all," Dempster replied. "All facts are true, but not all truth is fact."

"Now, that don't make no sense at all."

Dempster chuckled. "Oh, it makes a lot of sense," Dempster said. "Sometimes if the facts are stacked against you when you are pleading a case, truth is the only weapon you have."

"Lord have mercy, Dempster, are all lawyers that strange?"

"Most of us," Dempster agreed with a chuckle.

"Anyhow," Powell said, getting back to his story, "we heard him called Poke while he was in here, and the marshal over at Risco said that his name was Poke Gillespie. And like I said, Puckett said for sure that it was the same person that was in here, arguin' with Seth."

The bartender had been pouring the residue from abandoned whiskey glasses back into a bottle when Matt first stepped up to the bar. He pulled an expectorated quid of tobacco from one glass, dropped the quid into a spittoon, then poured the whiskey back into the bottle. Matt held up his finger.

"Yeah, can I help you?"

Matt's intention had been to order a whiskey, but seeing the bartender's action caused him to change his mind.

"I'll have a beer," he said.

The bartender turned to the beer barrel, pulled the spigot handle, and filled a mug. He slid the mug across the bar to Matt. "That'll be a nickel," he said.

"I'd like it in a clean glass."

"A clean glass? What do you need a clean glass for?"

"Carl?" someone from the other end of the bar called.

Carl held his hand out toward the customer, indicating he wasn't yet finished with his discussion.

"There don't nobody else ever complain about the mug I give them. What makes you any different from them?"

"Carl?" the customer said again with a little more urgency.

Carl picked the mug up. "Now, if you want it, give me your nickel. Otherwise, this goes back in the barrel."

"Carl, damn it! You'd better come down here, and I mean now!" the customer yelled this time.

"What the hell are you yellin' about, Logan? Can't you see I'm busy here?"

"Come here," Logan said.

With a sigh of frustration, and still holding the beer, Carl walked down the bar to the insistent customer. The customer whispered something in Carl's ear, and Carl blanched, visibly. Quickly, he poured the beer he was holding into a slop bucket, then got another mug and showed it to Matt.

"What about this mug, Mr. Jensen? Is it clean enough?" he asked solicitously.

"Yes, that'll do fine, thank you," Matt said.

"You shoulda said somethin'," the bartender said

as, with a shaking hand, he held a new mug under the beer spigot. "You shoulda tol' me who you was."

"You mean if I were someone other than Matt Jensen, I would have to be satisfied with the dirty beer mug?"

"Yes, sir, well, like I said, there don't nobody else ever complain about it. But anytime you want a clean mug, Mr. Jensen, why, you just ask me and I'll make certain you get one."

All the conversation halted as the entire saloon looked at the man nearly everyone in the room had heard of. Matt looked back at them without comment. Then he slapped his nickel on the bar and reached for his beer.

"No, sir, your money is no good in here," Carl said. "The beer is on the house, on account of you chose this side of the street."

That was the third time someone had mentioned the "side of the street" as if it were significant. Matt wanted to ask about it, but figured that if he stayed here long enough, he would find out.

"Thanks, for the beer," Matt said, picking up the nickel and pocketing it. He drank the beer in about three long drinks, then set the empty mug on the bar. "Can a fella get anything to eat in here?"

"Bacon, beans, and fried taters," Carl said.

"I'll go along with that. Any biscuits to go with them?"

"Biscuits? Mr. Jensen, you ain't never even tasted

biscuit, 'til you eat one of 'em that my wife bakes. Yes, sir, we got biscuits."

"Sounds good. With another beer."

"Yes, sir, you just go find yourself a table," Carl said.

A large man with heavy brows and a bulbous nose had been sitting by himself in the back corner of the room, but he looked up when he heard Matt's name.

So that's what the son of a bitch looks like, he thought, not speaking the words aloud. He continued to nurse his beer in silence as he watched Matt carry his second beer to an empty table. He listened in on the conversation at the next table.

"Do you think Matt Jensen has come to join up with Poindexter?" Powell asked the others at his table. He spoke quietly, because he didn't want Matt to hear him.

"He's on this side of the street, ain't he?" Bivens said.

"Reckon he'll go after Bodine?" Powell asked.

"I expect he will. I mean, I figure he'll at least try."

"Try? What do you mean, try? Are you tellin' me that Matt Jensen can't handle the likes of Lucien Bodine?"

"I don't know, but it would sure be a fine gunfight to watch, though, wouldn't it? Matt Jensen and Lucien Bodine?"

"Wonder how many men Bodine has kilt?" Bivens asked.

"Don't nobody know, because, truth to tell, I don't know that anybody really knows that much about Bodine. I mean, I never heard of him 'til he come here. But Strawn knows all about him, and Strawn said that Bodine has kilt himself a bunch of men."

"If he's kilt all that many men, I wonder why it is we ain't never heard of him?"

"It ain't the ones you've heard of that you have to worry about. It's the ones you ain't heard about."

"Well, I've heard of Sam Strawn, and I'll tell you true, he scares the hell out of me, for all that he is on the right side."

"Maybe," Dempster said. It was the lawyer's first contribution to the discussion.

"Maybe what?"

"Maybe Strawn is on the right side."

"Well, he's on the side of the Tumbling P, ain't he?"

"Yes, and Bodine is on the side of the BR. But if you notice, the killing didn't actually start until Bodine and Strawn showed up."

"You're thinkin' maybe they started all this, do you? Maybe to settle some score between the two of them?"

"It could be. What troubles me more is in trying to ascertain Jensen's side in this."

"What do you mean?" Powell asked.

"Think about it. He is the one who killed Poke Gillespie, and, according to you, Mr. Powell, Gillespie is the one who killed Seth Miller, one of the BR men.

So if Jensen is here to support the Tumbling P, why did he shoot someone who may have been acting on behalf of Morgan Poindexter?"

"Yeah," Powell said. "Yeah, I see what you mean. I didn't think about it like that."

Matt couldn't hear exactly what the men at the distant table were talking about, but he wasn't unaware that he was the subject of conversation. That was easy to tell because, during the conversation, more than one of them would steal a glance Matt's way.

Carl brought his supper to him.

"Thank you, Carl," Matt said.

Hearing Matt Jensen actually call him by name caused a big smile to spread across Carl's face.

"Yes, sir, anything I can do for you, why, you just let me know," Carl said.

The big man who was sitting back in the corner all by himself drained the rest of his beer, then left.

Chapter Twenty-one

Supper was pretty good, though Matt was certain that his hunger was the predominant spice. After supper, Matt left the saloon.

"Yes, sir," he heard someone say behind him as he stepped through the batwing doors. "That fella there, if he was to go after Bodine, or Strawn, either one, that would be somethin' to behold. Folks would come from miles around just to see somethin' like that."

Matt knew Strawn, and thought of his near encounter with him back in Pecato. The name Lucien Bodine wasn't one he had ever heard before, but most of Matt's travel and experience was considerably north, in Colorado, Wyoming, and even Montana. If a man named Lucien Bodine had made his reputation down here, it was quite possible Matt had never heard of him, no matter the notoriety he might have established. He started back toward the hotel, when he heard a woman's voice call out to him.

"Look out!"

Almost on top of the warning, Matt felt a blow to the side of his head. He saw stars, but he didn't go down.

When his attacker swung at him a second time, Matt was able to avoid him. With his fists up, Matt danced quickly out to the middle of the street, avoiding any more surprises from the shadows. It wasn't until then that he saw his attacker, a large man with heavy brows and a bulbous nose.

"Mister," the man said with a low growl, "you kilt my brother and I aim to settle accounts for him."

"Fight!" someone shouted. "They's a fight in the street!"

Almost instantly, it seemed, a crowd was gathered around Matt and the man who had come at him out of the shadows.

"Who was your brother?"

"That's just like you, ain't it?" the big man said, moving his fists in small circles as he looked for another opening. "You've kilt so many men that you don't know all their names, have you?"

"I know their names," Matt said.

"Yeah? Well, here's a name for you. Billy Carter. I'm Frank Carter and Billy was my brother," the big man said.*

"I remember your brother," Matt said. "I remember that he was trying to kill me. What was I supposed to do?"

*Matt Jensen, the Last Mountain Man: The Eyes of Texas

"What you was supposed to do was let him kill you, you son of a bitch."

The big man swung wildly at Matt, but Matt slipped the punch easily, then counterpunched with a quick, slashing left to Carter's face. It was a good, well-hit blow, but Carter just flinched once, then laughed a low, evil laugh.

"You might wonder why I didn't just shoot you when you come out of the saloon. I didn't shoot you, 'cause I plan to beat you to death with my bare hands." Carter swung again and missed, and again Matt counterpunched, but with little effect.

"Yes, sir," Carter said. "I aim to enjoy this."

"Five dollars says Carter whips him," someone said.

"This is Matt Jensen we're talkin' about," another said.

"Yeah, but this here ain't a shootin' now, is it? No, sir, it's bare-knuckle fightin', and I say Carter will whip 'im."

"I don't know, I've seen men who look like this fight before. They ain't all that big, but they're tough as rawhide. I'm going with Jensen."

With an angry roar, Carter rushed Matt again, and Matt stepped aside, avoiding him. Carter, unable to adjust his charge, slammed into a hitching rail, smashing through it as if it were kindling. He turned and faced Matt again.

A hush fell over the crowd now, as they watched the two men with a great deal of interest. Matt was six feet tall, and powerfully built, but Carter had him by at least four inches and forty pounds, none of it fat. It was obviously going to be a test of quickness and ability against brute strength, and they wanted to see if Jensen could handle Carter. Matt and Carter circled around for a moment, holding their fists doubled in front of them, each trying to test the mettle of the other.

Carter swung another club-like swing, but by now Matt had managed to gauge the timing, so that he was able to avoid Carter's efforts with little difficulty. Matt counterpunched and again he scored well, but again, Carter laughed it off.

"I'm willin' to take ever'thing you can throw at me 'til I get the openin' I'm lookin' for," Carter said.

As the fight continued, it developed that Matt could hit Carter at will, and though Carter laughed off his early blows, it was soon obvious that there was a cumulative effect to Matt's punches. Both of Carter's eyes began to puff up, and there was a nasty cut on his lip. Then, when Matt caught Carter in the nose with a hard right jab, he felt the nose go under his hand. Carter's nose started gushing blood, which ran across Carter's teeth and chin.

Matt looked for another chance at the nose, but Carter started protecting it. Matt was unable to get it again, though the fact that Carter was favoring it told Matt that the nose was hurting him.

Except for the opening blow, Carter hadn't connected. The big man was throwing great swinging blows toward Matt, barely missing him on a couple of occasions, but, as yet, none of them had connected.

After four or five such swinging blows, Matt noticed that Carter was leaving a slight opening for a good right punch, if he could just slip it across his shoulder. On Carter's next swing, Matt threw a solid right, straight at the place where he though Carter's Adam's apple would be. He timed it perfectly and had the satisfaction of seeing Carter put both hands to his neck as he gasped for breath. Then, with Carter leaving his head unprotected, Matt sent a powerful right jab to his jaw. Carter dropped to his knees, still clutching his Adam's apple.

Carter was vulnerable, and Matt could have finished him off, but he just stood there, looking down at him.

"Carter, you aren't responsible for your brother," Matt said. "You can't be blamed for anything he did, and you don't owe him anything now."

Carter didn't respond, except for a few audible gasps.

"Eat only soft food for the next few days. Your throat is going to be sore, but you'll live through it. You have a choice now. We can call this finished, or you can come after me again. And if you come after me again, I might have to kill you. So, which will it be?"

Carter was still unable to vocalize any answer, but, while still on his knees, he extended his hand, offering it as a handshake. Matt took it.

"Good choice," he said, as he shook Carter's hand.

Matt looked around at those who had gathered to watch the fight, then addressed two of the men who were the closest. "Help him up," he said.

The two men moved quickly to Carter and, with one on either side, helped him regain his feet.

As a result of the initial blow, Matt's right eye had been swelling all during the fight. He walked over to a nearby watering trough, stood there with his hands resting on the edge of the trough as he leaned against it, breathing hard to recover his breath. He looked at his reflection in the water and saw that, by now, the eye was swollen completely shut. He shut both eyes.

As he stood there with both eyes closed, he felt something cool and damp pressed up against his swollen eye. When he opened his good eye he saw that a woman was standing next to him, holding a damp cloth over his eyes. It was one of the women he had seen earlier, standing out on the upstairs balcony of the brothel.

"Thanks," Matt said.

"Do you have a hotel room?" she asked.

"Yes."

"Too bad. But, if you'll allow me, I'll walk you to your room."

"I appreciate that."

* * *

It was quiet where Shardeen, Cates, and Dagan waited in the rocks. They could hear crickets and frogs, a distant coyote and a closer owl, but nothing else. Then, they heard the sounds of approaching men, the drum of horses' hooves, the rattle of the saddle and tack.

"Here they come," Shardeen said. "Get ready for 'em." He pulled his pistol and checked his load, then waited.

The riders continued their ghostly approach, men and animals moving as softly and quietly as drifting smoke. Then, four riders appeared in the moonlight. They were completely unaware of what awaited them.

Shardeen, and the men with him, cocked their pistols and waited.

"Now!" Shardeen shouted. "Shoot 'em down!"

Gunfire erupted in the night, the flashes of the muzzle blasts illuminating the rocks like lightning. Shardeen, Cates, and Dagan were well positioned in the rocks to pick out their targets. The four riders, on the other hand, were astride horses that were rearing and twisting about nervously as flying lead whistled through the air and whined off stone.

The deadly ambush was over within half a minute and it was quiet, the final round of shooting now but faint echoes bounding off distant hills. A little cloud of acrid-bitter gun smoke drifted up over the deadly battlefield and Shardeen walked out among the fallen men cautiously, his pistol at the ready. With Shardeen's white skin gleaming in the light of the full moon, he looked like a ghost, moving through the night. He kicked at each man to see if anyone was still alive.

It wasn't necessary. All four men were dead and the entire battle had taken less than a minute.

"Who were these men?" Dagan asked as he watched Shardeen move from man to man.

"It doesn't matter who they were," Cates answered.

"Then why did we kill them?"

"We need the killing to spread beyond the two ranches. We need to get more people involved."

"Why?"

"You said you wanted in, didn't you? You wanted to make a lot of money?"

"Yes."

"Then you don't need to understand."

The next morning, Matt stood at the window of his hotel room, looking out onto Central Street. The morning commerce of the town was under way, and as he watched he saw that there was definite separation, with men and women moving up and down the boardwalks on one side or the other. Not once did he see anyone cross the street.

He heard the sound of the bed behind him and, looking back, saw that Lois, the woman who had walked him to his hotel room last night, had changed position. Her movement had caused the sheet to pull back from her shoulder, exposing a bare breast. He went over to pull the sheet back up.

Without opening her eyes, Lois smiled. "It's a

little late to be worryin' about my modesty now, isn't it?"

"I suppose it is," Matt admitted. "But you were asleep, and I don't like to take advantage of anyone who is vulnerable."

"Yes, I saw that yesterday when you let Mr. Carter go."

"Did you now?"

"Oh, my goodness," Lois said. "You should see your poor eye."

"Yeah? Well, if you think it looks bad from over there, you should see it from my side."

Lois laughed. "Does it hurt?"

"It's not the best feeling thing I've ever had," Matt replied. "At least the swelling is gone and I can see out of it now."

"It sure is black."

"Don't remind me. Listen, I'm hungry. What do you say we go downstairs and have breakfast?"

"Oh, honey, I'm not sure I'd be welcome there," Lois said. "In case you haven't figured it out yet, I'm what they call a soiled dove."

Matt chuckled. "You mean it wasn't my handsome looks and sparkling personality that attracted you?"

"Well, yes, it was," Lois said. "That and the five dollars," she added with a chuckle.

"Come on, you'll be welcome. You'll be with me."

"All right, if you say so," Lois said a bit apprehensively.

* * *

There were a few stares when Lois stepped into the dining room, but when Matt offered her his arm, no one progressed beyond what were obviously disapproving stares.

Matt led Lois to a table, and even held the chair for her as she sat down.

"Did you see that, Martha?" some man hissed. "That man held the chair out for that whore, just like she was a lady or something."

Matt heard the remark, and he looked at the speaker with an intimidating glare.

"Let's go, Martha," the man said to his wife.

"Go where? Marvin, I haven't even finished my breakfast," Martha said.

"Let's go," Marvin repeated, more urgently this time. Taking his wife by the arm, he physically removed her from the dining room.

When Marvin and Martha left the dining room, Marvin left back a copy of the newspaper, and excusing himself for the moment, Matt walked over to pick it up.

Four Citizens Murdered in Cold Blood

Bodies Found on the Road

Keith Ziegenhorn, Dewey Gimlin, Walter Bizzel, and Tom Dunaway, all good and upstanding citizens of our fair city, were found murdered. Their bodies were discovered early this morning by Mitchell Phelps as he was driving his freight wagon to Valencia to pick up a load from the railroad terminal.

It appeared as if they had been set upon by men so foul as to defy description, for all four had been shot many times, the pistol balls taking terrible effect.

It is not believed that these murders are connected with the ongoing feud between the BR Ranch and the Tumbling P, as none of the men were employed by either ranch. Their deaths however, cannot but add to the melancholy that has settled upon our town with the previous demise of Seth Miller and Jimmy Patterson.

As Matt was reading the newspaper, three men, Alan Blanton, Jack Martin, and Bob Dempster, were meeting in the newspaper office. They were meeting there because Alan Blanton, who was the mayor of the town, was also the editor of the newspaper. They were discussing the four bodies that had been found on the road.

"Why were they killed?" Martin asked. "I know that none of them had anything to do with the BR or the Tumbling P."

"That's the mystery of it," Blanton said. "For some reason this feud seems to be expanding, and we need to find out why."

"We need to do more than that," Dempster said. "We not only need to find out why, we need to find some way of dealing with it."

Blanton shook his head. "There's no way Hunter can deal with it. Even if he could, he couldn't, this happened outside of town."

"It's going to spread into town, and it's going to do that soon, if we don't do something about it," Dempster said.

"Do what about it? Do you have any ideas?"

"Yes," Dempster answered. "I do have an idea."

Chapter Twenty-two

Matt was enjoying his breakfast with Lois, and was now on his second cup of coffee and a second batch of pancakes when three men approached the table. All of them were wearing suits, none were wearing guns.

"Do you know them?" Matt asked.

"The short, baldheaded man is Alan Blanton. He is the editor of the newspaper, and the mayor of the town," Lois whispered. "The tall, thin man is Jack Martin. He owns a hardware store. The fat man with a round face and glasses is Bob Dempster. He is a lawyer."

"Yes, I saw Dempster in the saloon yesterday. Do you think they are a committee come to talk to me about the company I keep?"

"No, I don't think so," Lois said. "From time to time, the mayor has been . . ." Lois paused, looking for the word, before she finished her sentence. "A guest of mine," she concluded.

Matt smiled. "That's good to know."

"Mr. Jensen, please excuse us for disturbing you at your breakfast, but I wonder if we might have a few words with you?" Blanton asked.

"Go right ahead, Mayor," Matt replied. "As long as the young lady and I don't have to stop eating."

Matt carved off a large piece of ham and stuck it in his mouth.

"I was just wondering . . . that is, we were wondering, how long you are planning on staying around our town?"

Matt took a swallow of coffee to wash down the ham, and he studied the mayor and his delegation over the cup rim.

"Are you telling me that you want me to leave your town?" he asked, calmly.

"What? No!" the mayor barked. "Heavens, no, nothing like that. I hope you wouldn't think that."

"Well, normally when a mayor and a delegation make a special visit to see me, then ask how long I'm planning to stay, their next comment is a suggestion that I leave. You asked me how long I was planning to stay—what did you expect me to think?"

"I'm sorry. I meant in no way to infer that."

"All right. Then, just what is it you want?"

"The way things are in this town, now, Marshal

Hunter has more than he can handle, and that leaves us, virtually, a town without law. And no town can afford to be without law," Dempster said.

"Marshal Hunter is doing the best he can, under the circumstances," Martin added. "But the problem with Hunter is the same problem that any local resident would have. You may not realize it, having just arrived in town, but we are a town divided."

"Yes, so I have noticed. You are divided by the north and south side of the street," Matt said.

"Yes, so you do know."

Matt shook his head. "No, I don't, not really. I know there seems to be some significance as to whether someone is on the north or the south side of the street, but I don't know what is so important about that."

"We are a town at war with itself," Dempster explained. "Our two most substantial citizens are in the midst of a feud that goes back well over twenty years. And, in the last few weeks it has gotten worse. Much worse."

"Worse in what way?"

"Well, as of last night, the total number of killings has risen to six," Blanton said.

"Six?" Lois said, surprised by the information. "I know that one of Mr. Ross's men, Seth Miller, was killed. And I know that young Jimmy Patterson, from the Tumbling P was killed. You're saying four more were killed last night?"

"Yes."

"Well, which ranch were they from?"

"That's just it. None of them were riders for either Ross or Poindexter. In fact, all four of them worked in town. Ziegenhorn, Gimlin, Bizzel, and Dunaway.

"Gimlin? Dewey Gimlin?"

"Yes."

"Oh, he was such a nice man," Lois said. "But I don't understand. What did any of them have to do with the feud?"

"That's just it," Blanton said. "They didn't have anything to do with it at all. It's now gone beyond the two ranches."

"How long has this feud been going on?" Matt asked.

"Twenty years. But up until the last few weeks, it had just been that. A feud. Oh, there have been a few fistfights now and then, but nobody had ever been killed before."

"And you say this increase in activity has just happened?" Matt asked.

"Yes, and that's what's so strange about it. I mean, why now, after all these years?"

"There's some skullduggery going on somewhere, that's for sure," Martin said. "And I'm not all that sure that Ross or Poindexter are even behind it."

"If you ask me, it's Bodine and Strawn," Dempster said.

"Strawn? Would that be Sam Strawn?" Matt asked.

"Yes, do you know him?"

"I've met him," Matt said.

"Well, here's the thing. Bodine and Strawn are

bitter enemies. They are about as bitter as Ross and Poindexter," Dempster said. "And as Bodine is working for Ross, and Strawn is working for Poindexter, I wouldn't be in the least surprised if they weren't carrying on their own personal battle, just using the feud between the BR and the Tumbling P as an excuse."

"What do you mean, working for them?" Matt asked. "You don't mean they are cowboys, do you?"

"Ha! No, sir, nothin' like that," Martin said. "They're callin' themselves cattle detectives. But the truth is, they ain't nothin' more'n hired guns."

"When did these cattle detectives begin? It can't be too long ago, because it wasn't more than a few weeks ago that I saw Strawn."

"It's only been for a few weeks," Blanton said. "Bodine started for Ross at the same time Strawn started for Poindexter."

"That's a little strange, don't you think? I mean that they have no history of using hired guns, then they both hire someone at about the same time."

"Well, yes, I suppose so," Blanton said. "On the other hand, if one of them took on a hired gun, then I guess the other one would just about have to."

"Anyway," Dempster said, "you can see where that leaves the county, and most of all, where that leaves Thirty Four Corners. If this thing breaks out into an all-out shooting war . . ."

"And it spreads into the town . . . ," Martin added.

"A lot of innocent people could wind up getting killed," Dempster concluded.

"And that's why we have come to you," Blanton said.

"Why have you come to me? What do you expect from me?" Matt asked. "Are you asking me to be a deputy to Marshal Hunter?"

"No, sir, that wouldn't give you any authority beyond the city limits, and you'd be as limited in what you can do as the marshal is now," Dempster said.

"So what we have done is, we have spoken to Sheriff Bill Ferrell, and he has agreed to appoint a deputy of our choosing," Blanton said.

"And we choose you," Dempster said. "That is, if you will accept the position. And as a deputy sheriff, you will have authority throughout all of Valencia County. That takes in the BR, the Tumbling P, and Wedge Hill."

"Wedge Hill?"

"It's a much smaller ranch that is sort of tucked in between part of the two big ranches," Martin said.

"Which side is Wedge Hill on?" Matt said.

"Neither side. So far, Kyle Stallings has managed to maintain a relationship with both ranchers."

Matt nodded. "That's good information to know."

"So, what do you say, Mr. Jensen? We come to you in good faith. Will you accept our offer?"

"When you say 'we come to you in good faith,' what 'we' are you talking about?" Matt asked.

"We, meaning the three of us," Blanton replied. "We are the town council. Mr. Dempster and Mr. Martin are two of the four members of the council."

"That's only half. What about the other members? What do they say?"

"I've spoken with the other members of the council, and they, too, support this," Dempster said.

"But it wouldn't matter whether they did or not," Blanton said. "Because if it actually came down to it, as mayor, I could break a tie vote."

"Let me ask you this. Which side of this feud are you three on? If I am perceived as allying myself with one side, how effective could I be?"

"That is a very good question," Blanton replied. "As the editor of the newspaper, I have tried to stay out it."

"My law office is on the north side of the street," Dempster said.

"And I own a store on the south side," Martin added.

Blanton smiled. "So you see, it is a bipartisan committee that has come to you."

"What can you tell me about Lucien Bodine?"

"You mean you don't know him?" Blanton asked.

Matt shook his head. "I've never heard of him. I've heard of Strawn, I've seen Strawn. But I've never seen nor heard of anyone named Lucien Bodine."

"I wish I could tell you something about him, but I don't know anything about him either," Blanton said.

"What about Marshal Hunter? Does the marshal know Bodine?"

"No," Blanton said. "I was with the marshal when we were trying to find out something about him. Whoever he is, and wherever he is from, he has managed to stay out of the newspapers, and off any wanted markers. There is absolutely no paper out on him at all."

Matt drummed his fingers on the table for a moment. The last thing he needed was to get involved in someone else's feud. He was about to say no; then he thought about Rufus Draco.

Matt had lost all track of Rufus Draco, though he had trailed him to within a few miles of this place. And, if there was some skullduggery going on, some means of using this feud to make a dishonest dollar, Matt was sure that Rufus Draco would be right in the middle of it.

"Have any of you gentlemen ever heard of a man name Rufus Draco?" Matt asked.

The three men looked at each other.

"I've heard of him," Blanton said. "I've even run a few articles in my paper about him. Why do you ask?"

"I've been looking for Draco," Matt said. "He murdered some friends of mine and I trailed him down here to New Mexico before I lost track of him. If there is skullduggery going on down here, I wouldn't put it past Draco to be a part of it."

Blanton shook his head. "No, I don't think he has anything to do with it."

"Would you recognize him if you saw him?" Matt asked.

"Yes, I think I would," Blanton said. "I remember his trial from a few years ago, when he killed that mill worker. I covered the trial and I saw him in court every day for a week. Yes, I would recognize him if I saw him again."

Matt had served as a lawman before, including as a deputy United States marshal. And if he had the cover of the law here, it might help him continue his search for Draco.

"All right," he said. "I'll do it."

"Fine, great, wonderful!" the three men said, all speaking at once. Then, one by one, they extended their hands to shake hands with Matt.

"The sheriff will be here about noon," Blanton said. "Come on down to the newspaper office, and we'll swear you in."

"You haven't even asked how much the job will pay," Dempster said.

"I don't care what it pays," Matt replied.

Lois had been quiet during the entire meeting between Matt and the officials of the town. Not until after the three officials of the town left did she speak.

"I hope you don't take your job of being a deputy sheriff too seriously," Lois said.

"What do you mean?"

"What I, and my friends, do, is against the law," Lois reminded him.

Matt chuckled. "Don't worry, I have no intention of closing down bawdy houses. You and your friends are safe with me."

"Will you want the same arrangement that Marshal Hunter has?" Lois asked.

"Arrangement? What sort of arrangement would that be?"

"You know," Lois answered with a coy smile. "An . . . *arrangement*." She came down hard on the word arrangement.

"Oh, yes, I think I do see," Matt replied. "But that won't be necessary."

Chapter Twenty-three

It was after 9:00 P.M. and dark when Rex Ross crossed from BR Ranch property onto Wedge Hill land. It was fairly easy to do. There was no barbed-wire fence that separated the two ranches, and Kyle Stallings didn't waste any man hours keeping an eye on the separation between his land and BR land.

Rex rode as quietly as he could, staying also in the shadows so that if one of the Wedge Hill riders happened to pass by closer than he anticipated, there would be less chance they would actually see him. He crossed over the wedge, reaching the side that bordered onto the Tumbling P without incident.

Now it was time for a decision. Did he stay mounted? If he was seen, he would have a better chance of escape by galloping away. On the other hand if he went the rest of the distance on foot, he would have a better chance of not being seen at all. Rex decided to go the rest of the way on foot, and he tied his horse to a shrub down in an arroyo so it wouldn't be seen.

It was about a two-mile walk from here to the big house, and there was always the possibility that he would be seen by some of the nighthawks. It would be bad enough to be seen by some of the regular cowboys, but if any of the new men Poindexter had hired were to see him, he knew that he would be shot.

"I am an absolute idiot for doing this," he told himself. "So, why am I?"

He didn't have to answer the question. He knew why he was doing it. He was doing it because he wanted to see Sylvia again. Would she see him, or would she refuse? And if she refused, would that be the end of it? Or would she tell her father and her brother that he was there?

"I can't believe I'm doing this!" he said.

But he didn't turn around.

In her upstairs bedroom, Sylvia Poindexter sat in the dark, looking out toward the full moon. What was it about her and men? First there had been H. M. Hood, who had not only broken their engagement, but had had the audacity to ask her to be his mistress.

And now, after having come to New Mexico, she'd met a man who could easily make her forget Hood, only to find out that he is the son of her father's bitterest enemy. Sylvia moved to the window and lifted it, enjoying the feel of a cooling night breeze.

"Why did he have to be a Ross?" she wondered, speaking aloud, though so quietly that no one could hear her.

From the bunkhouse she heard someone playing a guitar, the chords a steady beat, the single-string melody working its way through the piece like a thread of gold in a rich tapestry. She wondered how a cowboy could play so beautifully, and wondered why he wasn't a musician to share his talent with others.

"Sylvia?"

The name was so softly spoken that at first, she wasn't sure she even heard it.

"Sylvia?"

Now she knew that she had heard her name. Putting her hands on the windowsill, she leaned out into the night.

"Who calls?"

"I am here, by the hackberry tree."

Looking in the direction of the tree, she saw Rex Ross. At first her heart leaped in excitement, and she smiled broadly at the thought that he was here. Then she felt fear for him.

"What are you doing here? Are you insane? Someone is going to see you!"

"Not if you let me into your room," Rex said.

"No, impossible! How would you get into my room, anyway?"

"I'll climb in through your window," Rex said.

"I . . . all right, but hurry!"

Earlier that day Matt had made arrangements to attend the showing at the Birdcage Theater. Like the livery stable, the church, and the doctor's office, the Birdcage Theater was an establishment that served both sides of the town. But, like the livery, and the church, it was laid out in two halves, north and south.

The theater was often the scene of gunplay, though so far the gunplay had been the result of drunkenness and overexuberance. There had been no shots exchanged between the BR and the Tumbling P riders, and no one had been killed. However, the curtains and screens around the stage had more than one hundred bullet holes, and a particular target was the huge seminude portrait of a belly dancer, where some of the better marksmen had strategically placed holes in three obvious locations.

"Why do you let them bring guns into the theater?" Matt asked Marshal Hunter.

"I've thought about not letting them, but so far nobody has been killed. And to be honest with you, Matt, I'm not sure I could enforce it."

"Do you mind if I try?"

"No, no, be my guest," Marshal Hunter said. "I would love to see guns banned from the theater."

* * *

That evening Matt put a sign at the door informing all patrons to check their firearms before entering the theater. And having done so, he was now leaning against a post at the rear of the theater, looking out over the boisterous crowd. He smiled and tipped his hat to one of the girls he recognized from Diamond Dina's Pleasure Palace. She was hanging onto the arm of a visiting drummer.

Jack Martin came up to talk to him. "Deputy, I just thought you might like to know that there are some men on the south side, passing a bottle around and taunting the people on the north side."

"Are they heeled?" Matt asked.

"I think they are," Martin said. "None of them are wearing holsters, but I do believe a couple of them have pistols stuck down in their waistbands."

"Where are they?"

"They are in the very back row, nearest the aisle," Martin said.

"All right, I'll just mosey over there and stand near them," Matt suggested.

At that moment the band played a fanfare and, amidst shouts, hoots, and whistles, the theater owner walked out onto the stage. He stood in front of the closed curtains and held his hands up, asking for quiet.

"Ladies and gents," he called.

"There ain't no ladies present!" someone from

the audience yelled, and his shout was greeted with guffaws of laughter.

"Oh, yeah? Well, what do you call me, you slack-jawed, weasel-faced son of a bitch?" Sunset Lil shouted back.

There was more laughter, but the theater owner finally managed to get them quiet again.

"Honey, don't you go puttin' on like you're a lady. Don't forget, you used to work for me," Diamond Dina said, and there was more laughter.

"Ladies and gents," he repeated. "Here, lovers of the theater from both sides of any issue may come together in peace to enjoy quality entertainment. Welcome to the Birdcage Theater. Tonight I am pleased to say that we have an especially thrilling show for you."

"It's the same show tonight that it was last night, ain't it?" someone shouted, and again there was laughter.

"To be sure," the interlocutor said, smiling, without missing a beat. "And you enjoyed it last night, so shall you tonight. We begin our show with six of the loveliest girls to be found anywhere west of the Mississippi. I give you, the Mystic Beauties!"

Amidst a great deal of whistling and stamping of feet, six beautiful and scantily clad young women began the show. After the girls performed, there was a comedy act between a mustachioed man and a beautiful, innocent young girl.

MUSTACHIOED MAN: My dear, did you hear
     about the dog who has no nose?
YOUNG GIRL: My goodness, how does he
     smell?
MUSTACHIOED MAN: Awful.

A cymbal clash followed the joke, and the audience howled in laughter.

There were a few other jokes of that ilk, then a man billed as the "World's Greatest Magician" made his appearance.

"To prove that everything I do is authentic, and not merely the trick of a charlatan, I shall need the assistance of some brave young lady from the audience. You, young lady, would you come up here?"

He pointed to a woman who was sitting in the front row.

"Me?" she said, as she stood. "But, I know nothing of show business."

"All the better, my dear."

When the woman, stepped up onto the stage, she was wearing stage makeup, and looked very much like one of the Mystic Beauties.

"And now, friends, I shall perform an illusion with the help of this lovely volunteer, whom I have never seen before. Have we ever met, Annie?"

"No, Paul, we have never before met," Annie replied.

"Hey! How do you know her name then?" someone

shouted from the audience, but most recognized it for the humor that was intended.

"I have here a dagger," Paul said, holding up a knife. "This lovely young volunteer, whom I have never seen before, is going to thrust this dagger deep into my heart. Are you ready, my dear?"

"Why, I couldn't do that," Annie said.

"Oh, but you must."

"All right."

Paul clasped his hands behind his back, and Annie thrust the knife into his chest. Immediately blood began to spill from the "wound."

"Oh! Something went wrong. This wasn't supposed to happen!" Annie shouted, as Paul staggered around the room, his hands over the knife that was protruding from his chest. Many of the women in the audience screamed.

Paul fell to his knees.

"Get a doctor. Oh, someone get a doctor please!" Annie shouted.

"No!" Paul said holding out a hand toward her. Then, using both hands, and giving the illusion of a great struggle, Paul pulled on the knife. It came out, the blade red with blood, and Paul stood up. With a fanfare from the band, he made a sweeping bow.

Matt knew how the trick worked. The knife had a blade that collapsed into the handle, and Paul had a packet of blood just inside his shirt. But Paul and Annie had pulled off the trick with aplomb, and the audience had enjoyed it.

Suddenly, someone on the south side of the divided audience stood up and pointed a revolver toward the stage.

"See if you can do that with a bullet, professor!" he shouted.

Matt managed to reach him just in time to deflect his shot, while the terrified magician and his assistant hurried from the stage to the guffaws of the audience. Matt knocked the cowboy out, with one blow from his big fist; then he turned to the others and held out his hand.

"If any of you gents are carrying a gun, you'd better give them to me now."

Two other cowboys looked at each other for a moment, then, with hangdog looks on their faces, they pulled pistols from their waistbands and handed them over.

"What about you men on the north side? If you are carrying a gun, you had better hand it over now. If you don't, and I find that you are armed, I'll throw you in jail."

Two men from the north side turned over their guns.

The show continued until the curtain came down, with no further incidents.

The moon was shining brightly, sailing high in the velvet sky. It spilled a pool of iridescence through the window and onto the bed, bathing Sylvia in a soft, shimmering light. She wasn't asleep but she was breathing softly, and Rex reached over gently to put his hand on her naked hip. He could feel the sharpness of her hip bone, and the soft yielding of her flesh. The contrasting textures were delightful to his sense of touch, and he let his hand rest there, enjoying a feeling of possession.

"Rex," Sylvia said. She was practically whispering the word, but Rex could hear it quite clearly, because they were lying in bed together and her lips were but an inch from his ear.

"Yes?"

"You aren't just . . ." She started the sentence, but couldn't finish it."

"I'm not just what?"

"You aren't just using me as you would a prostitute, are you?"

Rex raised up on his elbow and looked down at her. "Sylvia, if I had been seen coming across Tumbling P property tonight, I could have been shot and killed. If I am seen going home tonight, I could be shot and killed. A man doesn't take risks like that just to . . . lie with a woman. There has to be something more."

"I'm glad," Sylvia said.

Rex smiled, and put the tip of his finger to her lips. "You mean you are glad I wasn't killed tonight?"

"Yes," Sylvia started to say—then she gasped. "Oh! Rex, you must go! Please, go now, and be careful! If something happened to you tonight because you came to see me, I couldn't live with myself."

"I'm glad to know you care," Rex said. "I'm so happy I could sing out loud!"

"No!" Sylvia said. She grabbed him and kissed him to keep him quiet.

"I like the way you have of shutting me up," he said.

"We can't meet here like this again," Sylvia said.

"Huh-uh. I've just now found you. I'm not going to let you go."

"I'll come up with a way," Sylvia promised.

"All right. I'm going to hold you to that promise."

Rex got dressed; then, with one final kiss, he climbed out her window, dropped to the ground, and ran across into the trees.

Chapter Twenty-four

It was just after midnight on that same night when Strawn, Meeker, and Wallace, riding quietly, approached one of the BR Ranch line shacks. They stopped on a low hill and looked down at the small cabin, clearly visible in the moonlight.

"Does Poindexter know we're a-doin' this?" Meeker asked.

"No, he don't know," Strawn said.

"Shouldn't we have told him?"

"Why should we tell him?"

"'Cause we're workin' for him, ain't we?"

"No, we ain't workin' for him, Meeker. We're workin' for ourselves, remember?" Wallace asked.

"Yeah," Meeker said, smiling at the thought. "Yeah, you're right. We're workin' for ourselves."

There was no movement in or around the cabin, which was good. "All right, Wallace, you know what to do," Strawn said.

Wallace dismounted and handed the reins of his

horse to Meeker. Then, taking down a can he had tied to his saddle, he started walking toward the line shack.

"Hurry up. Me 'n' Meeker, will keep you covered," Strawn said.

Strawn and Meeker pulled their rifles from the saddle sheaths, and watched as Wallace picked his way, carefully, down the side of the hill. When he reached the cabin he began splashing the liquid onto to the wide, weathered boards. That done, he tossed the empty can aside, then lit a match and held it against one of the soaked boards. The kerosene caught quickly and flames spread up that board, then leaped over to the other boards that had been splashed with the kerosene. Dropping the can, he turned and ran back up the hill toward his horse and the other two riders.

"Ian!" someone shouted from inside the cabin. "Ian, wake up! We're on fire!"

"What the hell?" Ian's voice replied. "Och, mon, how'd we catch on fire?"

"Hell, I don't know, but we got to get out of here!"

By now, smoke was pouring into the cabin and Strawn and the other two riders could hear the cowboys inside coughing.

"Get ready," Strawn said.

As Strawn had expected, the two men, both still wearing long-handle underwear, came running outside, coughing and wheezing.

"Now!" Strawn shouted, and all three of them

opened up, shooting rifles toward the two BR Ranch cowboys. Both cowboys went down.

When the firing stopped, Strawn walked down to where the two bodies lay, both bloodied with multiple gunshot wounds. Taking a sheet of paper from his pocket, Strawn wrote a message and placed it on one of the bodies, holding it down with a rock.

> **Don't be tying up any more of our men with barbed wire.**

"Let's get out of here," Strawn said. "Someone's goin' to see the fire and that'll draw 'em here like pissants to a doughnut."

The three men rode away, leaving the burning shack and the two bodies behind them.

Rex Ross had cut safely through the Wedge Hill Ranch and was heading back to the big house, when he saw the fire. Curious and concerned, he galloped toward it.

"Hold it right there, or I'll shoot you dead!" someone shouted, and Rex recognized Lou Turner's voice.

"Lou! No, wait! It's me! It's Rex!"

"Oh, gee, I'm sorry!" Lou said.

Rex rode up to the burning cabin where he saw Lou, Dean Kelly, his father, Bodine, Dooley, and Massey. He also saw two canvas-covered lumps on the ground, illuminated by the flickering orange light of the still burning cabin.

"What happened?" Rex asked.

"What happened? Ian and Harry have been killed, that's what happened," Ben said. "Where the hell have you been?"

"Nowhere in particular."

"Nowhere in particular at midnight?"

"I couldn't sleep," Rex said. "I've just been riding around. What happened here?" he asked again.

"It looks like some riders from the Tumbling P paid us a visit," Bodine said. "They burned the line shack and killed two of your men."

"How do you know whoever did this was from the Tumbling P?" Rex asked.

"Who else could it be?" Ben asked, showing Rex the note they found with the bodies.

"Mr. Ross, you give me the word and me 'n' my two men will take care of this for you," Bodine said.

"Take care of it how?" Rex asked.

"Take care of it a way that will keep you out of it," Bodine replied.

"I'm not convinced that any of Poindexter's regular riders did this," Rex said.

Bodine took his hat off and ran his hand across his bald head. "What do you mean you don't believe it? There's the burning line shack, and there are the two dead bodies. What is there not to believe?"

"I don't believe anyone from the Tumbling P did this."

"Then who do you think did?"

"Hasn't Poindexter hired some . . . *detectives* . . . like we have?" Rex set the word detectives apart from the rest of the question to express his disdain.

"So what if he has? That would be the same thing, wouldn't it?"

"Pop, how did you feel when everyone said that we were the ones who killed the Patterson boy?" Rex asked.

"What do you mean, how did I feel? We didn't do it."

"You know it, I know it, and I suspect everyone on our ranch knows it. But that didn't stop everyone else from believing that we did it. I'm just saying that I don't think we need to be jumping to conclusions here."

Ben stared at his son for a long moment, but said nothing. Then he looked over at his foreman.

"Get Ian and Harry into town first thing tomorrow morning."

"Yes, sir," Dean replied.

"So, what about this?" Bodine asked, taking in with a wave of his hand, the bodies and the shack, which had, by now, been almost totally consumed by the fire. "Do you want me and my men to take care of it?"

"No, don't do anything," Ben said.

"You're making a big mistake."

"It's my mistake to make."

* * *

Two days later, practically the entire town of Thirty Four Corners had turned out, the Ross supporters lining one side of the street and the Poindexter supporters on the other. They watched a wagon being pulled down the middle of the road. In the wagon were two coffins, and on the side of the wagon was a sign.

IAN MACDONALD
HARRY BUTRUM
Murdered by Cowards
who work for the Tumbling P

The wagon was followed by a carriage in which Ben Ross was riding. On horseback, behind the carriage, were Ben's son, Rex, and the ranch foreman, Dean Kelly. Behind them rode every other cowboy from the BR ranch.

Nate Poindexter was standing just inside the Brown Spur Saloon, holding a beer as he peered out across the batwing doors at the funeral cortege passing by.

Matt Jensen came up to stand beside Nate, and to look out onto the somber scene.

"You're Nate Poindexter?" Matt asked.

"Who wants to know?"

"I want to know," Matt replied.

Nate turned toward him, and saw the star of a deputy sheriff penned to Matt's vest.

"You're the law?"

"Yes, I'm the new deputy sheriff. The name is Matt Jensen."

"What can I do for you, Deputy Jensen?"

"For a start, you can tell me what you know about the killing of those two men."

"I don't know anything about it."

"What do you know about this?" Matt asked, showing him the note that had been found with the body. "This note does refer to one of your men, doesn't it?"

"He was hardly a man. He was fourteen years old, Deputy," Nate said.

"I'll admit that was a tragedy," Matt said. "But why extend the tragedy by killing two more men?"

"Are you accusing me of killing those two men?"

"No, I'm just asking you what you know about it?"

"I don't know anything about it." Nate ran his hand through his hair and sighed. "Deputy, I wish I could tell you with absolute authority that none of our men were responsible, but I can't. I will tell you that, if any of Tumbling P riders did it, they were acting on their own . . . not with the authority, the permission, or even the knowledge of my father, me, or our foreman. And to show you the sincerity of our cooperation, I will invite you to visit the Tumbling P, and question anyone you wish."

"All right," Matt said. "I appreciate your cooperation. I'll be out there in the next day or so."

"I'll be there," Nate promised.

With a nod, Matt left the saloon, then went out

to the cemetery to watch the burial of the two BR riders. He stood as unobtrusively as he could in the background, listening to the conversations.

Two coffins lay next to the two open graves, which were themselves next to the freshly turned dirt that marked the grave of Seth Miller. The BR riders were gathered around the graves, as were some of the bar girls and prostitutes who knew Harry Butrum and Ian MacDonald. Because the bar girls and prostitutes had been invited to the funeral, the Reverend Charles Landers had refused to perform the burial rites and give the accusatory sermon he had given at the burial of Seth Miller. Most of the cowboys thought his absence was a positive.

The task of actually "saying a few words" fell upon Rex Ross, and he moved over to stand by the two coffins.

For the moment, the coffins were open, and Ian and Harry, wearing suits that they had never worn during their lifetimes, lay in the coffins, their eyes closed, and their arms folded across their bodies, with their hands clasped. Both men were cleanly shaved, their hair was neatly combed, and none of their wounds were visible.

Rex cleared his throat, and began to speak.

"I have been asked to say a few words about Ian MacDonald and Harry Butrum. I do so willingly, considering it a great honor. Ian and Harry not only worked with us, they were our friends.

"Both of Harry's parents are dead, and he had

no brothers and sisters. We were, literally, the only family he had. The same could almost be said for Ian. He did have family, but they are all in Scotland, and that made us his family.

"So that these two men . . . our friends, and members of our family, not be forgotten, I want to share a few memories with you, memories that, as long as they be kept green, will mean that Ian and Harry are still with us.

"Who can ever forget Harry's skill at the fandango? I think all the young ladies here will attest to the fact that no one was any better at that dance than Harry Butrum."

Several of the women, their eyes welled with tears, nodded in the affirmative.

"Och, mon, and Ian's Scottish brogue stirred the hearts of many a lad and lassie." Rex perfectly imitated Ian's brogue, and it brought smiles, and even a few chuckles, to the mourners.

"And so we are here to lay our friends to rest, knowing that they are going to a better place . . . and that they'll be keeping each other company until they are reunited with old friends and family, and make new ones."

Rex nodded at the undertaker, who, quickly, put the tops on the coffins and nailed them shut. Then the two coffins were lowered into the ground by ropes. Once they were at the bottom of the graves, first Rex, then several others, dropped a hand full of dirt onto the wooden lids. That done, the grave diggers began shoveling dirt into the holes.

"You would be Matt Jensen?" Ben Ross said, coming over then to speak to Matt.

"Yes."

"I've heard you're the new deputy sheriff."

"That's right."

"Whose side are you on?"

"I'm not on anyone's side," Matt insisted.

"You say that, but are you not staying in a hotel that's on the north side of Central Street?"

"I am."

"That puts you on the side of the Tumbling P."

"No, Mr. Ross. It puts me on the north side of Central," Matt said. "If it makes you feel better, it so happens that I'm boarding my horse in the stalls that are on the south side of the livery."

Ross stared at Matt for a moment; then, unexpectedly, he broke out into laughter.

"Good enough, Deputy, good enough," he said. "In the meantime, will you be finding out who killed my two men?"

"I intend to," Matt said. "I would also like to know who killed Jimmy Patterson."

"Yes," Ross said. "I expect that you would. But I swear to you, Deputy, I had nothing to do with it, and I don't know who did."

"I'm going to go out to the Tumbling P tomorrow to see what I can learn. Nate Poindexter has offered full cooperation. If I come to visit the BR, can I expect the same thing from you?"

"Of course you can," Ben said. "I swear to you, Deputy, Poindexter and I have kept this feud going for well over twenty years without anything like this ever happening before. I don't know what has happened lately to bring on all this killing, but it has me greatly disturbed."

"Disturbed enough to establish peace between you?"

Ben pointed toward the two graves, which were now being closed. "How can I have peace when something like this happens?"

Chapter Twenty-five

Tumbling P Ranch

"There was another funeral in town," Morgan said.

"Yes, a couple of our boys went," Gabe said.

Morgan looked up in surprise.

"They stayed out of the way, and didn't cause any trouble. But they said they used to be friends with Harry before he started workin' for Ben Ross. I hope you don't mind."

"No, of course I don't mind. I just don't want any more trouble, if we can help it. What about Strawn? I haven't seen him in a few days. Have you?"

"Actually, he's out in bunkhouse, right now, playing poker," Gabe replied. "Do you want to see him?"

"Yes, send him up to the house, would you? I'd like to talk to him."

"All right." Gabe started toward the bunkhouse; then he stopped and looked back toward Ben.

"Ben, you think maybe he had somethin' to do with killin' those two BR riders, do you?"

Morgan was surprised by Gabe's question. "Why do you ask? Do you think he might have?"

"I've given it some thought," Gabe admitted.

"I sure as hell hope he didn't have anything to do with it," Morgan said. "But I want to hear him tell me, himself, that he didn't."

A few minutes later, Strawn came up to the big house, his steps heavy on the porch. He knocked loudly, and Morgan answered the door.

"Mathis said you wanted to see me," Strawn said.

"Yes, please, come in. Would you like some coffee?"

"No, thanks, I just had me some. Is someone givin' you trouble somewhere that you want me to take care of?"

"Not that I know of. Strawn, what do you know about MacDonald and Butrum?"

"MacDonald and Butrum? Who are they? Someone that's wantin' to work for you? You want me to check 'em out for you?"

"No, haven't you been into town? Haven't you heard anything about them? That's all anyone has been talking about for the last few days."

Strawn shook his head. "I ain't been off the ranch since I come to work for you. I figure I'm drawin' wages to look out for you, and your hands and cattle, then the least I can do is stay here and do my job without gallivantin' off somewhere. What about these two you're askin' about? Who are they?"

"Yes, well, they are . . . that is, they were, riders for

Ben Ross over at the BR. But a couple of days ago, in the middle of the night, someone burned the line shack they were in and shot both of them dead."

"You don't say."

"You wouldn't know anything about that, would you, Mr. Strawn?"

"No, I don't know nothin' about that. I never even heard about them until you just told me. But that sure does give you a good reason for keepin' me 'n' my men around."

"What do you mean?"

"What if someone was to do somethin' like that to you? You know, like to get back at you?"

"Why would they? I mean if we didn't have anything to do with killing MacDonald and Butrum, why would they want to get back at me?"

"Well, the thing is, they probably don't know who done it, so that means they'll figure you done it. Looks to me like I'm about to earn my pay."

"How is that?"

Sylvia heard a conversation going on between her father and another man, so she started down the stairs to see who it was. When she saw Strawn, she gasped. With the terrible scar and deformed eye, he had to be the ugliest man she had ever seen.

Hearing his daughter on the stairs, Morgan

looked up toward her. He hoped that she hadn't overheard too much of the conversation.

"Sylvia, this gentleman is Sam Strawn," Morgan said. "I know you haven't met him since you returned, but he has come to work for us. Mr. Strawn, this is my daughter."

"Pleased to meet you, ma'am," Strawn said, his voice a wheeze.

"I thought I had met all the cowboys since I came back," Sylvia said.

"Oh, honey, Mr. Strawn isn't a cowboy," Morgan said quickly.

"He isn't? Well, what will he be doing?"

"You do remember the incident on the road, don't you? When three of Ben Ross's men accosted us? They were going to take you with them, and hold you for ransom."

"Yes, of course. How could I forget something like that?"

"Mr. Strawn's . . . specialty . . . is in seeing that nothing like that happens again. You might think of him as a private detective, hired to keep our ranch safe."

"Anytime you've a notion to go travelin' somewhere, ma'am, why, you just let me know and I'll make sure you get there 'n' back, all safe and sound," Strawn said.

"I . . . I thank you, but I'm sure that won't be necessary," Sylvia said. Turning, she went, quickly, back upstairs.

Morgan watched his daughter run back upstairs, then turned back to Strawn. "I suppose there is something to what you are saying, about possible retaliation. So, over the next several days, I will expect you to be particularly vigilant as you go about your duties."

"All right," Strawn said. "I'll be wantin' bonuses," he added.

"Bonuses? For what?"

"Let's say that some men from the BR Ranch come onto the Tumbling P for no good reason, and when I challenge 'em, why there is a shoot-out. And, let's say that in that shoot-out, durin' which I'm riskin' my life, that mayhaps I might kill one of 'em. I think if somethin' like that was to happen, what with me riskin' my life 'n' all, well then maybe a hunnert-dollar bonus wouldn't be too much to ask for."

"Are you asking me to pay you a hundred dollars to kill someone?" Morgan asked.

"Yeah."

Morgan frowned. "Look here, Mr. Strawn, I do hope that you don't think I hired you for such a purpose. And if I were to pay a bounty on men that you might kill, it would make it appear that I am endorsing the killing. In fact, quite the opposite is true. The reason I hired you is the thought that having someone like you to provide security would cause the BR riders to think twice before there is any more mischief. I'm hoping that having you around will help to keep the peace."

Strawn stretched his face into what might have been a smile.

"I think you got the wrong idea of what I was sayin', Mr. Poindexter. It ain't as if I'm plannin' on just goin' out and shootin' people for no reason. But if comes down to it, and I wind up havin' to shoot someone, say, to save your life, or the life of your daughter, or mayhaps the life of one of your riders, I was just thinkin' that maybe a little bonus might be called for."

Morgan stroked his chin for a moment before he responded.

"All right, Mr. Strawn. If you put that way, I suppose I could, if the occasion warranted, pay a bonus."

Strawn smiled again, and extended his hand. "I thought you might see it that way. And I want you to know that as long as I'm on the job, then neither you, nor your son, nor your daughter, have got a thing to worry about."

A few minutes after Strawn left, Sylvia came back down, dressed in riding clothes.

"Are you going somewhere?"

"I'm going to visit Linda Stallings this afternoon," Sylvia said.

"Oh, darlin', given the circumstances, I'm not sure that is a very good idea."

"What circumstances?"

"You did hear that two of Ben Ross's riders were killed, didn't you?"

"Yes, but I don't see what that has to do with . . ." Sylvia stopped in midsentence. "Papa, we didn't have anything to do with that, did we?"

"No!" Morgan said instantly. "At least, I certainly didn't have anything to do with it, and I'm equally certain that no one who works for me did."

"Then why should that have anything to do with whether or not I can visit Linda?"

"I suppose it has nothing to do with it," Morgan said. "But please, do be careful."

Rex was leaning against a fence watching the farrier use a hoof pick to clean stones from a horse's hoof before replacing the shoe.

"Mr. Ross?"

Turning, Rex saw Andy Warren from the Wedge Hill Ranch. For just a moment, Rex felt a twinge of apprehension. Had he been seen crossing the ranch the other night?

"Hello, Andy. What brings you over here?"

Andy pulled an envelope from his saddlebag and handed it down to Rex. "Miss Stallings give me this letter to give to you," he said.

"Thank you, Andy. Oh, the cook made sinkers this morning. Step into the cookhouse and have a couple, with a cup of coffee, before you start back."

Andy smiled, and nodded. "Thanks, I'll just do that."

Curious as to why Linda Stallings would send

him a letter, Rex waited until Andy had ridden away before he opened the envelope.

I shall meet you at one o'clock tomorrow afternoon at the old springhouse on Wedge Hill Ranch.

Sylvia

Rex smiled broadly, then folded the letter and stuck it down into his pocket.

There were two horses tied up outside the springhouse when Rex arrived, and for a moment he was confused. Why were there two horses? Had someone found out that Sylvia sent a letter to him? Was this a trap?

Cautiously, he approached the little, low-lying stone house, then examined the horses. One had a tilted P as its brand, the other had two-piece brand. The first mark was an angle on its side, the second a triangle with the point up. Wedge Hill.

Linda Stallings appeared in the doorway.

"Hello," she said.

"Hello," Rex replied, still curious about what was going on.

Sylvia appeared then.

"Oh, I'm so glad you could come!" she said, excitedly.

Smiling, Rex dismounted, and was surprised when Sylvia rushed into his arms and kissed him in front of Linda. He looked toward Linda.

"Oh, don't worry about her. She knows all about us," Sylvia said. "Don't forget, she's the one who set up this meeting for us."

"I'm going to take both of your horses with me," Linda said. "I think that if someone happened to be riding by and saw two horses outside a building that has been abandoned for several years, they might get a little curious." Linda smiled. "And though it isn't any of my business, I think you probably aren't going to be interested in curious visitors for the next hour or so."

"Did you eat lunch?" Sylvia asked.

"No. You said to meet you at one, I didn't want to take a chance on being late."

"Good. I have fried chicken, biscuits, and potato salad. We'll have a picnic lunch."

"Oh, a lunch sounds heavenly!" Linda said.

"Get your own lunch," Sylvia replied, not taking her eyes off Rex's face.

"I can take a hint," Linda said. "I'll be back by three o'clock. I hope you two can find some way to entertain yourselves until then," she teased.

"I'm sure we'll find something," Sylvia said.

Tome

Of all the little settlements in Valencia County, Tome was the most Mexican in character. Bodine, Strawn, and Shardeen were in the Vaquero Cantina. At the moment, they were the only ones in the entire cantina who were speaking English.

"I think we've just about got everything in place," Bodine said. "Once we take care of this little job tonight, it's going to bring it all to a head. I expect we'll be at an all-out war within a couple of days."

"Tell me, how are we going to steal cows from the middle of a battle?" Strawn asked.

"We ain't goin' to be in the middle of the battle-field, 'cause the battle is goin' to be takin' place downtown. We'll be out on the range takin' cattle."

"By the way, Draco, I supposed you've heard that Matt Jensen is in town."

"Don't call me that!" Draco said sharply as he stroked the red stubble of what had once been a red beard. "My name is Bodine now. The last thing I need is for that son of a bitch to be breathing down my neck."

"You know he's goin' to find out who you are," Shardeen said.

"Who's going to tell him? You are the only two who know."

"It just seems to me like it's goin' to get out," Shardeen said.

"If it does, I'll take care of it then. For now, and until our plan is carried out . . . I'm Bodine. To everyone. Do you understand?"

"Sure, Bodine, whatever you say," Strawn said.

"You want me 'n' Cates 'n' Dagan to do the raid tonight," Shardeen asked.

"No. Like I said, it's time to get this spread out beyond the two ranches. I've got Dooley in town now, recruiting the men we'll need for the task tonight."

"You think he can get enough people to go along with him?" Strawn asked.

"Yeah."

Sitting at another table, but close enough to overhear the conversation, was Frank Carter, the man with whom Matt had fought several days earlier.

Chapter Twenty-six

Rex pulled his boots back on. "I'm going to go see your pa," Rex said. "I'm going to tell him that I want to marry you."

"No!" Sylvia said, quickly.

"No? You mean you don't want to marry me?"

"Of course I want to marry you. But now is not the time to ask Pa. There's too much going on between the two ranches. I know he wouldn't agree to it, and I don't even know how safe it would be for you to come on to the ranch like that."

"Sylvia, I have found you, I love you, and I don't plan to let you get away," Rex said.

Sylvia took Rex's hand and lifted it to her lips. "I'm not going anywhere," she said. "We just need time to work things out, that's all. Please, don't just rush in."

"All right, if that's the way you want it. But, Sylvia, don't keep me waiting too long. Patience is not one of my virtues."

"Hello inside!" Linda's voice called. "Are you still here?"

"We're still here, Linda. Come in!" Sylvia called back.

Tumbling P Ranch

When Matt rode out to the Tumbling P, he was met by Nate Poindexter, who introduced him to his father, and to Gabe Mathis, the foreman.

"I would be willing to bet everything I own that none of our men had anything at all to do with killing MacDonald and Butrum," Gabe told Matt. "But I do know that they were awful upset over the way the BR men drug Jimmy behind a horse like they done. And they wasn't none too happy about someone from the BR tryin' to snatch Miss Sylvia, either."

"Who is Miss Sylvia, and what do you mean someone tried to snatch her?" Matt asked.

"Sylvia is my daughter," Morgan said. "She has been back east with my sister for a while. I picked her up in Los Luna and was bringing her home when three masked men stopped us on the road. They were going to take my daughter and hold her until I paid a ransom to get her back.

"But someone, I don't know who, shot one of the three men, and the other two left."

"Do you know who they were?" Matt asked. He realized, even as Morgan started to tell the story, that this was the incident he had happened onto, but he decided it would be best not to say anything about his participation in it.

"Well, like I said, they were all three wearing masks, but when I asked if they were from the BR, one of them said that I wasn't as dumb as I looked. So, in my mind, that told me that's where they came from."

"Or, perhaps that's where they wanted you to think they came from," Matt suggested.

"The truth is, this feud that's goin' on between the Tumblin' P and the BR has turned just full-time mean," Gabe said. "And whenever things are full-time mean, there's just no tellin' what's goin' to happen next."

"Deputy Jensen, you can go anywhere on my ranch you need to go, talk to anyone you need to talk to," Morgan said. "I want to get to the bottom of this as much as you do."

"I appreciate that," Matt said. "Oh, and I wonder if I could have a letter from you to that effect. Some of the men might be a little hesitant to talk to me if they don't know that you are fully supportive."

"I'll write you the letter," Morgan said. He chuckled. "Not sure how much good it'll do you though. About a third of my men can't even read."

As the men were talking, Sylvia came riding up.

"Hello, darlin'! Did you enjoy your visit with Linda?" Morgan said when he saw his daughter.

"Yes, very much," Sylvia replied.

"Deputy, you asked about Sylvia a few minutes ago. Here she is, my pride and joy," Morgan said.

"Sweetheart, this is Deputy Sheriff Matt Jensen. He's trying to get to the bottom of all the killing."

"I hope he can do more than just get to the bottom of it. I hope he can stop it," Sylvia said.

"I'm going to try, Miss Poindexter. I'll give you my word, I'm going to try."

Thirty Four Corners

"Twenty-five dollars apiece," Shardeen told the six men who were sitting around a table with him at the Black Bull Saloon.

"What do we have to do for the twenty-five dollars?" a man named Fillion asked.

"Help us get revenge for MacDonald and Butrum," Shardeen replied.

"How we goin' to do that?"

"An eye for an eye," Shardeen said. "The Tumbling P burned out a cabin where MacDonald and Butrum were staying, then shot them down when they came outside. We're goin' to do the same thing."

"How will we know who it was that shot MacDonald and Butrum?" Coombs asked.

"What difference does it make if they are the same people or not?" Shardeen replied.

"What do you mean what difference does it make?" Coombs asked, surprised by Shardeen's answer.

"It's a war," Shardeen explained. "When you are at war, you don't always shoot the same people who shot people on your side. When you are at war, everyone is fair game."

"That's true," Fillion said. "My pa was in the war. He said he just shot at men that was on the other side, and he didn't know any of 'em. So I reckon when you are at war, it don't really matter none."

"But we don't none of us ride for the BR," Coombs said.

"You see how this town is laid out, don't you?" Shardeen asked. "Ever'one on this side of the street is on the side of the BR Ranch. Ever'one on the other side is for the Tumbling P. That's how wars is. You take sides, 'n' that's the side you fight on."

"This here is more of a feud than it is a war, ain't it?"

"It was a feud, 'til Seth Miller, Ian MacDonald, and Harry Butrum got themselves shot and kilt," Shardeen said. "Then it became a war."

"Yeah," Fillion said. "Me 'n' Butrum was good friends, too. And I don't like Poindexter, or any of those sons of bitches that ride for him, either. You can count me in."

"What about the rest of you?" Shardeen asked.

"Twenty-five dollars?" one of the other men asked.

"Yes."

"Hell, twenty-five dollars sounds pretty good to me right now. I'd shoot my own brother for twenty-five dollars, iffen I had a brother."

The others laughed, then one by one agreed to go with Shardeen on what he was calling a "revenge raid."

"Meet me at four o'clock this afternoon, at the Bluewater Creek crossing," Shardeen said

"We'll be there," Fillion replied.

Shardeen stood up, then handed out a five-dollar bill to each man. "You'll get twenty more dollars tonight, after the deed is done," he said.

"Damn! I'm goin' to pay me a visit to Diamond Dina," Fillion said with a big smile as he scooped up the bill.

The sun was setting.

"I'm comin' with you," Stoddard said.

"You can come with me, but you have to get your own woman," Fillion said.

"Of course I'm goin' to get my own woman. What the hell, do think I was just comin' along to watch?"

"I'll let you watch for a dollar," Fillion teased, and the others laughed.

Tumbling P Ranch

Having been given absolute freedom to go anywhere and talk to anyone on the Tumbling P, Matt had spent the entire afternoon exploring the ranch and discovering for himself just how large it was. At nightfall he found himself in the most remote line shack on the ranch, and thought this might be a good place to spend the night.

"Hello the house!" Matt called before he dismounted.

The door opened and a man looked out. "Who are you?"

"The name is Matt Jensen."

"What do you want?"

"I'm just looking around the ranch. I've got a letter of introduction here, from Morgan Poindexter."

"That don't mean nothin'. I can't read."

"Oh, well, in that case I can read it to you, and make it say anything I want, can't I?"

For a second the cowboy looked confused. Then he chuckled. "Yeah, I guess you could at that. I'm just about to cook up some bacon and beans. Climb down and come in. The name is Jesse. Jesse Billings."

"Glad to meet you, Jesse."

"Damn, Jensen, are you the law?" Jesse asked, noticing for the first time the star on Matt's vest.

"Yes, but it isn't a permanent condition," Matt said.

"What do you mean, it ain't permanent?"

"I've just signed on to help Sheriff Ferrell out for a while. Also, to be honest with you, I'm after someone. I've been following a man named Rufus Draco, and it has led me here. I thought that packing a star might help me find him."

"What are you looking for him for?"

"He and a couple of other men murdered a friend of mine. They also raped and murdered my friend's wife and daughter. Only they didn't just rape them, they butchered them." Matt went into some detail about the condition in which they had left the mother and daughter.

"How come you're only lookin' for this feller,

Draco? How come you ain't lookin' for the other ones?"

"I found the other ones," Matt said, cryptically.

"Damn, I ain't never heard of Draco, but if I ever do, I'll be sure to let you know. Someone like that don't deserve to be runnin' around free. It'll be gettin' dark in another hour or so. You plannin' to stay the night here?"

Matt smiled. "Now that you mention it, I was hoping I would get an invitation to do so."

"Consider yourself invited. Do you play checkers? It gets kind of lonesome out here, and truth to tell, checkers ain't all that fun when you play yourself."

"You play yourself?"

"Yeah, and when I play myself . . . I cheat. And damn, I hate playing a cheater."

Matt laughed. "I won't cheat."

"I won't either, seein' as I only cheat myself. Oh, and you can take your horse around and tie him in the lean-to," Jesse suggested. "There's hay and water for him back there."

"Thanks."

"I'll start supper."

Matt took Spirit around to the lean-to, where he saw another horse. He tied Spirit to the hitching rail, then returned to the cabin. By the time he stepped inside, he could smell the aroma of frying bacon.

"I made biscuits this mornin'. Still got some left if you don't mind eatin' 'em cold," Jesse said. "I only like to bake once a day 'cause the oven heats up the house too much."

"That'll be fine. There's nothing better than a cold biscuit and a hot piece of bacon," Matt said.

It took but a few minutes to prepare lunch, since the beans came from a can and only had to be heated to eat.

"So, tell me, Sheriff . . ."

"I'm the deputy."

"Deputy. Other than lookin' for Rufus Draco, who I ain't never heard of 'til you mentioned his name a while ago, what else brings you way out here?"

"I'm sure you heard of the two BR riders who were killed a few days ago."

"Yes, and Seth Miller before them." Jesse was just in the act of lifting a fork of beans to his lips, but he stopped midway. "Wait a minute. Look here, Deputy, you ain't a-thinkin' that I done that, are you?"

Matt shook his head. "No, I have no reason to believe that you did. But I am trying to find out who might have done it."

"Well, if you're thinkin' any of the men who ride for Mr. Poindexter might have done it, you're barkin' up the wrong tree, I can tell you that right now. I know ever'one that rides for the Tumblin' P, and there ain't a man of 'em who would do a dirty trick like was done to Butrum and MacDonald."

"Did you know Butrum and MacDonald?" Matt asked.

Jesse was quiet for a long moment before he answered. "You've heard about the fight between me 'n' MacDonald, haven't you?"

"No, I haven't heard anything about a fight. Was there one?"

Jesse chuckled. "Yes, sir, there was a jim-dandy of a fight betwixt us. And I whupped him, too. Ever'one who seen the fight said that I whupped him." He looked at Matt. "So, if I whupped him, why would I want to kill him?"

"No reason at all," Matt said. "I was just wondering what you thought about the two men?"

"Truth is, I actually thought they was pretty good men. If we had happened to be ridin' for the same spread, why then there ain't no doubt in my mind but that we woulda been pretty good friends. But, bein' as they rode for the BR, and I ride for the Tumblin' P, well . . . you know how it is."

Unseen by Matt or Jesse, Shardeen and the six men he had recruited were approaching the small line shack.

"You think there's anyone here?" Fillion asked.

"If there ain't nobody here, we'll burn the shack anyway," Shardeen said.

"They's somebody here," Coombs said. "They's a couple horses out back."

"All right, boys, it's time for you to earn your twenty-five dollars," Dooly said.

Inside the shack Matt had just lifted a fork full of beans to his mouth when a fusillade of shots rang out, crashing through the two windows and the door.

"Get down!" Matt yelled, though his warning wasn't necessary as Jesse was already on the floor, gun in hand, crawling toward one of the windows. Matt crawled to the other and the two men began returning fire.

"I ain't no good with a pistol," Jesse said. "I gotta get my rifle." He stood up and started toward his bunk.

"No, Jesse, keep down!" Matt shouted, but even as he was calling out his warning he saw a mist of blood fly up from Jesse's chest as he was hit.

Jesse fell and Matt crawled over to him, and the two men lay on the floor as the bullets continued to come through the windows, the glass totally shot out.

"Damn! Damn, that was a dumb thing for me to do!" Jesse said, his voice strained with pain.

"How badly are you hit?" Matt asked.

"Bad enough, I reckon," Jesse replied. "Seein' as I'm dyin'."

More bullets slammed against the outside wall, but because the walls were made of thick logs, the only ones that got through were the ones that came crashing in through the window.

"Deputy, would you take my confession?" Jesse asked, exerting himself to talk.

"Jesse, I'm not a priest. I'm not even Catholic."

"That don't matter. I'm dyin'. All you got to do is listen. It's important to me, Deputy. I don't want to go see God without confessin'."

"All right," Matt said. "If all I have to do is listen."

Jesse crossed himself, then began speaking, the pain evident in his voice.

"Father forgive me for I have sinned. It's been two years since my last confession. I've done things, I've drunk too much, I've laid with whores, and that twenty dollars that Billy Largent lost, and I was helpin' him look for, well, I found it, only I didn' tell 'im I found it, and I kept it for myself. So, truth to tell, that means I stole it. Amen."

"Amen," Matt added, though he didn't know whether or not that was appropriate.

"Deputy, will you tell Billy that? Tell 'im I'm sorry. An' tell 'im he can have anythin' of mine that's worth twenty . . ." Jesse stopped in midsentence, gasped a couple of times, then quit breathing.

"I'll tell him," Matt said, though he knew that Jesse could no longer hear him.

"Are you both dead in there? Or are you just out of ammunition?" a voice called from outside.

Staying low, Matt crawled back over to the window then looked outside. He saw someone rise up to get a look, and Matt fired, then saw the man he shot at fall back.

"Son of a bitch! They got Finley!" he heard someone yell.

Matt's shot had the effect of bringing on another fusillade.

Matt raised up and fired three more times, primarily just to let them know that there was still someone left and that he still had ammo.

He opened the cylinder and punched out the three empty cartridges, then replaced them. Now his pistol was fully loaded, but he had no more bullets except for those in his saddlebags, which were in the lean to out back. And there was no way he could get to them.

"Looks like they still have some fight left," Shardeen said.

"Yeah, but it don't seem like there's as much shootin' as there was," Fillion said.

"Coombs, there ain't no windows on the back side of that cabin. You think you can get around behind it, and set fire to it?" Shardeen asked.

"It depends," Coombs replied.

"Depends on what?"

"On whether or not I get the twenty dollars that was goin' to Finley."

"You get that fire goin', 'n' the twenty dollars

that was goin' to Finley will go to you," Shardeen promised.

Coombs nodded, then, carrying a can of kerosene with him, started out, running behind the ridgeline so as not to be seen from the shack. He lit the fire, then ran back around the ridgeline to rejoin Shardeen and the others. Now only Shardeen, Stoddard, Coombs, and Fillion were left of the seven who had come to attack the cabin. By the time Coombs got back, the little line shack was fully engulfed with flames.

"Anybody come out yet?" Coombs asked.

"No, but it's only a matter of time," Shardeen replied. "The way it's burnin', there can't nobody stay in there now."

Chapter Twenty-seven

Matt was trapped. There were only three ways out of the shack: the front door and the two front windows. And he couldn't go out that way without being shot. But it was equally obvious that he couldn't stay in the house. By now, the smoke was getting unbearable and he had to get down on his stomach and keep his nose to the floor in order to breathe. He moved to the back corner of the house, though he knew there was no place he could actually go.

Then, as he lay there, he saw an iron ring on the floor and, curious, he pulled on it, and was surprised to see that it was a trap door in the floor. Lifting it, he saw that was an opening to the ground underneath the house.

Matt crawled back across the floor and, grabbing Jesse by his legs, pulled him back to the open hole, then pushed him through. He didn't intend to leave Jesse in the house to burn, even though he was already dead. Matt dropped down as well. Then, wriggling on his belly, he dragged Jesse's body out from under the house on the opposite side from where his attackers were, his escape from the burning house unobserved by them.

The four attackers were standing in the open now, waiting for someone to come bursting through the front door, out of the smoke-filled cabin.

There was a dry arroyo behind the house, and Matt pulled Jesse down into it. Then he stood up, the arroyo deep enough that he wasn't exposed. He stayed there for moment breathing hard, not so much from the exertion, as from trying to replace the inhaled smoke with clean air.

Finally, his breath recovered, Matt moved down the gully for some distance, then he climbed back up to look over the lip of the arroyo. From there he had an excellent view of the house, which was now nearly one hundred percent engulfed with fire. He also saw four men standing about fifty yards away from the house, watching it burn. All four were holding pistols in their hands, waiting for someone to try and escape.

Matt dropped back down into the gully and moved farther down, then crawled up for another view. This time he saw that he was exactly behind the four men. He climbed out of the draw and, quietly, began walking toward them.

"Think they're dead yet?" one of the four men asked.

"Ha. If they ain't dead, they gotta be hurtin' somethin' awful."

"I think they must be dead. Else they woulda come out by now."

"I hope they ain't dead yet," Stoddard said. "I want 'em to burn."

"Yeah, like they're in hell," Coombs added.

"Speaking of hell, that's exactly where I'm about to send you four," Matt said.

Startled, the four men turned around.

"Matt Jensen," Shardeen said.

"Hello, Shardeen," Matt said. "I guess it looks like you and I may have that little showdown you ran away from back in Geseta, doesn't it?"

Shardeen smiled. "It looks like we might at that. Boys, put your guns away. I'll handle this. You three can be my witnesses. Emmett Shardeen, the man who killed Matt Jensen."

"You sure about this, Shardeen?" Fillion asked.

Shardeen's smile turned into a chuckle. "Oh, yeah, I'm sure. You see, I'm going to keep a little edge here. I'm not going to put my gun away. I'm just going to keep it handy. What do you say about that, Jensen?"

"I say it doesn't matter whether you put your guns away or not. I'm going to kill all four of you."

"Well now, would you like to tell me just how the

hell you are going to do that, with your gun still in your holster?" Shardeen asked.

"I think I'd rather show you," Matt replied.

Before the last word was out of Matt's mouth, the gun was in his hand. Not one of the four had even raised their pistols yet, thinking they had the advantage. Not one of them managed to get off a shot.

Morgan and Nate Poindexter, as well as Gabe Mathis, Strawn, Meeker, and Wallace were at the burned-out line shack. Except for Jesse's body, which had been pulled out of the arroyo and covered with canvas, the bodies of the men who had come to attack Jesse and Matt lay where they had fallen.

It was dark, but Gabe had brought a kerosene lantern, and he carried it with him as he examined the bodies.

"I'll be damn," Gabe said.

"What is it, Gabe?" Nate asked.

"I know these men. I know all of 'em, Gabe said. "Except for that pasty-faced son of a bitch there."

"His name is Shardeen," Matt said. "Emmett Shardeen."

"The way they're layin' here, looks like all four of 'em was killed at the same time," Gabe said.

"Nearly the same time," Matt agreed.

"They all got their guns in their hands, and they was all shot in the front. You done this, didn't you?"

Matt didn't answer.

"Yeah, well, my question is, what were these men doin' out here? There don't none of 'em ride for the BR, and I know that to be a fact."

"No doubt they were hired by the BR," Strawn suggested. "Give me the word, Poindexter, and I'll pay 'em back in kind."

"It would look to me like they've already been paid back in kind," Morgan said. "There are seven bodies here. And, like Gabe said, not a one of them came from the BR."

"We don't know that they didn't come from the BR."

"No, but what we do know is that you and your men weren't doing the job I hired you for, though, were you?"

"Poindexter, you've got two hundred and fifty thousand acres here. How the hell do you expect just three of us to be everywhere at once?"

"Strawn, did you kill MacDonald and Butrum?"

Strawn looked over at Matt, who was looking directly at him, waiting for his response.

"No," Strawn said.

"Well, whether you did or not, I won't be needing you here, anymore. I want you and the two men you brought with you off the Tumbling P by tomorrow morning."

"You're making a big mistake, Poindexter," Strawn said. "Especially after this. This here feud you got with Ross has turned into a war, and you are goin' to need someone like me more than ever."

"I've gotten along without anyone like you for twenty-five years," Poindexter said. "I think I can do without you a little longer."

Wedge Hill Ranch

Although Rex and Sylvia were lying together on the small bed that was in the springhouse, they were both fully clothed. Sylvia's head was nestled on Rex's shoulder.

"Maybe the fact that not one of the men came from our ranch will prove that we had nothing to do with it," Rex said. "Just as I believe that nobody over at the Tumbling P had anything to do with killing MacDonald and Butrum."

"Rex, I know there has long been a feud between Papa and your father. But it was never like this. What happened while I was gone? When did all this start?"

"It just started," Rex said. "And I don't have any idea what started it."

"What's going to happen?" Sylvia asked.

Rex tightened his arm around her shoulders.

"To us," she said.

Rex kissed her.

"Are you going to town for Mr. Billings's funeral?" Sylvia asked.

"I would, but I'm sure I wouldn't be welcome."

"Please come," Sylvia said. "If you aren't welcome, then neither am I."

Rex raised up on his elbow and stared down at Sylvia. "Are you sure you want me to come?"

"I think it's time we told Papa," Sylvia said.

A broad smile spread across Rex's face. "I'll be there," he said.

Tome

At the same moment that Rex and Sylvia were together in the springhouse on Wedge Hill Ranch, Bodine, Strawn, Dooley, Massey, Meeker, Wallace, Cates, and Dagan were gathered in the Vaquero Cantina.

"It was Matt Jensen that kilt Shardeen and the others," Meeker said.

"One man kilt all of 'em?" Dooley asked.

"I don't know about all of 'em, but he kilt at least four of 'em. We found Shardeen and three more of 'em lying out together, like they was all shot down at once. And get this . . . all four was holdin' guns, and all four had only one bullet hole in 'em."

"There ain't nobody that good," Massey said.

"Matt Jensen is," Strawn said. "I seen him in action when he kilt my pard, Vargas. I'm afraid Jensen is goin' to cause us problems."

"No he ain't. He ain't goin' to cause us no trouble at all."

"What do you mean he ain't? How can you say that, Bodine? Hell, so far he's kilt seven of our men," Strawn said.

"I can say that because tomorrow is the day we

finish this. And my name isn't Bodine. It's Rufus Draco."

"Draco? I thought you told us you didn't want to use that name no more," Meeker said.

"That's behind me now," Draco replied. "Tomorrow, Matt Jensen dies." Draco's lips stretched into a demonic smile. "And I want the son of a bitch to know who killed him."

"You said we are going to finish this tomorrow. How are we going to do that?" Strawn asked.

"Tomorrow is the buryin'," Draco said. "We're goin' to be in town early, before anythin' starts, so that we can get into position. Strawn, you, Meeker, Wallace, and Cates are going to be in position on the south side of the street. Dooley, you, Massey, and Dagan will be with me on the north side. Spread out all up and down the street, and find you some place where you can't be seen, on top of buildings, behind corners, anywhere that keeps you out of sight. Then, once you have your place, just wait for my signal."

"Wait for your signal to do what?" Meeker asked.

Draco smiled again. "To start the war," he said.

Thirty Four Corners

"No!" Morgan Poindexter said, resolutely, when, just before Jesse Billings's funeral the next morning, Sylvia approached him with the information that Rex Ross was going to attend the funeral with her.

"I can't believe you would even ask that."

"Papa, I love Rex."

"What?" Morgan gasped. "How can that be? You've only been home for a month! You haven't had time to know whether or not you love anyone, let alone Rex Ross."

"Papa, how long did you know Mama before you and she were married?"

"What? That . . . that has nothing to do with this!"

"It seems to me like it has everything to do with this," Sylvia said. "Is, or is not, the fact that you ran away with Mama—on the very day that she and Mr. Ross were to be married—the cause of this twenty-five-year-long absolutely foolish feud?"

"You don't understand," Morgan replied. "I tried to make up with Ben. I went to him, hat in hand, apologized for what I did, and offered him my continued friendship. He is the one who said no."

"Nevertheless, that was your generation. This generation belongs to Rex and me. We are in love, and we intend to be together."

Morgan closed his mouth so tightly that his lips formed only a thin line, and his temple throbbed in anger.

"Then you'll be together somewhere else," he said. "Not in my house, and not in this funeral."

Tears sprang to her eyes.

"Then so be it. Good-bye, Papa," Sylvia said, spinning on her heel, then walking away, quickly.

That conversation had taken place in front of the church where Jesse Billings's funeral was to take place. Landers was not conducting the funeral; it was to be conducted by a Catholic priest who had come over from Tome. Morgan had made the arrangement to use the church by donating five hundred dollars to Lander's discretionary fund.

"Where is Sylvia going?" Nate asked, coming out of the church just in time to see Sylvia walking away.

"It doesn't matter," Morgan said. "Let's get inside. The priest can't stay here all day."

Matt Jensen was in the Black Bull Saloon, nursing a beer, when he saw a big man coming toward him. The man was Frank Carter, the same man Matt had fought with several days earlier. Matt tensed as Carter approached.

"Jensen?" Carter said.

Matt turned to face him. "What do you want, Carter?"

"You've been lookin' for a man named Draco?"

"Yes."

"It's Bodine."

"What?"

"It's Bodine. His real name is Draco. And he plans to start somethin' today."

"What do you mean he plans to start something today? And how do you know this?"

"I know it, 'cause I was in Tome 'n' I heard him 'n' Strawn and some others talkin'. They said they was goin' to start a war today. And Draco said he was goin' to kill you."

"Why are you telling me this, Carter?"

"I don't know. Maybe it's cause when me 'n' you fought, you whupped me fair and square. And you coulda done more. You coulda kilt me, but you didn't. You treated me right, so I figure I owe you."

"Thank you, Carter, I appreciate that."

Carter nodded, then looked toward Hodge. "I'll have a bottle of whiskey," he said.

Hodge handed him the bottle, and a glass.

"I won't need no glass," Carter said, pulling the cork with his teeth, then spitting it out. He carried the bottle with him to a table in the back of the saloon, then sat there.

Rex Ross was waiting for Sylvia just inside the Birdcage Theater. He didn't have to ask how Sylvia's meeting went. He could tell by the tears in her eyes, and the look on her face, that it hadn't gone well.

"I'm sorry," he said, opening his arms to her.

"It doesn't matter. I belong to you now. Forever," she said, and they shared a deep kiss.

Jesse had a funeral, but there was no funeral for the seven men who had come to kill him. Clergymen weren't present for their burials, nor were they asked for. Because of the uniqueness of the situation, being that the pallbearer would be burying Jesse Billings, as well as the men who had killed him on the same day, he kept some separation between the actual burials. Jesse's funeral concluded with graveside rites. Then, even before the mourners left the cemetery, the mass burial of the seven other men began. It was preceded by a somber cortege of four wagons, two bodies in each of the first three wagons and only one body, Shardeen's, in the last wagon.

Six of the men were well known in town, having lived in Thirty Four Corners for some time. Because of that, the entire town turned out to watch the doleful parade of charnel wagons.

"How come Billings got a funeral, and our men didn't?" someone shouted from the south side of the street.

"Because your men are murderers!" the shout came back from the north side.

"Like your men weren't when they kilt Miller, MacDonald, and Butrum?"

The man who yelled the last remark stepped down from the boardwalk on the south side of the street and lifted his clenched fist over his head to express his anger.

Draco was lying of the roof of the leather goods store, and because of its location, it gave him a field of fire to either side of the street. He aimed his rifle at the man who had yelled, and pulled the trigger.

The man Draco shot went down. That was just the opening shot. It was followed immediately by other shots as, up and down Central, on both sides of the street, gun fire erupted. Bullets flew, windows crashed, women screamed, and men, women and even children went down under the fusillade.

The drivers of the charnel wagons jumped down and ran for cover, The horses pulling the first two wagons were hit and they fell, but not before they staggered off, effectively blocking the street.

Sunset Lil had been standing on the balcony of her Parlor of Delight watching the burial procession when the shooting started, and Matt Jensen, who had left the Black Bull after hearing the first shot, saw a mist of blood from the side of Sunset Lil's head. She fell over the bannister, and landed in the street below. Matt also saw where the shot came from that killed her, and aiming his pistol, he fired. The man who had shot Sunset Lil had been standing on top of a mercantile store on the south side of the street, and dropping his gun, he clutched his chest, then tumbled down from the roof.

Even as that man fell, Matt saw someone with a gun peer around the edge of the false front of the North Star Saloon, and one more shot dropped him. Matt ran down to the livery, thinking that if he could get up into the loft, he would be able to see where all the shooting was coming from.

Dooley and Meeker had beaten Matt to the position, and both were already in the loft of the livery.

"Hey, Meeker, ain't that Matt Jensen?"

"Yeah," Dooley said. "I expect Draco will give us a bonus for killin' him."

Dooley and Meeker, both of whom had rifles, stood in the open door of the loft. Matt didn't see them at first, but when Meeker's shot whizzed by his ear, it got his attention. He fired two quick shots, and both Meeker and Dooley fell.

"Son of a bitch!" Cates said, shouting from the second-floor balcony of the hotel, down to Dagan, who was behind the corner of the apothecary. "He's done kilt four of us! Quit shootin' at the others! Shoot at Jensen!"

Cates shot first, and the bullet hit the edge of the door of the livery, just before Matt stepped inside. Turning, he saw someone standing on the hotel balcony, and another near the corner of the druggist, both men aiming rifles in his direction.

They were out of pistol range, so Matt reached down to pick up one of the rifles dropped by the two men he had just shot. Bending down at that precise moment was a fortuitous move for him, because a bullet took off his hat. Had he not bent down exactly when he did, the bullet would have crashed into his head.

Matt jacked that lever down. It ejected a live cartridge, but it was necessary to reassure him that the rifle was loaded and cocked. Raising the rifle to his shoulder, he aimed at the man on the ground, deciding he could more easily get cover than the man on the hotel balcony. He squeezed the trigger, then jacked a second shell into the chamber and brought the rifle to bear on the man the balcony. He didn't even check the first man. He knew, without looking, that he had hit him, and he knew, without looking, that he had killed him.

He fired a second time, and the man on the balcony turned a flip in midair as he fell, landing on his back on the boardwalk below.

By now, the cowboys from both ranches had armed themselves, and they reappeared on both sides of the street, with weapons in hand.

"No! No! Stop! Stop!" Sylvia shouted, running out into the street between the two groups of armed men. "Stop the shooting!"

"Sylvia! No! Come back here!" Rex shouted, running out after her.

Draco watched the two run out into the street, and, looking toward Strawn, who was on top of the feed store, he pointed toward Rex and Sylvia. Lifting his rifle, he aimed at the girl, and pulled the trigger.

Sylvia went down.

"Sylvia, no!" Rex screamed in agony. The next round dropped him.

The cowboys—from both ranches—were stunned by what they just saw, and not one shot was exchanged between them.

Matt ran out into the street, then looked back, trying to determine the origin of the shots, but he saw nobody.

Rex got to his hands and knees and crawled toward Sylvia, who was still alive, but barely.

"I love you," he said, wrapping his arms around her. She returned the embrace.

"Sylvia!" Morgan shouted, running toward his daughter.

"Rex!" Ben called, running from the opposite side of the street, toward his son.

The cowboys from both ranches, their guns put away, moved silently toward Rex and Sylvia, who were on the ground, locked in embrace.

Morgan dropped to his knees beside them, and reached out for his daughter.

"Sylvia! Sylvia!" he called in anguish.

"I . . . love him . . . Papa," Sylvia said, the words barely audible.

Gently, Rex put Sylvia's hand in her father's hand. There was no life left. Rex looked at Morgan, then at his father. He shook his head sadly, then took his last breath.

"My God," Ben Ross said. "What have I done? What have I done?" He looked at Morgan. "Morgan, I have been such a fool all these years, and look now, what it has done."

"We have both been fools," Morgan replied.

"What now?" Strawn asked. "Jensen has kilt all our men. We sure as hell can't steal a thousand head by ourselves."

Strawn and Draco, having left their firing positions, were now on the ground behind the feed store.

"The bank," Draco said.

"What?"

Draco smiled. "Right now, the whole town is in such an uproar that there won't be nobody payin' attention. We can go into the bank and clean it out. And there won't be no cows to herd."

"Yeah," Strawn said. "Good idea!"

Matt knew that the shots that killed Rex and Sylvia had come from First Street, and because he had heard the two shots coming from two different locations, he knew there were at least two shooters left. He studied all the buildings hard to try and find their location. That was when he saw Wes Gregory, the hostler, standing just inside the livery. Gregory was trying to get his attention.

"The bank," Gregory said when Matt approached. "Bodine and Strawn just went into the bank."

"Thanks," Matt said. He moved quickly to the side of the Birdcage Theater, which would allow him to approach the bank without being seen. Then, reaching the bank, he looked in through the window.

There was only one teller in the bank and he was shirtless. He was shirtless because, under the guns and watchful eyes of the two robbers, he was putting bound stacks of bills onto the shirt.

Matt recognized both men. One was Strawn and the other, as Carter had said, was Rufus Draco. He felt a sense of satisfaction at having, at long last, caught up with him.

"How much money is there?" Draco asked.

"Fif . . . fifteen thousand," the teller said, stuttering in his fear.

"Ha!" Draco said. "And only two of us to divide it up."

Matt opened the front door and stepped inside.

"The money isn't going to be divided," Matt said.

Startled, the two robbers turned toward him.

"Jensen!" Draco said.

"Hello, Draco," Matt said.

Both Draco and Strawn fired. Matt returned fire, getting off two shots so fast that it sounded like one.

Draco and Strawn missed.

Matt didn't.

Epilogue

There were so many to bury over the next few days that Tom Nunnlee had to send out for help, and other undertakers and grave diggers arrived from Tome, Las Luna, Valencia, and even as far away as Albuquerque. Counting Jesse Billings, and the seven others who had been in the process of being buried when the war had started, there were a total of twenty-one to be buried.

But that twenty-one did not count Rex and Sylvia, for whom special arrangements were being made.

"Are you sure this is what you gentlemen want?" Nunnlee asked. "A special casket built large to hold both of them?"

Ben Ross and Morgan Poindexter were standing together.

"Yes," Ben said.

"But this is most unusual. I don't think I've ever

done anything like this. Nor have I ever even heard of it. Burying two people in the same casket. Especially a man and woman who aren't even married."

"Don't worry. They will be married."

"What do you mean, they will be married?" Nunnlee asked. "How can they possibly be married?"

"God will marry them," Morgan said.

Matt stood at the edge of the cemetery. The day before, there had been funerals for six innocent citizens of the town, three men, two women, and a child. But there had been only burials for the fifteen outlaws, including Draco and Strawn, who had, ultimately, been responsible for the mass slaughter.

Today, the cowboys from both the BR and Tumbling P were gathered around the gravesite, along with more than half the town, as the specially constructed and oversized casket was lowered into the double grave. The cowboys from the two ranches had approached each other, made new friends, and renewed old friendships.

Morgan and Nate sat under a canopy with Ben and his wife, Nancy, sitting beside them.

Marshal Hunter came up to stand beside Matt.

"I . . . uh . . . wasn't much help to you," Hunter said.

"You got the people off the street, didn't you?"

"Yes. But that's all I did."

"You probably saved ten or fifteen lives by doing that," Matt said. "So don't sell yourself short."

"Thanks."

Matt took off the star and handed it Marshal Hunter. "If you would, please give this badge back to Sheriff Ferrell. I won't be using it anymore."

"All right."

Matt turned to walk back toward Spirit, who was tied to a nearby hitching rail.

"I suppose we'll never see you again, will we?" Marshal Hunter asked.

Matt lifted his hand in a wave, but he didn't turn around.

"Never is a long time," he said.

J. A. Johnstone on William W. Johnstone
"When the Truth Becomes Legend"

William W. Johnstone was born in southern Missouri, the youngest of four children. He was raised with strong moral and family values by his minister father, and tutored by his schoolteacher mother. Despite this, he quit school at age fifteen.

"I have the highest respect for education," he says, "but such is the folly of youth, and wanting to see the world beyond the four walls and the blackboard."

True to this vow, Bill attempted to enlist in the French Foreign Legion ("I saw Gary Cooper in *Beau Geste* when I was a kid and I thought the French Foreign Legion would be fun") but was rejected, thankfully, for being underage. Instead, he joined a traveling carnival and did all kinds of odd jobs. It was listening to the veteran carny folk, some of whom had been on the circuit since the late 1800s, telling amazing tales about their experiences, which planted the storytelling seed in Bill's imagination.

"They were mostly honest people, despite the

bad reputation traveling carny shows had back then," Bill remembers. "Of course, there were exceptions. There was one guy named Picky, who got that name because he was a master pickpocket. He could steal a man's socks right off his feet without him knowing. Believe me, Picky got us chased out of more than a few towns."

After a few months of this grueling existence, Bill returned home and finished high school. Next came stints as a deputy sheriff in the Tallulah, Louisiana, Sheriff's Department, followed by a hitch in the U.S. Army. Then he began a career in radio broadcasting at KTLD in Tallulah, which would last sixteen years. It was there that he fine-tuned his storytelling skills. He turned to writing in 1970, but it wouldn't be until 1979 that his first novel, *The Devil's Kiss*, was published. Thus began the full-time writing career of William W. Johnstone. He wrote horror (*The Uninvited*), thrillers (*The Last of the Dog Team*), even a romance novel or two. Then, in February 1983, *Out of the Ashes* was published. Searching for his missing family in the aftermath of a post-apocalyptic America, rebel mercenary and patriot Ben Raines is united with the civilians of the Resistance forces and moves to the forefront of a revolution for the nation's future.

Out of the Ashes was a smash. The series would continue for the next twenty years, winning Bill three generations of fans all over the world. The series was often imitated but never duplicated. "We all tried to copy the Ashes series," said one publishing executive, "but Bill's uncanny ability, both then and now, to predict in which direction the political winds were blowing brought a certain immediacy to the table no one else could capture." The Ashes series would end its run with more than thirty-four books and twenty million copies in print, making it one of the most successful men's action series in American book publishing. (The Ashes series also, Bill notes with a touch of pride, got him on the FBI's Watch List for its less than flattering portrayal of spineless politicians and the growing power of big government over our lives, among other things. In that respect, I often find myself saying, "Bill was years ahead of his time.")

Always steps ahead of the political curve, Bill's recent thrillers, written with myself, include *Vengeance Is Mine, Invasion USA, Border War, Jackknife, Remember the Alamo, Home Invasion, Phoenix Rising, The Blood of Patriots, The Bleeding Edge,* and the upcoming *Suicide Mission.*

It is with the western, though, that Bill found his greatest success and propelled him onto both the *USA Today* and the *New York Times* bestseller lists.

Bill's western series include *The Mountain Man, Matt Jensen, the Last Mountain Man, Preacher, The Family Jensen, Luke Jensen, Bounty Hunter, Eagles, Mac-Callister* (an Eagles spin-off), *Sidewinders, The Brothers O'Brien, Sixkiller, Blood Bond, The Last Gunfighter,* and the upcoming new series *Flintlock* and *The Trail West.* May 2013 saw the hardcover western *Butch Cassidy, The Lost Years.*

"The Western," Bill says, "is one of the few true art forms that is one hundred percent American. I liken the Western as America's version of England's Arthurian legends, like the Knights of the Round Table, or Robin Hood and his Merry Men. Starting with the 1902 publication of *The Virginian* by Owen Wister, and followed by the greats like Zane Grey, Max Brand, Ernest Haycox, and of course Louis L'Amour, the Western has helped to shape the cultural landscape of America.

"I'm no goggle-eyed college academic, so when my fans ask me why the Western is as popular now as it was a century ago, I don't offer a 200-page thesis. Instead, I can only offer this: The Western is honest. In this great country, which is suffering under the yoke of political correctness, the Western harks back to an era when justice was sure and swift. Steal a man's horse, rustle his cattle, rob a bank, a stagecoach, or a train, you were hunted down and fitted with a hangman's noose. One size fit all.

"Sure, we westerners are prone to a little embellishment and exaggeration and, I admit it, occasionally play a little fast and loose with the facts. But we do so for a very good reason—to enhance the enjoyment of readers.

"It was Owen Wister, in *The Virginian* who first coined the phrase *'When you call me that, smile.'* Legend has it that Wister actually heard those words spoken by a deputy sheriff in Medicine Bow, Wyoming, when another poker player called him a son-of-a-bitch.

"Did it really happen, or is it one of those myths that have passed down from one generation to the next? I honestly don't know. But there's a line in one of my favorite Westerns of all time, *The Man Who Shot Liberty Valance,* where the newspaper editor tells the young reporter, 'When the truth becomes legend, print the legend.'

"These are the words I live by."

Turn the page for an exciting preview!

THE UNTOLD SAGA OF SHAWN O'BRIEN

From acclaimed storytellers William W. Johnstone
and J. A. Johnstone, who brought us
The Brothers O'Brien, comes an explosive new series
featuring the gunslinging O'Brien who brought
peace, law, and order to the American frontier . . .
one bullet at a time.

A MAN WHO TAMED THE WEST—
ONE TOWN AT A TIME

Unlike his brothers, Jacob, Sam, and Patrick,
Shawn O'Brien isn't content to settle down on the
family ranch in New Mexico territory. With his razor-
sharp eye, lightning-fast draw, and burning thirst for
justice, Shawn is carving out a reputation of his own.
As a town tamer, he takes the most dangerous,
lawless towns in the West and makes them safe
for decent men, women, and children.
When a stagecoach accident leaves Shawn stranded
in Holy Rood, Utah, it doesn't take long to realize
he's landed in one ornery circle of hell.
Ruled by a cruel and cunning crook turned
merciless dictator named Hank Cobb, Holy Rood
is about as unholy a place as any on the frontier.
Anyone who breaks Cobb's rules is severely
punished. Anyone who defies Cobb's hooded
henchmen dies by rope, stake, or guillotine.

But Shawn O'Brien isn't just anyone.
He's the town tamer.
And this time, *he's going to paint the town red . . .*

SHAWN O'BRIEN, TOWN TAMER
by WILLIAM W. JOHNSTONE
with J. A. Johnstone

On sale March 2014, wherever
Kensington Books are sold.

Chapter One

Hours of jolting, swaying misery ended suddenly as the stage came to a harness-jangling halt. It remained still until the following dust cloud caught up and covered the four passengers inside with a coat of fine, mustard-colored grit.

The driver climbed down, stepped to the window, and stuck his shaggy head inside. A patch made from a scrap of tanned leather covered his right eye.

"Town coming up, folks, but this stage don't stop there," the man said. "Fact is, no stage stops there. We go on through Holy Rood at a gallop, so hold on tight an' say your prayers if you got 'em."

Shawn O'Brien had been lost in thought, deep in heartbreaks of the past, but now he stirred himself enough to say, "Why is that? Why all the hurry?"

"Because Holy Rood is a downright dangerous place to be, young feller," the driver said. "Especially if you got a sin to hide."

"Hell, we've all got a sin to hide," a passenger said.

He was a pleasant-faced man who wore the broadcloth finery and string tie of the frontier gambler, his black frockcoat now a uniform tan from trail dust.

"Then repent for yer sins an' hold on like I told you," the driver said. "This here stage is barrelin' through that damned town like a deadheading express."

"Oh dear," said a small man with the timid, downtrodden look of a henpecked husband. "When we left Silver Reef, Wells Fargo didn't inform me that my life would be in such peril."

"Hell, they never do." The driver grinned. "Holy Rood ain't on the map as far as Wells Fargo is concerned."

The gambler smiled at the little man. "What sin are you hiding, mister?" The humor reached his eyes. "Looking at you, I'd say whiskey and women are your downfall."

"Good heavens no," the man said. "My lady wife would never allow it. She bade me promise on our wedding eve that my lips would ne'er touch ardent spirits nor my loins join in unholy union with those of another woman." The little man seemed to shrink into his seat. "She's a stern, unbending woman, my wife, much given to the virtues of holy scripture and liberal doses of prune juice."

"Then I guess you've nothing to fear," the gambler said. "Hell, man, you're a shining example to all of us."

His eyes moved to the girl sitting next to the little man. She'd seemed pretty in the Silver Reef boom town, but hours in the stage had taken its toll. Now she looked weary, hot, and uncomfortable and smelled muskily of perspiration and stale perfume.

"What about you, missy?" the gambler said. "You got a little sin to confess?"

A hot breeze gusted through the stage window, carrying dust and a faint odor of sage and mesquite.

"I don't think that's an appropriate question to ask a lady," Shawn O'Brien said. "I reckon you should guard your tongue, mister."

The gambler had to crane his head to look at Shawn. And when he did, he wished he hadn't.

The young man's handsome, well-bred face bore a mild, almost amused expression, but the gambler read a hundred different kinds of hell in his blue eyes. He'd seen eyes like that before across a lot of card tables, the I-don't-give-a-damn look of the seasoned gunfighter.

By the nature of his profession the gambler was a cautious man and he tacked onto a more favorable course.

To the girl he said, "The gentleman is correct, of course. I'm sorry if I said anything to offend you, ma'am. That was far from my intention."

The girl had a beautiful smile, white teeth in a pink mouth. "No offense taken," she said. "You asked a most singular question, sir, and my answer to it is that I cuss sometimes."

"I rather fancy that any cuss from lips as sweet as yours, must be mild indeed," Shawn said.

"Well, I do say hell and damn when the occasion demands it," the girl said.

"And I say a hell of a lot worse that that, young lady," the stage driver said. "And you'll probably hear it when we hit the main street through Holy Rood. So hang on, everybody, and let's git this here rig rolling."

He rubbed a gnarled hand across his mouth. "You see a poor soul with his head on the chopping block, don't look no further, huh? It ain't a sight fer good Christian folks."

Without another word, the driver disappeared and the stage creaked and lurched as he climbed into the box. A whip cracked and the six-mule team shambled into motion.

"Yeeehah!"

The whip snapped again and the mules took the hint and stretched into a gallop.

"What did he mean about a poor soul's head on a chopping block?" the little man said. "That was a most distressing thing to hear."

His voice hiccupped with every jolt of the stage and his knuckles were white on the carpetbag he held on his lap.

"I wouldn't worry about it," the gambler said. "Stage drivers are like ferrymen, crazy as bullbats. I ain't never met a sane one yet."

"It was a strange thing to say, all the same," Shawn said.

"I'll allow you that, mister," the gambler said. "'Twas a strange thing to say . . ."

A couple of minutes later it was the girl who first saw them . . . the yellowed skulls that grinned atop tall timber posts bordering both sides of the wagon road.

The girl opened her mouth to say something, but the words bunched up in her throat and wouldn't come.

The timid little man spoke for her.

"My God, what kind of town is this?" he said, his voice breaking. "It's signposted by the devil himself."

Shawn stuck his head out the window.

Skull after skull flashed past, most yellow, a few still red and raw, a macabre march of the mutilated dead.

The driver stood in the box, his whip cracking over the backs of the straining mules, and the stage rocked and pitched like a barque in a storm.

Shawn tried to count the skulls, but soon gave up. There were just too many of them.

Gunshots slammed beside him, and the girl let out a high-pitched shriek of surprise and fear.

The gambler was leaning out the window and cutting loose with a short-barreled Colt. After the hammer clicked on the empty chamber he sat back in the seat and said, "That isn't decent, the skulls of dead men lining the road. I tried to shoot some of them off."

"Hit any?" Shawn said.

"Not a one."

Above the rumble of the wheels and the pound of the mules' hooves, the driver yelled, "Town comin' up! Hang on, folks!"

Shawn looked out the window again. A dozen yards in front of him a large, painted sign read:

WELCOME TO HOLY ROOD
A Blessed Place
~
Come Worship with Us

Then the stage hammered into the town's main drag, its attendant dust cloud rolling along behind, trying desperately to catch up.

Shawn was aware of a wide street lined on both sides with timber buildings, all of them painted white, and the strange fact that there was not a soul around.

Then disaster struck . . . an unforeseen incident that would soon plunge Shawn O'Brien and the other passengers into a living nightmare.

Chapter Two

As the thundering stage took Holy Rood's main street at a gallop, the cussing driver stood in the box and frantically cracked his snaking whip, urging the mules to go faster . . . and faster. . . .

The town's buildings flickered past like runaway slides at a demented magic lantern show . . . and then catastrophe.

The big meat hog that charged out of an alley, fleeing a butcher, weighed a little over three hundred pounds. It was solid enough and fast enough to slam into the left lead mule with the force of an out-of-control freight train.

The mule went down, screaming, like a puppet that had just had its strings cut. Panicked, the rest of the team swerved to their right. Too late! The following mules crashed into the downed animal and then hit the ground in a tangle of kicking legs and jangling traces.

Rocking violently, the stage couldn't right itself,

tipped over on two wheels and then crashed onto its side.

The driver was thrown clear, but his neck broke when the back of his head slammed into the board-walk. He died within seconds, soundlessly and without movement.

But the scene inside the stage was as chaotic as the tangle of kicking, screaming mules.

As the stage filled with dust, Shawn was thrown on top of the gambler and the timid man was lost under a flurry of the girl's white petticoats.

"Hell, mister, you're crushing me to death," the gambler said, gasping for breath. "Git off me!"

"Sorry," Shawn said. "I'm going to move and get the door open."

"Then move carefully, for God's sake," the gambler said. "I'm dying here."

"I'll try," Shawn said.

The girl had managed to squirm into a sitting position on the little man's chest, and he wailed in protest.

"Are you all right?" Shawn said to her. "No broken bones?"

The girl nodded. "I don't think so."

"I can't breathe," the little man wailed. "I'm getting crushed to death. Oh, my poor wife."

"Hold on. I'll get you out of there," Shawn said.

But before he could make a move, the stage door was thrown open and a man's head appeared.

"Is anybody hurt?" he said.

"I don't think so," Shawn said.

"Then praise the Lord," the man said. "His sweet mercy has spared you."

A moment later two sets of hands reached into the stage and Shawn said, "Get the girl first."

"Grab my hands, young woman," the rescuer said.

The girl was hauled out and then the little man, who staggered a little and declared that this entire experience was an "outrage," and that Wells Fargo and this benighted town would "pay for his terrible injuries."

"I need to stand on you," Shawn said to the gambler. "I'll try not to step on your face."

"Just . . . do it," the gambler growled, his distorted cheek jammed against the other door. "And be damned to ye for weighing more than my ex-mother-in-law."

Using the gambler as a step, Shawn clambered though the open door and onto the street. The gambler got out a few moments later, bleeding from a cut on his forehead, his eyes blazing and some sharp words for Shawn on the tip of his tongue.

But then, like the intended target of his wrath, he could only stand openmouthed and silent, stunned by what he saw . . .

Five men wearing monkish black robes and flat-brimmed, low-crowned hats of the same color, stood around the stage. All wore belted Colts and carried Winchesters. Nowhere was a smile to be seen.

Shawn pegged them as hard cases in monk's

clothing, and a couple of them had the look and arrogant attitude of Texan hired guns.

A couple of shots rang out as someone killed the injured mules, and then one of the five men spoke. He had ice-blue eyes and a black, spade-shaped beard.

"Your driver is dead," he said. "You will stay here in town until your fate is decided."

"Now see here," the little passenger said, puffing up a little. "My name is Ernest J. Pettwood the Third and I'm a senior representative of the Miles and Anderson Ladies Corset Company of St. Louis. I demand that you arrange transportation to my original destination. And I mean—instanter!"

The bearded man stared at Pettwood as though he were a slimy thing that had just crawled out from under a rock.

His face like stone, he raised his rifle and shot the little drummer in the chest.

Pettwood staggered back and fell on his butt. He glanced down at the scarlet flower blossoming on his chest with a mix of surprise and shock, then keeled over onto his side and lay still.

The girl ran to the dead man and took his head in her arms. Her hands bloodstained she glared at the drummer's killer and said, "You damned animal!"

"Anybody else got a demand they want solved instanter?" the bearded man said.

"Damn you for a murdering rogue," Shawn said. "I'll see you hang for this."

He took a step toward the bearded man, then

stopped when four rifles rattled as they swung in his direction.

"His was an obscene profession," the bearded man said. "Such as he can't be allowed to live and pollute the very air we breathe in this fair town."

"I've seen you before, mister," Shawn said, his anger barely under control. "I can't remember where, but I'll swear it was on a wanted poster."

The man made no answer, but he turned to one of the others with him.

"Brother Melchizedeck, search the men for firearms," he said.

The gambler opened his coat with his left hand. "Take it," he said. "In the shoulder holster."

Brother Melchizedeck took the gambler's Colt, then said to Shawn, "Where is your gun."

"I don't have one," Shawn said.

"Search him, brother," the bearded man said. "He has a dishonest face and a mocker's tongue."

Shawn opened his coat, and the man named Melchizedeck patted him down. "He has no gun, Brother Uzziah."

The bearded man nodded. Then, to the gambler, he said, "By what name do you call yourself?"

"I call myself by the name my parents gave me. What misbegotten son of a whore gave you yours?"

"You wear the garb of a professional card player, and are thus already suspect," Uzziah said. "Best you keep a civil tongue in your head."

"Or what? You'll murder me like you did the drummer?" the gambler said, anger flaring his cheeks.

"I must tell you that I believe that your fate may already be sealed," Uzziah said. "Look to the church and tell me what you see?"

The gambler eyes shifted to the steepled church at the end of the street. Even at a distance the preacher could be heard roaring at the faithful inside.

"Damn you, it's a gallows," the gambler said. "What kind of people put an obscenity like that at the door of a church?"

The man called Uzziah smiled without humor. "It's a guillotine," he said. He tucked the butt of his rifle under his arm and bladed his right hand into the open palm of his left. "It removes the heads of the sinful and dispatches them to hell. Instanter, as the drummer said."

"Mister," the gambler said, "you're a sick man and this is a sick town."

"No, it's a peaceful town, and prosperous," Uzziah said.

A dust devil reeled in the street, then collapsed in a yellow cloud.

"He's not a sick man. He's a hired gun and a woman killer," Shawn said. He stared at Uzziah, a hard blue light in his eyes, "As I recollect, his name is Sheldon Shannon from down Nogales way with time out for a five-year spell in Yuma. I reckon he was spawned with a price on his head. A far piece off your home range, aren't you, Shel? I never knew you to operate north of the Red."

"And who might you be?" Shannon said. "Or do you know?"

"Name's Shawn O'Brien from the Glorieta Mesa country in the New Mexico Territory."

Recognition dawned in Shannon's eyes. "Your pa's the bull o' the woods down that way an' you got a brother, Jacob. Big man, plays the piano real good."

"My father, Colonel Shamus O'Brien, is the biggest rancher in the territory," Shawn said, his face stiff. "As for my brother, Jake, he plays the piano, among other things."

"He's a rum one, all right, is Jacob," Shannon said. "I was there the night he killed Everett Wilson down Austin way. You heard of him?"

"Yes. I've heard of him."

"Wilson was no bargain."

"So Jake told me."

"Judging by your kin, I reckon you're gun slick, O'Brien. Strange thing in a man who doesn't carry a pistol."

"You should be in Yuma, Shel. But I don't see you carrying chains."

Shannon nodded. "You have a quick wit, O'Brien. Well, I don't know how long you'll live, but you call me Shel Shannon just one more time and your life ends right here."

"So what do I call you, besides son of a—"

"You call me Brother Uzziah. Get it right next time, O'Brien, or I'll kill you."

"What do we do with them?" Brother Melchizedeck said.

His eyes still burning into Shawn's face like branding irons, Shannon said, "Take O'Brien and the gambler to the prison. They'll be put to the question later."

"And the girl?"

"The hotel. Once the church service is over, two holy and righteous women of the town will examine her for the witch's mark."

"Brother Uzziah, look!" one of the other men yelled. He pointed to a rock ridge above the town, where a man sat a white horse in front of a stand of aspen.

Shannon scanned the ridge, then screamed, "Damn him! Damn him to hell!"

He threw his Winchester to his shoulder and levered off several shots at the rider on the ridge. The man didn't flinch.

"Is it him?" Shannon yelled, lowering the rifle. "Is it the shifter?"

"It's him all right," Melchizedeck said, a strange, stricken fear in his eyes. "It's Jasper Wolfden as ever was. He's come back from the grave." Then, "My God, Uzziah, look at that!"

The rider leaned from the saddle and hefted a long pole that seemed heavy for him because of the human head stuck on the axe-shaved point.

"Who is it?" Shannon shrieked. "Damn you, whose head is that?"

"It's Mordecai," a young, towheaded brother said.

"Are you sure?" Shannon said, his voice ragged with near hysteria. "Damn you, are you sure?"

"Yes, it's Brother Mordecai. I can make out the black powder burn over his left eye."

Shawn studied Shel Shannon. The gunman was a cold-blooded killer, lightning fast on the draw and shoot, but his hands trembled and he continually swallowed as though his mouth was filled with saliva.

"He's a shifter," Shannon said. "You can't kill a shifter."

His eyes keen, Shawn directed his attention to the horseman on the ridge.

The man held his macabre trophy high. By the look of the head, its late owner had died recently. Shawn guessed within the past couple of hours.

He had no idea who Jasper Wolfden was, but dead men don't sweat. Dark arcs showed in the armpits of the man's shirt and his hat had a salt-crusted stain around the crown.

Wolfden had not returned from the grave, but spook or not, shifter or not, he'd put the fear of God into Sheldon Shannon . . .

. . . a man who didn't scare worth a damn.